THE SIREN

USA TODAY & WSJ BESTSELLING AUTHOR

giana darling

"The Night We Met"— Lord Huron
"Come Fly With Me" – Frank Sinatra
"Lover Undercover"— Melody Gardot
"Broken Strings"—James Morrison
"Dead Hearts" — Stars
"Black Mambo"— Glass Animals
"Love Love Love" – Of Monsters & Men
"Pleasure This Pain"—Kwamie Liv, Angel Haze
"Open" —Rhye
"Can't Help Falling In Love"—Ingrid Michaelson
"New Amsterdam"— Pink Martini
"Transformation"—The Cinematic Orchestra
"This Is What It Feels Like"— BANKS
"Le Vie En Rose" — Edith Piaf
"Leave Your Lover" – Sam Smith
"One Last Night" —Vaults
"Ne me quitte pas" — Carla Bruni
"Non, Je Ne Regrette Rien" – Edith Piaf
"Bleeding Love" —Leona Lewis
"Broken Strings" — James Morrison, Nelly Furtado
"Are You Hurting The One You Love?" — Florence + The Machine

"I Get Along Without You"— Chet Baker
"Dead Hearts" – Stars
"Baby I'm A Fool" — Melody Gardot
"Only You" – Matthew Perrymen Jones
"Painter Song" – Norah Jones
"Toes"– Glass Animals
"All About That Bass" – Meghan Trainor
"Desparado" —Diana Krall
"To Love Somebody"— Lindi Ortega

To everyone who read The Frenchman and understood that love is complicated and all the more beautiful for it.

Everything carries
Me to you
As if everything
That exists,
Aromas, light, metals,
Were little boats that said
Toward those isles of yours
That wait for me.

Pablo Neruda

Chapter One

The waiting area in front of the arrival gates at JFK airport was crowded with people waiting for loved ones. Before I was even fully past the sliding glass doors, a wonderful voice—rich and decadent like a spoonful of chocolate ganache—called out to me.

"Giselle, *mi amore!*"

Cosima Lombardi was one of the lucky ones. Easily the most beautiful person I had ever seen, she crossed the crowded space with strong strides, her waist-length onyx hair floating behind her and attracting the glances of everyone in the terminal. Oblivious to it, she enveloped me in her long, thin arms and pressed me close to her body so that I was flush against her famous curves. This was the way a woman like Cosima

Lombardi hugged – no boundaries and no embarrassment, just passion.

She pulled back to regard me with startlingly long-lashed eyes the color of melted butter. "I've missed you, *bambina*."

It was still hard to believe a woman like this could be my sister.

"I missed you too, Cosi." I dragged in a deep breath of her spicy scent and instantly felt at ease. "But you didn't have to pick me up. I thought you had some work thing tonight?"

As one of the hottest young models on the fashion scene since Karl Lagerfeld championed Cara Delevingne, she was constantly working.

She swished one caramel hand through the air, the gold bangles on her wrist just as musical as her mild Italian accent. "My sister comes before work, Gigi. You should know that. I haven't seen you in seven months and two weeks." Her frown was fierce, and it was obvious to me why photographers loved her face as devotedly as they did.

"Excuse me." A teenage girl, no older than fifteen, approached us with barely concealed excitement, dragging her embarrassed father behind her. "Are you Cosima Lombardi?"

My sister smiled genuinely at them and extended her long-fingered hand. "Hello, darling."

She winked at the awkward father and leaned over to give the strange girl a kiss on each cheek.

"Wow," the teenager gushed, and I smiled as my sister obligingly took a picture with both father and daughter.

There was no one in the world I loved more than my sister. It felt good to watch her interact with the people who approached her for her face and fame only to become enchanted with her warmth.

I was still smiling when she returned to my side and pressed a kiss to my cheek. "I'm sorry about that. Now, tell me absolutely *everything* I've missed in the past seven and a half months."

The shadow of Christopher crossed my thoughts, but I stubbornly refused to acknowledge it. There were only two other people in the world who knew the truth about why I was moving to New York after years abroad, and I intended to keep it that way, no matter how much I loved my sister.

"Your life is much more interesting, Ms. Sports Illustrated."

Cosima laughed at my teasing, and it felt good when she took my arm in hers to march me over to the baggage claim.

Yet I found myself casting my gaze around the airport in search of a certain man with electric blue eyes. I knew that he wasn't on the same flight, but I had done three laps of the plane just to make sure. For the rest of the journey, I had alternated between staring blankly at the seat in front of me and bursting into intermittent tears. The poor man beside me hardly fared better than Pierre on the flight from Paris. At least this time, the Dramamine tablets I had taken kept me from throwing my guts up. Still, I knew my eyes were probably still red from crying, and I was pale from lack of sleep. Thankfully, Cosima was too excited to see me to notice the telling signs.

"It was very weird," Cosima was saying. "The fact that people pay me just to pose for a camera is still strange to me. Do you know how much I got paid for that shoot?"

"Do I want to?" I winced, thinking about how much my studies at *L'École des Beaux-Arts* cost. Though I had been slowly climbing my way to success in the Parisian art scene, uprooting my life cross continents was bound to take its toll, and I was reluctant to rely once again on my sibling's generous financial support.

"Probably not," she agreed cheerfully and casually reached out to smooth my wayward hair. "Let's just say it was enough to put a down payment on a two-bedroom apartment in Tribeca!"

It still surprised her, I knew, that her face could buy such an opulent lifestyle for herself and our family. I would never understand what it had been like for her, running away to Milan from our small town in Southern Italy in order to raise enough money for us to leave our impoverished life behind. Sometimes, there was sadness in her eyes that I knew no one would ever reach.

"That's amazing, but you know I'm not surprised. You work so hard."

She made an unattractive sound and easily swept my luggage from the carousel. "Modeling isn't work. At least compared to what you do. I loved the print you sent me for my birthday. It's in the office of my new apartment."

We pushed out into the parking lot, and I was hit with a burst of bracing air. Greedily, I gulped in deep breaths because I knew the quality of the city air would be far from this clean, far from the pastry-scented, Seine-flavored breeze of my beloved Paris.

"I'm thrilled you're home, Gigi, but I think I should warn you." Cosima peeked at me from the corner of her eye as she handed my bags to a cab driver. He was an older, East Indian man with a particular smell and lovely brown eyes who stared at my gorgeous sister with nervous appreciation. "Elena is going to come down on you like the hammer of God for not coming home in four years."

"I saw her two years ago," I protested weakly, but I couldn't meet her eyes as we got into the yellow cab because I knew that was a lame excuse and so did she.

"I know you two have..." Cosima struggled for diplomatic words, but they did not come easily. "A distance between you, but you are sisters, and it hurts her that you never come home."

"I'm home now." But I leaned my head against her thin shoulder and sighed because I knew though she was talking about Elena, she was really speaking on behalf of the whole family. Four years was far too long, especially for a family as close as ours. "And I brought Elena her only vice, Bonnat chocolates. I took the train to Voiron for the weekend just to pick some up for her."

Our eldest sister was one of those women whose work was their life, which was the main reason, I think, that she liked America so much more than our native Italy. She had enrolled in law school as soon as the twins had enough money to bring her over from the motherland, and now, only four years later, she was an associate for one of the top firms in the country. For her to take time out of work to make room for a man in her life was a pretty big deal.

"So I guess she and this guy are pretty serious," I said with a massive yawn.

Cosima clucked and took my hand in her bronze one. We looked so dissimilar that no one ever believed we were related. The twins, Cosima and Sebastian, were mirror images of each other while Elena hovered somewhere in the middle with deep red-brown hair and stormy gray eyes similar to my own.

Cosima snorted inelegantly. "They've been together for nearly the entire time you've been gone. Elena wants them to adopt a baby."

"What about marriage?" I sat up, startled.

Marriage was a huge thing for our very traditional Italian mother. I couldn't imagine her reaction to a baby born out of wedlock.

"Daniel doesn't believe in marriage." She shrugged, but the sadness flashed in her eyes, and I wondered what she knew about the mysterious Daniel. "Mama might not understand that, but she loves Daniel enough to forgive him for it. Besides, it's already hard enough for Elena. You weren't here, but she had a meltdown when they realized she couldn't have children."

I pursed my lips and looked out the window at the passing blur of lights in the night. Elena had always wanted to be a mother. Of all of us, she was the most traditionally Italian, lusting after the family life at the cornerstone of the culture. It was ironic, I had always found, that she was the least maternal person I knew. Despite my reservations about my older sister, I felt deeply ashamed that I hadn't been there for her.

"Ah, the city." Cosima tugged my hand. "She won't welcome you, *bambina*, but I promise you, in time, you'll come to love her."

I sighed and rested my head against the stale-smelling headrest to watch the vibrant lights of New York City come at me. I had the feeling that Cosima was talking about more than the city. I hadn't realized until now how much I had missed in the past four years, and maybe, how hard it would be for me to come home.

*M*y anxiety fled the moment Cosima and I pulled up to Mama's townhouse on the border of Soho and Little Italy. It was an old brick affair with black trim and red flowers in the window boxes. Mama had lived there since she and Elena had moved to America four years ago, but I had only been inside once when Cosima had flown me in for Mama's restaurant opening.

As soon as Cosima opened the door, we were hit with the pungent smell of Mama's Italian cooking and the warmth of many bodies. We shuffled through the small entrance area and into the long living room where, to my slight horror and surprise, a small gathering of people stood and yelled, "Surprise!"

I laughed delightedly at Cosima as she propelled me into the many waiting arms. "I can't believe you did this!"

"Giselle."

My mother's voice, the thickly accented, heavy sound of it, froze me in my tracks, and without knowing why, tears came to my eyes. Hers was the only face I saw in the crowd, and I realized with sadness that I had forgotten what she truly looked like. The twins had inherited her coloring – the inky waves, and caramelized skin – but her figure, a classic hourglass like Sofia Loren but softened with good food and kind age, was like mine. A silent sob escaped me when she wound me up in her warm arms, and the scent of rosemary and sunshine enveloped me.

"Giselle, my French baby," she murmured over and over as she held me, her fingers pulling gently through my tangled hair.

"Mama," I breathed once before tucking my face into her hair.

We stood like that in the middle of a room full of people for a few minutes before I could compose myself. Though we had talked almost every day on the phone or by email, it felt unspeakably good to be with my mother again. As with my other siblings, she was everything to me, and it astonished me —now that I was home—that I could have ever been comfortable staying away.

"Quit hogging her, Ma." A rich voice, the male equivalent of Cosima's, but deeper, darker, resounded throughout the room, and with a shriek of joy, I threw myself from Mama's arms into Sebastian's.

He chuckled as he caught me and lifted me easily into his arms. "You've grown, *mia sorella*, and your hair..." He tugged a piece. "I think this is the first time I've seen you red since you were twelve."

I pulled back and smiled into his ridiculously handsome face. "God, I missed you."

Mama tapped me on the bottom and *tsk*-ed at my use of God's name, but Sebastian and I only laughed as he placed me once more on the floor.

Seb had visited me last year in Paris while he shot a movie, and it still wowed me that my two younger siblings were doing so well in their respective careers. Two years ago, Sebastian had written and starred in a low-budget indie movie about an impoverished Italian immigrant in New York during the 20s. It had won three awards at the Toronto International Film Festival, and now, my baby brother, the same person who used to run naked through the grimy streets of our home in Napoli, was a burgeoning movie star.

"I missed you too, *bambina*." Though I was older than the twins, they both called me baby because I was decidedly shorter than their towering heights.

"I like it better this way." Elena stepped forward, suddenly in front of me, her hands awkwardly extended for an embrace. "Your hair, I mean."

My eldest sister shared my coloring but little else. Her auburn hair was darker than mine, a red so black it was the color of wine, cut short and chic around her angular face, showcasing a creamy expanse of freckle-free skin and sloe eyes the color of storm clouds. Her body was lean and small-boned where mine was softer, curved like the other women in our family, and I knew, as her eyes fell over my breasts and tucked waist, that she felt a pang of isolation at seeing me again.

Whereas I took comfort from knowing that we looked at least vaguely similar, Elena saw only the things in me that made her different. She was the spitting image of our father, and we all knew that was hard on her, but I always found her heartrendingly beautiful anyway, somehow sharp and romantic all at once.

And though she was also the smartest person I knew, and despite my deep respect for her, our embrace was awkward. Something between us had wilted years ago, and I was still unsure how to recover it.

"You look beautiful too, Elena."

We both took a large step back after our hug, but the twins and Mama filed in around us.

Though I was tired and still mildly queasy from the long flight, it felt good to spend time with my family and the close group of friends they had made over the years. I met Sebastian's girlfriend, Kayla, who I had recognized immediately as a model for Calvin Klein. It wasn't serious, Seb assured me later as he refilled my wineglass, but she was a good lay.

There were also my mama's three best friends, all chefs like herself, and Cosima's friend, Erika, a Dutch model with cheekbones that could cut glass, and Elena's assistant, Beau, whom I had known for years and was closer to than Elena herself.

"So," Cosima began as she caught my arm and spun me through the doorway into a dark room off the main hall.

I had only visited the house once on my prior trip to America after the twins had officially moved Mama and Elena here three years ago, so the layout was still unfamiliar, but I thought we were in the guest bedroom.

"Tell me how things ended with the Frenchman," she said before she flicked the light on and gracefully collapsed on the deep red covered bed, patting the space next to her so that I would sit.

I sighed and placed my head next to hers on the pillow,

comforted by her spicy scent and the way she casually took my hand in hers. "I left."

"Oh?"

"I left before he woke up this morning. I just couldn't say goodbye. What was I going to say? Thanks for the hot sex and amazing adventures. I love you. Catch you never?"

I held myself still in the ensuing silence and resisted the urge to turn over to look into her expressive face for her response. Cosima was careful with her words—when she wasn't in a rage—and I knew she was meticulously shifting through them like individual grains of sand.

"I was worried you would love him. You didn't tell me much about him. I don't even know the mystery man's name, but I know you." Her thumb swept back and forth over my palm. "And intimacy for one so passionate cannot be untangled from love."

I scoffed. "You're the passionate one, Cosi."

She propped herself up on one elbow in order to glare down at me. "Can there be only one passionate woman in this family?"

I pursed my lips but said nothing.

"Exactly. Now tell me why you left like this. You took away his chance."

"His chance to what?" Break my heart in person?

"To ask you to go home with him."

She said it as if it was a simple choice, as if it was only natural that he would want to take a complete stranger home with him.

"He didn't know anything about me." But I winced even as I said it because I knew it wasn't true.

"You can know a person without knowing the trivialities."

"I don't even know where he lives. That's a pretty big omission."

She snorted inelegantly, and I couldn't help but smile at her.

Before Sinclair, I had never loved another human being like I loved Cosima. To me, she was the essence of beauty and life, full of volatile emotions and overwhelming love.

"You would have liked him."

Her expression softened, and she smoothed a piece of hair away from my face. "I'm sure I would have."

We both turned to look at the door as it creaked open, revealing Elena, who blinked owlishly at us cuddled on the bed before muttering an unintelligible apology as she closed the door.

"Get in here, Elena," Cosima scolded and jumped up to tug her forcibly into the room.

Our eldest sister looked uncomfortable but allowed herself to be maneuvered by Cosima so that we lay in a row with Cosima at our center, connecting us but tactfully giving us the space we needed from each other.

"We were talking about men."

"Ah."

"Giselle had a little fling in Mexico."

"Really?" Elena's brows almost touched her hairline. "That doesn't seem like you."

Anger rushed through me like a brush fire before I settled it with a deep, careful breath. "It isn't, but I'm glad I went through with it. I want to be bolder."

"There's a thin line between bold and reckless," Elena said in her schoolmarm voice, the same tone I had heard countless times as a child and the same tone I still heard every time I faced a potentially thrilling situation, always cautioning me to stay safe.

"Oh come on, Lena, it's only a harmless fling." Cosima winked one of her golden eyes at me. "And besides, you of all people can't blame a girl for falling for a pretty face."

"True."

"Daniel was a model for a few years." Cosima laughed at

the expression of prudish disapproval on our sister's face. "That's how we met."

I remembered Sinclair's terse expression when he brought up his own short-lived modeling career, and even though I didn't know his foster parents, a flare of hatred burned up my throat. I was grateful to Mama for not pressuring Cosima into the profession, but that didn't mean my little sister didn't carry invisible scars on her pretty gold skin.

"Wait till you meet him. Over the past few years, he's become even more stern." Cosima made a face, comically constipated looking, before dissolving into laughter. "If Elena didn't make him have Bran cereal every morning, I'd think he was having serious issues."

I laughed, scooting from the bed as I did so. I indicated pouring some wine and moved toward the door when I got their nods of approval. It was a rare conversation amongst our family that didn't include a bottle of wine.

"Very funny." Elena smiled indulgently at our favorite sibling. "I should get out there. He'll be here soon."

"Where was he this time?" Cosima asked, idly running a hand through Elena's short, elegantly curled tresses.

"Mexico," she said as I closed the door behind me and made my winding way back into the large kitchen at the front of the house.

It was an open space punctuated with a large wooden island over which Mama's prize copper pots and pans resided on a sort of rustic trellis. The cabinets were an unfinished birch, and the gleaming countertops were cool under my questing fingers as I sought out the clay pitcher of red wine Mama kept filled at all times.

I smiled at the sounds of laughter from the main room, and for the first time that night, I relaxed enough to stop worrying about Sinclair. The decision to leave him without a word would plague me for the rest of my life, I knew, but at least for this first month in a new city, surrounded by my loving family, I would have plenty of opportunities to take my mind off it.

I was pouring out three glasses of wine when I felt the prickle of awareness race up my spine. There was the soft fall of shoes crossing the wooden floors, and then the heat of another body pressed close to my back. Somehow, though I didn't know how it could be possible, when I turned around to face the stranger, it was my Frenchman.

"What are you doing here?" he snapped, his eyes blazing.

He looked at ease in the space. His crisp shirt was still pristine and tucked into his charcoal gray pants, but it was open at his throat to reveal a deep slice of brown skin. The cuffs were rolled hastily over his forearms, and his jacket hung across his shoulder casually as if he had just taken it off to relax. Even though I had just seen him this morning, the sight of him in my mama's kitchen threw into stark relief just how absurdly good-looking he was.

"Well?" he growled when I didn't immediately answer.

I couldn't believe he was here. My mind spun wildly, trying to confirm his presence. It seemed more probable that I was imagining him. I had the strongest urge to reach out and run my fingers through his glossy red-brown hair.

"What are you doing here?" I whispered, afraid he would disappear.

Confusion crossed his face but something like horror came over his features, and he croaked, "Elle... Giselle Moore."

I opened my mouth, but no noise would come out, probably because my thoughts kept running into themselves and collapsing. I cleared my throat, about to ask *something,* when Elena came in from the hall, obviously looking for him. "Oh good, you're here."

She walked briskly over to him and planted a perfunctory kiss on his cheek. He was still staring at me, wearing a stunned expression on his arresting features. And as Elena tucked herself into his side, I finally understood why.

"Giselle, this is my partner, Daniel Sinclair." Her voice was cool, carefully devoid of the Italian accent the rest of the family still maintained.

A loud sound thrummed through my ears, a crackling, creaking, and thunderous noise akin to a burning building falling in on itself. I hadn't known that heartbreak was audible, but—I swallowed hard against the rise of sobs in my throat—I discovered that, apparently, it was. I didn't have time to fully absorb the behemoth emotion because Elena stared at me as if I had grown three heads.

An awkward moment ensued where we all stared at each other but finally, my face flaming with embarrassment, I stepped forward with my hand extended.

"It's a pleasure to meet you."

"You are supposed to be a scrawny brunette," Daniel asserted as he quickly took my hand in his.

Even though the connection was brief, desire vibrated through my core. Irritated, I took a step forward and fought the urge to bare my teeth. I couldn't believe this was happening.

Things like this didn't happen in real life.

My heart crashed against my ribs, and I gritted my teeth as I said, "When I was eighteen maybe."

He plucked a framed photo off the windowsill behind him, demonstrating a familiarity with Mama's house that unnerved me.

Thrusting it into my hands, he said, "Eighteen?"

It was a picture of me two years ago, the last time Mama and Elena had visited me in Paris. We stood before the Eifel Tower, and I had to admit, it was easy to mistake me for someone else. My first few years in Paris, alone, after everything that had happened, were hard on me. Though somehow the family had scrounged up enough money to send me to school, there was little else to spend frivolously on clothes and accessories. I'd always been shy and awkward in my body, the ugly duckling in the gorgeous Lombardi flock. As a result, the twenty-one-year-old me was too skinny, pallid, and adorned with hair dyed an unnatural shade of black.

"Twenty-one," I demurred, unable to look up into the blue eyes bearing down on me.

"She went through an awkward phase, Daniel." Elena took a fresh glass from the cupboard and poured wine as if she was completely oblivious to the tension between us. "All girls do."

She and Cosima hadn't, but I didn't bother to say that.

"I've never seen a picture of you," I spoke quietly, desperately wanting this to be a private conversation. "I don't have Facebook."

"Who the fuck doesn't have a social media account?" he growled, his voice low and dangerous.

Shame flared through me because it was an omission that my mentor at *L'École des Beaux-Arts* had harped at me about, but growing up in Italy hadn't instilled a great love of technology in me, and honestly, the current social media frenzy kind of freaked me out.

I opened my mouth to snap at him defensively when I noticed that we were close, only a step away from being pressed up against each other as if we couldn't stand the space between our bodies even as we reeled from the shock of our reunion. My heart was fluttering madly, but I wasn't sure if it was with desire or some heady mixture of anger and fear.

I raised my voice and felt it liquefy with rage. "So, Daniel, you've been with my sister four years. What an amazing *commitment.*"

Suddenly, he loomed over me, and I lost my breath when I saw the electricity in his eyes. Thrilled to be sparring, I looked up at him, ready to volley a return when Elena came between us. She pressed a wineglass into Daniel's hand, frowning at him when he didn't immediately take it. Finally, with a scowl, he took the glass, put it deliberately down on the table, and poured himself a tumbler full of the brandy Mama kept hidden behind the flour in the pantry.

Elena watched him with concern but didn't say anything. Instead, she tilted the bowl of her wineglass around and around so that it caught the light and cast a red-tinted gleam against the white wall.

"So, you're back for good," he muttered over the rim of the crystal glass as he came to stand before me once again.

I nodded, even more sure of it than I had been before this exchange. I was giddy with nerves, hot with shame and lingering desire for the man who had been my sister's for the past four years.

"And you are going to help make that happen," Elena reminded him with a gentle hand on his tense arm and steel in her tone. "You promised to introduce her to Rossi, remember?"

Daniel's features softened when he looked down at her, as did hers, and I was struck by how perfectly compatible they seemed. Obviously, they shared a powerful ambition and an iron-hard exterior that was impenetrable to most but the very, very lucky.

I swallowed hard. I knew Sinclair better than that.

"I'm sorry, Lena, I'm exhausted. Of course, I will." He patted her hand and smiled tightly.

Her smile was wider, and I noticed how full and red her mouth was. "Mexico was hard?"

He nodded and ran a hand through his thick russet mane. Just last night, my hands had pulled on those silky strands as I climaxed around him, hoarsely calling his name. "It was necessary."

"Well, I'm glad it's finished." She turned to me and stepped closer against his side for comfort. "It's so good to have you home after so many years, Giselle. But I have a case going into mediation tomorrow, and I'm afraid I have to be off."

We embraced each other again, and Daniel snared my gaze over her shoulder. We stared intently at each other with my heart thrumming against Elena's as if we could somehow discern the beginning of our inexplicable bond and sever it at the base.

"It really is nice to have you home," Elena murmured once more as she moved away, and I caught the flicker of insecurity in the quirk of her lips.

"I'll get your coat," Daniel offered, already strolling purposely across the room, but she stopped him with a tired wave.

"You just got back, Daniel, and Mama made your favorite Kobe meatballs. Stay." She walked over to him and placed a tender kiss on the corner of his lips. "I'll see you at home."

Daniel's eyes barely flickered my way, his intractable jaw clenched before he nodded and pressed a kiss to her forehead. "I won't be late."

She nodded. "I'll be up."

After a quick glance and half a step in my direction, she pushed her arms into a gorgeous black trench coat and left through the front door without looking back.

And I was left with the one man in the world I most wanted to avoid.

Chapter Two

Obviously, he wasn't pleased. He stared at me with a severe scowl, and it disturbed me that I felt a shiver bite into the sensitive skin at the small of my back. I could hear the murmur and explosion of passionate chatter from the other room, but it was muffled in my ears as I strained to remember every detail of our week together. There must have been clues, but my lust-saturated memories were hazy. The only thing that kept coming to mind was Sinclair, his laughter as we rolled through the waves, his cool commands as he directed me for his pleasure, the way he had held me so tenderly our last nights together. My eyes stung with tears and my throat burned, but I kept my jaw locked against the emotions, only taking a moment to acknowledge the irony of my constraint. I had learned it from Sinclair.

"Jesus Christ," Daniel Sinclair groaned. "I should have known."

"I can't believe this is happening," I murmured, and my voice came to me as if I was underwater.

He paced away from me, putting the counter between us before he faced me again.

"I don't know what to say."

"Then don't say anything," he growled, still unwilling to look at me. "This is too fucked for words."

My mind was whirring, stuttering, and smoking like a failing engine, making my eyes tear. I coughed to clear my throat and tried to assemble some rational thought. "I don't know what to say."

He spun around and swooped down on me, his fists clenched by his sides. "You ran off."

"Excuse me?"

"You left this morning without a word, Elle." His breath hissed through his clenched teeth, and he took a large step away from me. "Not a bloody word."

"I thought it would make it easier."

"And is this what you had in mind?" He glowered at me, those striking brows pulled low over his blazing eyes.

He took my breath away, even in moments like this.

"I didn't know." I shrugged, trying to ease the load of guilt off my shoulders. "I didn't expect to see you ever again."

Something powerful darkened those blue eyes I had grown to love so much, and I held my breath, wondering if my words had hurt him. But before I could say something, he was in front of me again, his cool mask in place.

"Giselle?" Sebastian called from the other room.

We leaped apart, and I let out a shaky laugh, pulling a hand through my hair self-consciously.

"Be out in a second!"

"We can't do this here," Sinclair said.

I fisted my hands on my hips and corrected him, "We can't do this *anywhere*. You are dating my sister!"

"I'm aware of that. But we need to talk about things before we pretend this never happened."

Never happened?

My heart faltered and almost gave out. How could I forget about him? I caught a glimpse of one of the many family photos lining the wall beside the massive dining room table. Sinclair stood with his arms around Elena and Cosima, his smile small and tight. Anger surged through my blood, but I was already so weak with guilt that my voice wasn't as condemning as I wanted it to be.

"You cheated on my sister, Sinclair. Or should I call you Daniel?"

"It takes two to cheat, Giselle."

His dark eyes narrowed, and I flinched away from the truth of his words.

"I'm not the one with the partner!" I bit out between my gritted teeth.

"Doesn't matter," he said in that damn slippery smooth voice. "You knew there was a woman. You just didn't know who it was."

Guilt surged through me, tripling my anger. I stalked toward him, my eyes glinting as I caged him in the corner of the kitchen.

"Are you saying this is some kind of lesson in karma?"

He cocked his head slightly, a piece of burnished hair falling into his eyes. "Yes."

"How can you be so fucking philosophical and calm right now?" I hissed.

I had never been so full of poison in my life. My thoughts were gathering speed, hurling into my conscience, sending straight shots of shame directly into my heart. I reached out to grab him and noticed my hand shaking.

He stared at it too before dragging his eyes across the rest of my body. My face flamed as each pass of his gaze evoked a memory of his skin against mine, and when his eyes finally met mine, they were bright with something other than hatred or horror.

The murmur of voices grew louder, and I heard Mama heralding people into the kitchen to search for me. Sinclair looked at the door, his jaw hardening again. He took a bold step toward me so that my breasts just brushed his lower chest. Despite myself, desire furled deep in my belly.

He stared at me for only a second, but to my sluggishly beating heart, it felt like a lot longer. I sucked in a quick breath when he lifted his hand and brought it with astonishing tenderness to my overheated cheek, dragging his knuckles down the slope of it in a gesture I had come to yearn for.

"I never stood a chance." He smiled thinly and brushed his lips against my forehead so lightly I couldn't be sure he actually touched me.

When he stepped away, I trembled with a heady combination of longing, regret, and anger, but before I had a chance to voice it, Sinclair was striding from the room. He collected his coat in the main hall, and I heard him run into Cosima. They spoke too swiftly to hear, in voices too low for me to understand. I was still standing there when the front door closed behind him, and Sebastian strolled into the room with Mama on his arm.

They both took one look at me and frowned. Mama rushed to my side and settled me against her soft body, cooing softly in familiar Napoli dialect while Sebastian immediately refilled the empty wineglass beside me on the counter. It was Elena's, but I didn't protest when he pressed it into my hand. My gut clenched when I realized how much more we had unintentionally shared. Now that Sinclair was gone, I felt hollow and rotten like an old house creaking in a tunneled wind.

Cosima swept into the room with a large smile that immediately dropped into a scowl when she took in the room's temperature. She glided over to my side and took my face between her warm, dry palms.

"She said something to you, didn't she?"

Oh God, I almost moaned. Of course, they would think Elena had said something to upset me. It was usually the case. But now, after what I had done, it hit me like Thor's hammer in the stomach.

"No." I tilted my face into her left hand and tried to smile. "Jet lag."

There was silence in the kitchen as my family debated whether or not to press me. They knew better than to believe my deception, but I was hoping they would accept it anyway.

Cosima pursed her lips and shared a look with Sebastian, but it was Mama who turned me in her arms and hugged me tight again.

"You go home with Cosima now, *bambina*, unless you want to stay here with me?" She pulled back to look down at me. Her beauty settled the turmoil currently twisting my stomach into knots.

"No," I murmured, because even though I wanted to be alone, I knew Cosima would be upset if I spent my first night home without her. "I'll go."

Mama nodded and pressed a kiss to each cheek. "You will feel better in the morning. Come by the restaurant when you have a minute, *si*?"

My acceptance turned into a squeak as Sebastian lifted me easily in his arms and squeezed me tight.

"I'm glad you're finally home, Gigi."

Tears pricked the back of my eyes, so I buried my face in his neck and clung to him hard before he let me down. He smiled down at me with those large amber eyes but I could tell it was just a mask so that I wouldn't pull away from his searching gaze. He wanted to know what was wrong, and it went against his nature not to question me further. The only reason he was letting me go at all was because he believed Cosima would press me for answers.

I said goodbye to the rest of the party, claiming jet lag as the cause for my early departure, and left with my sister. We were quiet in the cab, and Cosima's uncharacteristic silence made my distress all the more acute. A part of me wanted her to hit me so hard with questions that I cracked open and spilled all my secrets. It would feel so good to come clean, confess about the mess my life had become, but I knew that it would be selfish to indulge myself. Elena was our sister and expecting Cosima to keep my secret was asking her to pick sides.

Besides, I was more than a little afraid she wouldn't be on mine.

She watched me as we entered the tall, elegant building near Central Park West. I took in the sweeping lobby with caramel-colored marble floors, and the older man with brilliant white hair manning the desk. It was a soothing, sophisticated place that didn't seem to suit my sister, but I realized the last time I had really spent any quality time with her was back in Italy at our small house on a wild plot of salty land in Napoli. She was a model now and a successful one at that.

We traveled up to the eighth floor, and I knew she had made a deliberate choice to live on this level as it was her lucky number. For some reason, I held my breath while she opened the large door at the end of a short hall. I was worried that her apartment would be much like the building, aesthetically pleasing but impersonal, glossed over with glamour instead of warm with personality. The idea that I might not know my sister like I had always assumed made my skin prickle.

I let out a sigh of relief as soon as I stepped inside. Large black bookcases stuffed with novels sectioned off a small office behind the living room where twin chocolate brown leather chairs and a mahogany sofa bracketed a large fireplace. The walls were painted a deep warm red, and the dark wood floors extended all the way back into the kitchen, where I could see glass-fronted cabinets and a dedicated shelf overflowing with herbs. It was so true to the Cosima I knew, brilliant and warm and secretly introverted, that the sight of it instantly settled my stomach.

"You like it." She grinned at me and slipped off her ridiculously tall heels, putting them in the mirrored closet beside the door.

"I love it," I agreed.

"I bought it over a year ago, and I've been slowly trying to make it my own," she admitted. "I had to flirt shamelessly with the building committee in order to paint the walls—they were beige." She made a face, prompting me to laugh. "But I think it's coming along nicely."

She took my purse and jacket from me, hanging it up amid the myriad of designer items in the closet before taking my large suitcase in hand.

"Hades is around here somewhere," she said over her shoulder as she led me through the apartment to the hallway where my bedroom would be. "He can be a little hostile with strangers."

Hades was her black cat, a feline with more attitude than his mistress.

"Oh, Cosi." I gasped when I saw my room. Blues and lavenders dominated the scene, inspired by the massive painting over the white wrought-iron bed. It was one of my own pieces that I had sent to her after my first gallery showing. Tears brimmed over my lashes, my emotions unable to take another hit, no matter how slight.

"I decorated with you in mind. I know you want to find your own place, but I want you to feel at home here, and if you want to stay, well"—she shrugged—"that would be fine too."

I laughed weakly and hugged her. "*Sei carinissima.*"

"I'm not sweet at all. I just love you."

There was no *just* about it, so I squished her harder.

"And when you are ready to tell me what happened with you and Elena, I hope you'll come to me. No matter what, I'm yours. I'm here for you," she whispered, stroking a hand down my hair.

I only nodded as the tears came freely, dripping soundlessly down my face.

Chapter Three

I had made a list on the plane. A list of things I had to accomplish my first week in the city. But at eleven o'clock on my first day in New York City, I sat at Cosima's kitchen counter staring blankly at the paper, my eyes stuck on the first item lining the top.

Contact Elena's boyfriend about DS Galleries.

Cosima had left at the crack of dawn for a photo shoot in Central Park, her beautiful face bare of makeup but glowing even at four thirty in the morning. I had shuffled out of my room on two hours of restless sleep and pressed a kiss to her cheek. At the time, I was happy to have the morning to myself, but now, as the afternoon crept closer, I found myself still paralyzed in my chair.

I tried telling myself a million different things. That I

couldn't love a man I had only known for a week, that it didn't matter because I couldn't love him enough to hurt my sister, that even *that* didn't matter because he didn't feel the same way about me and how awkward would it be at family dinners knowing that he had done things to me and I to him that I had never dreamed about before meeting him.

I tried to luxuriate in the love I felt for my sister, but the material felt rough, abrasive against my skin. Elena and I hadn't been close in a long time, and I wasn't sure if that should alleviate my guilt or deepen it.

But it didn't matter, and honestly, I knew no rationale would make the problem go away nor my overactive feelings about it or him. I was stuck, well and truly stuck between a rock and a hard place.

I was just about to drag myself out of the apartment to walk aimlessly around New York, hoping to absorb my new hometown, when the landline trilled. I hesitated for a second before answering and immediately regretted it.

"Giselle Moore? This is Margot Silver." I recognized her professional disdain immediately—Sinclair's personal assistant was hard to forget. "I'm calling on behalf of DS Galleries. We would like to set up an appointment for you to meet with our curator Isa Rossi at your earliest convenience."

Was she going to pretend she didn't know who I was? I swallowed loudly before answering, "My schedule is relatively open as I've just moved to the city. I can be available whenever is convenient for Mrs. Rossi."

"Very well." Her tone had warmed fractionally. "She has a cancelation tomorrow at one o'clock. If you'll come to the gallery, she will see you then. Oh, and you may want to think about investing in a cell phone and joining the modern age so that it is easier to get in touch with you."

My hand was slightly unsteady as I replaced the old-fashioned phone back on its cradle. I let out a whooshing breath and dragged my hands through my hair. Sinclair had kept his promise to Elena to introduce me to the New York City art world, but he wouldn't be doing it himself, that much was sure. It was for the best, of course, but my heart still panged pitifully in my chest as I stalked into the bathroom to shower before lunch with my family.

The streets of New York were not at all like the streets of Paris. The French city was the most visited in the world, yet even at the height of tourist season in the summer, it did not feel half as crowded as New York City on any given day. I was thrilled by the bustle as soon as I descended from Cosima's quiet apartment. My senses tingled as they were assaulted with every smell from bagels to smoke and choking exhaust, and my eyes flitted across hundreds of beautiful, varied faces. My dilemma was momentarily trivial in comparison to the hugeness of New York, and I allowed myself to bask in humanity.

Unfortunately, as soon as I reached Osteria Lombardi in Soho, my good mood gave way to anxiety. I had been inside my mother's restaurant only once before when Cosima had flown me in for the big opening party. So, it felt strange to stand in front of the brick façade, staring at the family name I had forsaken scrawled elegantly across the massive glass window beside the red-painted door.

I wrung my hands together as I realized the truth of my situation. A childhood of poverty and frequent, violent visits from the mafia had adhered my siblings, Mama, and me together like paint on canvas, but after I left Italy years ago, I had purposely kept my emotional distance from them. I had needed the space to recover from Christopher.

Now, I was paying the price. I had no idea what was going on with my siblings, and worse, I hadn't even known Elena's goddamn boyfriend.

I dragged a deep handful of city air into my lungs and opened the door.

Soft Italian opera floated on the fragrant air, and the murmur of late lunch diners lent the rustic, elegant interior a homey feel. The exposed brick walls were lined with shelves full of Italian wines, and the wood-beamed ceiling perfectly matched the dark chocolate stain of the table and chairs.

Loud throaty laughter drew my attention to the back of the long rectangular room to the table where the Lombardi family sat.

"Giselle," the twins and Mama called out at the same time, their musical voices chiming.

Mama got up to wrap me in her sweet dough-scented arms, and I felt myself relaxing a bit. It had been a long time since my mother held me.

"I order for you," she said as I settled beside my brother.

He quickly placed a kiss on my hand in greeting. I watched him check the screen of his buzzing phone and smile roguishly.

Mama swatted at him with a fierce frown. "You know the rules, *patatino*. Phone down."

Seb chuckled, but his phone disappeared with a cool sleight of hand. "I'm a grown man, Mama. I think we can stop with the nickname."

I cocked my head playfully and squinted at him. "I don't know. You do kind of look like a potato."

He bristled because his beauty wasn't something he took for granted, but he surprised me by saying, "That is Mr. Potato Head to you. Who do you think they modeled those suckers from?"

Elena remained absent as the food was brought out, and we all tucked into Mama's delicious meal, but I decided not to remark on it. Instead, I teased Cosima about the makeup she still wore from her animal print-themed shoot in Central Park, and Sebastian told me about the development of a film he was intent on directing and starring in. After three glasses of wine and a heaping plate of Mama's pillow-soft ricotta gnocchi, I felt as if I had never left the family table.

"Where is she?" I asked because my tongue was loosened from the Chianti.

They didn't have to ask whom I was speaking about.

"Appointment with the adoption firm."

I looked sharply at Sebastian. How had I forgotten that Elena wanted to adopt? My stomach flipped, and I placed a hand over my mouth, certain I might be sick.

"How far along are they?"

I could feel Cosima's careful gaze as Seb answered. "Early days. They've been approved but no matches yet."

"No wedding?"

Cosima had mentioned over the phone that Sinclair didn't believe in marriage, but perversely, I wanted to hear them talk about him.

"He is a handsome man, but the family idea is"—Mama pursed her lips as she fought to translate her words into English—"broken. Marriage for him is a cage."

"And a baby isn't?" My voice was remarkably calm even though my heart thudded loudly inside my rib cage. Any sister would ask questions about the boyfriend, so I didn't think I was being too conspicuous.

Mama shrugged. "They do it differently in America."

"He's French," I automatically corrected her.

My nails dug into the skin above my knees as punishment for my stupidity.

"I know what you mean, though," Cosima said. Her golden stare made sweat fizzle under my skin. "Honestly, I think that he wants a baby to please Elena. He would do anything to make her happy."

I was careful to school my features into a pleasant but unconcerned expression and gave a noncommittal, "Mmm."

"I'm not a fan."

"Sebastian!" Mama scolded him, slapping the back of his hand even as her wide mouth smiled.

He winced and rubbed his hand dramatically, but I wondered if he wasn't delighted with her. He and Cosima had been without parents for so long that I thought it would either be irritating or incredible to have a mother, especially such an involved one like Mama, in their lives again.

"What? I don't. He does not know how to properly love a woman. If he did, Elena would be a much happier woman, no?"

"Have you ever thought that might be Elena's problem and not his?" I asked before I could help myself. When everyone's eyes swiveled to me, I swallowed harshly. "I mean, you can't rely on other people for your own happiness."

I really needed to try to remember that. I'd been walking around like my former self, the pre-Sinclair Giselle who smiled only timidly and still felt like a scrawny, unappealing youngster. Just because I couldn't have him didn't mean that I had to revert to that. I had fallen in love with two people that week in

Mexico, Sinclair and the new version of myself, one that I was genuinely proud of.

I sighed into the contemplative silence at the same time that Cosima did, and we both smiled at each other.

"I've known him for years. You forget that I introduced him to Elena, and I wouldn't have done that unless I had faith in his character," Cosima said as she glared at her male equivalent, but he only shrugged casually, throwing a wink my way when it only made Cosima more irritated.

"Me? I like him. He is very cold. I can say this? No hugs for him, you understand?" Mama tried to explain even as she stroked my hair, twirling it around her fingers and draping it against her palm. She had always loved my red hair, and I knew she was happy I had stopped dying it black.

I thought about the Sinclair I knew and tried not to take away too much hope that the warmth I had experienced with him was a one-off, reserved not even for his girlfriend but just for me, his weeklong mistress, his holiday affair. He had *wanted* me to love him, making love to me until the wealth of my affection for him was all I felt, all I could articulate. Why had he done it?

I couldn't decide now who the villain was. Me, for pursuing him, for allowing myself to love another woman's partner, or him, the gorgeous devil who had so thoroughly, so easily seduced the simple European girl on the way to a fresh start?

"I'm late," Elena announced by way of apology as she slid into the vacant chair at our table. The rich material of her cashmere coat whispered as she swung it off her delicate shoulders and around the back of the chair. In a high-necked lace blouse and stovepipe black pants, she looked like an Italianate Audrey Hepburn.

"Yes, and I don't believe I forgive you," Cosima warned.

A reluctant grin tapped Elena in the cheek as she immediately moved forward to place warm kisses on her youngest sister's cheeks.

"Better."

This time she actually laughed, a sound I was pretty sure I hadn't heard in years.

"You are such a dork." She shook her head and reached over to take Mama's hand in hers. "Seb, how are you and flavor-of-the-week?"

He snorted but didn't take offense. "How did you know her name is Flavor?"

"Easily, all your bimbos clearly had unintelligent parents. That kind of stupid is genetic."

"Just because they aren't rocket scientists doesn't mean they aren't highly imaginative in... other areas."

"Slut."

"Prude."

"*Ragazzi!*" Mama scolded tiredly. "Enough. I must go to the kitchen and help men there. You sit, Elena, and eat, *si*?"

"*Si, Mama,*" we chorused.

"What happened to Savannah? I thought I saw you two talking the other day outside your building." Cosima asked as she topped off our glasses of rich red wine.

Sebastian's reaction was immediate. His thick straight brows crashed down over his molten eyes like boots stomping out a fire.

"Nothing."

"Who is Savannah?" I batted my eyelashes at my brother. "Your lover?"

"Shut up."

"Oh, someone is touchy." Elena frowned at her nails, smoothing down a slightly ragged cuticle on her otherwise delicate and perfectly manicured hands. "And I don't see why. Savannah Richardson is one of the most well-respected women in the city, Sebastian, hardly a dirty little secret."

He bared his teeth, and—I almost couldn't believe it— growled.

"Oh right," Elena continued smoothly. "She is recently married, isn't she? To some hotshot Hollywood producer."

"Elena," Cosima warned softly, her shoulder pressed hard into Sebastian's side in an effort to stabilize him.

"Fine, I'll just say, it's probably for the best. She should be with someone her own age. Tell me, what is it like to have sex with someone the same age as Mama?"

"Elena," Cosima snapped this time, but it was too late.

Sebastian was out of his chair, looming over the table in Elena's calm face.

"I think you've proved to all of us that age doesn't equal maturity." He ripped the leather jacket from the back of his chair and took a moment to stare at her, his features softening slightly. "And you would not be nearly as cruel if you understood love yourself."

"Sebastian," I called after him as he stormed away from the table, the consummate actor, exquisitely dramatic.

"What is wrong with you?" Cosima asked, somehow keeping her irritation firmly under control. I was surprised, to say the least. The teenage girl I had lived with years ago was not capable of such self-restraint.

Elena shrugged, causing Cosima to bare her teeth and repeat her question with more force.

She sighed and scraped her dark hair behind her ears. "Daniel has been acting strange since he came back from Mexico."

I stilled, every muscle in my body paralyzed by my inner conflict, the half of me that wanted them to know and the other half of me that was terrified to death of the discovery.

"I'm not sure if he really wants this baby," she continued.

"Oh Lena." Cosima reached across the table and clasped her hands. "You know how Daniel is. He will love the baby just as soon as it arrives. Abstract thought isn't his biggest strength."

"True."

"He'll be a great dad."

My sisters stared at each other for a second before collapsing into giggles. I bristled a bit at their humor, though I *did* think Sinclair would be a great dad.

"What about you, Giselle?" Elena turned to me. "What was your first impression of my partner?"

Partner? What a stuffy way to refer to a lover, reducing it to something almost platonic and certainly boring. I took a deep breath, realizing that I was unfairly judging my sister for how she related to *her* boyfriend. Hers, not mine. It wasn't my place to even think about them, let alone allow my bias to further taint my strained relationship with my sister.

"He seemed..." I paused to consider—gorgeous, enigmatic, too controlled? "Professional, maybe a bit aloof."

Elena nodded, satisfied and maybe even a little proud of my impression, but Cosima scoffed. "If you met his parents, you would understand."

"His parents?" I assumed he no longer saw any of his foster parents.

"Willa and Mortimer Percy."

I frowned, the names tickling something half-forgotten at the back of my brain.

"Mortimer Percy is the governor of New York," Elena explained with quiet pride.

My mind bubbled and spun like soapy water between my ears. I took a breath and then another one. Had Sinclair *lied* to me?

"I thought, I mean, I think someone mentioned to me that he was in the foster system."

"Oh yes, until he was sixteen. They found him in France, you know? Willa is with Looking Glass Model Agency, and she spotted him on the streets of Nice. A few days later, they were taking him back home to America." Elena sighed happily. "It really is an amazing story."

And total bullshit. I was certain of it. Though it did make sense that this Willa woman would work in the fashion agency if Sinclair had been telling the truth about his time spent as a model.

"He modeled for a time, but after a year or so, the Percy's decided to adopt him."

"Elena's making it sound like this fairy tale, but really, they are not good in the heart, you know?" Cosima stroked the stem of her wineglass, staring into the bowl as if it were a crystal ball. "They found Cage too but didn't bring him back to America."

"Don't be so dramatic, Cosi. They paid for his living expenses and visited him. Cage is just ungrateful." Elena sniffed.

"I don't know what your problem is with Cage, but you need to get over it. He's practically family."

"Oh, so we are letting just anyone into the family these days?"

"Elena," I protested softly because I could see Cosima was gearing up for a throwdown.

Her lips thinned, and she reached out to pat my hand as she said, "I wasn't talking about you, Giselle. Obviously, the twins and Mama are very happy you're in New York now."

Her words slammed against the soft spot in my rib cage and cracked bone. My breath whooshed out of body, but I shook my head when Cosima leaned forward to take a bite out of our older, callous sister even though my own rage was burning the back of my tongue.

I knew there were reasons behind Elena's attitude; excuses and psychological scars that could provide invaluable context to her insults. I knew it, but I didn't care. The bottom line was, I didn't like her, and I could barely remember a time when I had.

When we were younger, it was easier for me to take the passive-aggressive put-downs, the scathing reminders of my flaws. But it was different now, not least of all because I was in love with her boyfriend.

It made the situation so messy I could only stare at it, unwilling to dirty my hands even if it meant cleaning it up. I hated my sister, and I was in love with her boyfriend. Even if the two had once been separate entities, they couldn't be mutually exclusive now that I had made their connection. Once combined, they yielded an infinite number of questions, but the most important one flashed before my eyes like a neon For Sale sign.

Was hating my sister justification for ruining her life?

Chapter Four

Osteria Lombardi was three blocks from DS Galleries, and I made it a point to walk past the artful stone façade on my way home from the restaurant. I even peered in the windows, but I told myself I wasn't looking for anything in particular. A massive abstract painting done in brilliant glistening oils hung over the reception, and before I had made a conscious decision, I was through the wide doors into the cool interior.

The receptionist smiled as I approached, but she left me in silence to stare at the piece for a moment longer.

Anyone who inquired at the front desk was immediately submerged in the painting. I was underwater looking up through layers of cerulean, lazuline, and pastel blues to the heart of the sky where it winked white and yellow as if behind a pane of mottled glass. It was deeply disorientating yet strangely serene, imbuing me with the kind of calm that comes from holding your breath underwater for a little too long.

When I finally blinked, surfacing with a physical shiver, the young woman behind the desk smiled kindly at me. It didn't surprise me that she was used to such a reaction. It was a stunning piece.

Since I was already there, I strolled through the gallery, a collection of large and larger rooms made cohesive by the exhibits on display. Though there were some stunning pieces, including an array of weepy watercolors depicting haunting scenes of solitude, there were no more paintings like the one in the reception.

"Who is the artist?" I asked when I rounded back to the front room.

The petite Asian woman smiled, but the sound of approaching footsteps distracted us both from her answer. I felt overheated and conspicuous in my green dress, like Gatsby's beacon. My embarrassment was short-lived, though, because it was true. I had come into the gallery hoping to see him, and my wish had been granted.

"Sinclair," I greeted calmly as I turned around, proud of my composure.

It shook dangerously when I took in the tall, cool sight of him standing before me with his hands in the pockets of his gray tweed pants. He was dressed casually, the sleeves of his oxford blue shirt rolled up, and his suit jacket disposed of to reveal a gorgeous flannel vest cut perfectly to his tapered torso. My mouth was parched by the time my eyes reached his, the blue of his irises smoky with an indecipherable emotion.

"I wondered if you might stop by."

I blinked, which only made his beautiful lips twitch slightly in amusement.

"Thank you, Eddie." He nodded toward the receptionist. "I'll take it from here."

Without turning to see if I followed, Sinclair strode briskly down the hallway that I had just emerged from. I hesitated. Now that I was actually in his presence again, my determination to tell him off wavered precariously. Just the sight of him, the feel of him in the same room as me, unbound me from the tight moral constraints I knew were necessary.

"He wants you," the Asian woman explained, startling me out of my blank stare.

"Excuse me?"

"He wants you to follow him," she explained kindly, and I realize she was probably used to clients staring dumbstruck after her hunky boss. "His office is on the top floor of the building. I'll let his assistant know you are on your way up."

"Isn't that office space?"

She smiled sympathetically at me. "Yes, for Mr. Sinclair's primary business, Faire Developments."

I felt nauseous. How could I know so little about him when every thud of my heart seemed to echo his name? I smiled tightly, thanking her in a small voice before following Sinclair's path down the hallway to the large chrome elevator.

The doors whooshed open on the sixtieth floor to reveal a large reception done in cool grays and blues and punctuated by the large glass-fronted desk displaying the name of the company in bold navy letters, *Faire Developments*.

It wasn't a genuine surprise. After all, I had known in Mexico that he was there to buy a failing resort, but every piece of information I garnered still felt like a nail in the coffin of our relationship. *Relationship*? God, who was I kidding here? There was no relationship between us, but foolish ex-lovers and a long future as potential in-laws stretched ahead of me. I placed a hand on my queasy stomach and straightened my spine, determined to bowl over the awkwardness between us no matter what.

His assistant, a surprisingly young man with brilliant red hair and a smattering of large russet freckles, waved me through with a large grin, and I wondered briefly where the frosty Margot was. I followed the fluid sound of Sinclair's voice around the corner to a set of slightly open frosted glass doors.

I hesitated in the doorway, watching him stare out the wall of glass at the street, the pale autumn light beautifully highlighting the planes of his face. He was speaking Spanish, and it took me a second to notice the black Bluetooth headphone in one ear. I was just about to leave, painfully uncomfortable, when those blue eyes punctured me, pinning me to the wall like a preserved butterfly.

"*Sit,*" he mouthed. And there was no room for disobedience in his stern expression.

I sat but made sure to level a hefty glare his way as I did so.

While I waited, I tried to distract myself by studying the office space. It continued in the modern aesthetic of the rest of the building, but there was warmth in the white, brown, and cream color scheme, the depth of the leather chairs, and matching low-level couch. The entire length of the far wall was glass as well as most of the back wall by the chairs. It offered a stunning panorama of the bustling city streets and made the office seem like the Crow's Nest of the civilized world. There was a conspicuously blank space suited for a painting behind his desk, and not a single photograph graced his work surface. I searched for any sign of the man I knew and found none.

I smoothed the hem of my short skirt over my thighs and tried to steady my breath. It was nerve-racking to sit in front of him like that as if I was a lowly student waiting for an interview and not an angry ex-lover with righteous concerns. But each moment I spent sitting there diluted my fury. I wondered if he had planned for exactly that.

When I tilted my head up to see if he had finished the call, he was looking at me with his hands folded across his desk. I didn't know how long he had been done with his conversation, but I also didn't really care. The moment our eyes met, whatever resolve I might have amassed went up in flames.

"Giselle."

Hearing his voice caress my full name did something funny to my pulse.

"Daniel," I said with considerably more venom.

He stared at me impassively from over his steepled fingertips, and I couldn't help but notice what a picture he made, the handsome prince on his urban throne. For some reason, the image made me remember my previous anger.

"So, you came to have a mature conversation about this."

My eyes bugged out of my head, and it took me a second to find my voice. "Are you kidding me? I came here to tell you to *go to hell!*"

His lip twitched infinitesimally, just enough to let me know he was joking with me.

"This is hardly the time to develop a sense of humor, Sinclair," I chastised him, but when he broke out in a small boyish grin, I couldn't help but smile back at him.

"There is a thin line between comedy and tragedy." He opened his steepled hands wide.

I shook my head. "I have no idea how you can be so calm right now. We betrayed Elena."

The light in his eyes flickered and dulled as his gaze turned out the window. He was silent for a few long minutes, but I didn't know what to say to fill the quiet.

When he finally turned back to me, Sinclair, the businessman, was gone, and I was once again faced with the man I had grown to know in Mexico.

"The irony isn't lost on me, Giselle, and of course, I know the information hurts you." He leaned forward, bracing his forearms on the desk, his eyes blazing. "You think it's easy for me? I feel the same guilt you do."

I was shaking my head without even realizing it. "Then how can you even ask me to be here?"

Didn't he feel the same physical ache that I did, looking at him, being in the same room, the same city, on the same god-forsaken continent?

I was speaking before I even fully understood what I wanted to say. "How is it possible that you didn't recognize me?"

I knew it wasn't fair to blame the situation on him, even though he had decided to cheat on Elena, but it felt good to unleash some of the raging emotions trapped in my chest.

"You were a scrawny, timid brunette in every family photo, and honestly, Elena doesn't speak about you very much."

I flinched from his words even though I should have guessed as much.

Sinclair's eyes were sharp against my skin, slicing through my mask until I felt raw and abraded. "I can live with the guilt, Giselle, and I know what I want. The only question is, what do *you* want?"

"What do you mean, you know what you want?" I whispered, almost afraid to ask but willing to delay answering his question by any means possible.

How was I supposed to respond to that, anyway?

Well, Sinclair, I love you, and the thought of spending the rest of my life seeing you with my sister, loving her, starting a family with her... I forcibly swallowed the sob that rose in my throat. No, of course I couldn't say that to him. Not only was he dating my sister, but even when I had bared my soul to him our last night in Mexico, he remained stoic. It was clear that he wanted to resolve the situation as quickly and cleanly as possible. I wondered, with sudden dread, if he would suggest I move back to Paris.

His lips flat-lined as he stared at me. "Why did you sneak out that morning?"

"It seemed like the easiest option," I muttered, suddenly embarrassed by my flight, especially in light of the fact that he was constantly questioning my maturity.

"I see." His words landed heavily on my ears. "Well, if you want things to be easy, Giselle, I have nothing to offer you but avoidance. Is that what you want? To coexist in this family, see each other at dinners and birthdays while ignoring the chemistry between us?"

No! my mind screamed, but I only shook my head slightly. "That does seem like the best option."

My eyes were clouding, but for a brief second, I thought I caught a flash of disappointment cross his stern features. But before I could double-check, Sinclair was back in control. He nodded curtly and leaned back in his throne.

"Fine. You will deal exclusively with my business partner then, and we will limit our interactions to polite small talk at family functions. Obviously, we will keep what happened in Mexico between us."

"I don't have anyone to tell."

The corner of his firm mouth softened momentarily. I straightened my shoulders before he could take pity on me.

"Well, thank you for making this as simple as it can be." I stood and smoothed my slightly shaking hands down my skirt, aware of his gaze taking in my every movement. "I just want to finish by apologizing for my behavior in Mexico. I knew you were involved, and even when you tried to leave me, I threw myself at you." I smiled slightly, black humor twisting my lips. "Maybe we even deserve this."

I heard his carefully controlled breathing, but I didn't have the strength to look up at him before I turned to make my way out of the office. My hand was on the door, my damp palms almost slipping off the handle when I felt him behind me. I tried to swallow the cry bubbling up from my chest, but a strangled moan escaped from my clamped lips.

"Oh, Elle." He sighed.

His hands clamped gently around my shoulders and slowly turned me around to face him. I kept my eyes trained on the floor, taking in his polished leather loafers. I knew if I looked up into his handsome face, I would lose it. He waited for my gaze before sighing, and when he didn't get it, carefully, as if I was made of tissue paper, he wrapped me in his arms. My head was tucked under his chin, my cheek pressed to the fabric of his blue button-up, and I could feel his heartbeat, slow and measured, beneath my touch. His scent overwhelmed me, and the feel of his hard lines cushioned by my curves reminded me of every touch and tryst we had shared in Mexico. My heart trembled, my resolve crumbling until finally, I shifted in his hold so that I could press my arms around his lean waist. We both let out another sigh as we melted into the embrace, and though it was just a hug, it was the most heartrending embrace I had ever experienced. My tears stained his expensive dress shirt, but I knew he wouldn't care.

This is going to be so hard, I thought.

Sinclair's arms tightened around me, and I realized I had spoken aloud.

"I don't want to hurt you."

"You promised me you would." I laughed weakly and tried to put some distance between us, but he only let me pull back slightly so that one hand could tilt my chin up to meet his gaze. Those blue eyes burned into me, making me shiver.

"Tell me this is what you want, Elle." His voice was hoarse.

Could he possibly want to be with me too? I allowed myself to think for one insane, amazing second.

"No," I murmured, honestly, "but I'm not willing to ruin my sister's life."

He raised his eyebrows. "And if it wasn't your sister you were hurting, what would you do then?"

I shook my head adamantly and tugged myself out of his grasp. "It is. There is no point in pretending otherwise."

This time, he let me open the door, and I was already halfway down the hall when his voice followed me.

"I'll miss you."

I didn't turn around to let him see how freely my tears fell, so I just paused and whispered, unsure if he could even hear me, unsure if I even wanted him to, "Me too."

Chapter Five

We managed to avoid each other for two and a half weeks. It's amazing how productive my period of misery became. Almost every day, I made an effort to paint or walk around the city with my camera, and coupled with long conversations and hours of reconnecting with the twins and Mama, I was able to maintain my façade as a content, single girl.

If Cosima noticed my misery at home, the effort it took me to rouse myself in the morning, the times my eyes unfocused as I was tugged into the current of my memories with Sinclair, she didn't say anything. She had always been perceptive, but I suspected she wasn't willing to talk to me about my private life because she wasn't ready to speak about hers. She spent very little time at the apartment, and sometimes, when she arrived home, she seemed hollow; her beautiful eyes like gold lame over her turmoil.

I also met with Sinclair's DS Galleries business partner, Rossi, surprised to find an incredibly friendly woman waiting for me at the chic French bistro where we had scheduled to meet. She was one of the most beautiful older women I had ever met, with fine light blond hair that softened her handsome face and large tilted eyes like a cat. Despite her inherent glamour, she was extremely well versed in the New York City art scene, and the tight ball of insecurity I felt about my lack of artistic abilities loosened under the weight of her professional wisdom. Eddie, the pretty Asian receptionist I had met the day of my confrontation with Sinclair, was often present at our discussions, and I found their odd couple chemistry—Ms. Prim and Proper and witty, coolly bored Eddie—refreshing.

Despite the distractions, it sucked not having someone to talk to about Sinclair. I knew where to find Candy now, and the temptation to make contact with her was strong, but I decided it wasn't fair to drag her into my mess, especially not when she worked with Sinclair. And I was convinced that he had told no one about the horrific connection we had. Which was why I was both suspicious and thrilled when I received a call on my new cell phone from Cage late one Friday afternoon as I was exiting the gallery.

"How's my beautiful European?" he asked into my shocked silence.

I cleared my throat and found myself looking around the busy street conspicuously as if even talking to Sinclair's best friend was a crime. "It's good to hear from you, Cage, but how did you get my number?"

There was a pause and my heart clenched in worry before he laughed. It was such a familiar and infectious noise that I found myself smiling.

"Sin might have slipped up a bit a few days ago, and you

know me, I couldn't lay it to rest until I found you, so"—I could hear the triumphant smile in his voice—"here we are."

"As good as it is to hear your voice, I don't think Sinclair, er, *Daniel*, would like it very much if he knew we were talking."

"That's probably true," he mused, and even though I knew I was right, disappointment settled in my chest. "Which is why we won't tell him about it."

"Cage..."

"Good, I'm glad that's settled. I'm starving. Meet me for an early dinner?"

"Cage—"

"*Génial*, there is a really great French bistro near the gallery. I'll meet you there in fifteen."

He rattled off the name and address before I could protest and hung up the phone.

I stared at the slim piece of technology for a few minutes, debating the pros and cons of meeting Cage for lunch. On the one hand, Sinclair would be furious if he ever found out, and it was definitely not fair of me to be seeing his best friend when we had agreed to stay out of each other's lives as much as possible. But on the other, I was desperate to talk to someone about him, and I didn't doubt Cage's sincerity or ability to lie to Sinclair.

Before I had even fully made up my mind, I looked up to find myself in front of the intimate French restaurant. Just as I was about to chicken out, I noticed the crowd of young women next to the entrance and the lovely sound of Cage's heavily accented but perfect English. Their bodies parted enough to reveal him in all his superstar glory, using his white teeth, deeply tanned skin, long braided hair, and formfitting leather pants to their distinct advantage.

He noticed me shyly lingering a few feet away, and his bad-boy grin stretched into a true smile. Excusing himself quickly from the giggling mass of breasts and hips, he strode my way.

Giddiness and genuine pleasure propelled me forward, sending me walking and then running into his arms.

He chuckled into my hair as he caught me and squeezed me tight. "It's good to see you too, Elle."

I pulled away, blushing with embarrassment, which made him laugh again.

"It's good to see you just the same as ever." He winked and threw an arm around my shoulders to usher me into the cool interior.

Even though I knew I shouldn't, I secretly delighted in the feel of Cage's arm around my shoulder, the security and the comfort it afforded me as we stepped into the trendy restaurant filled with the crème of New York society. The hostess smiled warmly at him and ushered us immediately to a table against the far wall. I was grateful too that he remained silent until we were seated.

"I hear you are settling in well," he began, but his eyes sparkled as if he were a kitten toying with a mouse before pouncing.

He sat easily in the chair, slouched slightly with his leather jacket open to reveal a tight gray T-shirt embossed with the name of his band in uppercase black letters. The end of his thick, perfectly mussed braid hit his sternum, and his slashing brows covered large, almond-shaped eyes that denoted him as something other than purely Caucasian. His body was massive, surpassing six feet by numerous inches, and the hand that tapped out a tune on the table was large and powerful. I almost snorted at my former analogy. Cage was nothing like a kitten.

"Oh, what leads you to say that, Cage?" I asked with a small smile because I had honestly missed his games. "In fact, if I remember correctly, I never gave you any of my information."

"I have my ways, Giselle." He winked and broke into a wide grin when I laughed. "Just as you have yours."

My smile dissolved into a sigh. "Sure, the ways of a freaking adulterer."

Cage's laughter prompted the tables closest to us to look our way, but my charming companion waved them away with a smile. "So hard on yourself, Elle. As they say, it takes two to tango."

"In this case, there were too many people on the dance floor," I muttered, playing with the short hem of my purple dress. Sinclair had loved me in purple; he once said it was the color of my scent. I swallowed hard and put on my auto smile for Cage. "I hope you didn't ask me to lunch to talk about him."

"No," he spoke carefully. "Not exactly."

The waitress chose that moment to take our drink orders, and I waited impatiently for Cage to stop flirting with her. His eyes twinkled as he did so, and I knew he took some satisfaction from annoying me.

When he was finished, he turned to me again. "You know, we have never spoken my language together."

"Non, je ne savais pas si tu aimeras cela," I said.

We grinned at each other.

"For future reference, I do like it. Sinclair and my bandmates are the only ones I know in America who speak French with me."

"How long have you been here? Despite all the time we spent together in Mexico, I don't know anything about you." I realized that with sadness. How could I have spent such an endless week with such fascinating people and know so little about them?

"And I, you."

My gaze snapped to his, and something locked in place with an almost audible click. It was a comforting thing, and I recognized it immediately as friendship.

Leaning across the table, Cage took my hand between his two large ones. "Sinclair is like a brother to me. I have known him through everything, and he will always be family. But that doesn't mean I don't have room for a friend."

The waitress arrived with the bottle of Burgundy we had ordered, and I grinned, ignoring her hostility, as I raised my glass. "I can toast to that."

A bottle and a half later, Cage and I were still sitting at the table, swinging from French to English and back as we imbued more of the heady French wine. The chef had even come out to see the faces of the couple that had ordered two main courses each, leaving it to him to decide what they were given. He was entirely too young and handsome to head up a successful restaurant, and I told him as much when he finally agreed to sit down for a moment.

"Ah, well, I was blessed with good luck," Chef Devereaux, or Dev as he had encouraged us to call him, said in an accent as thick as Cage's. "And even richer friends."

I laughed. "And rich friends make great investors."

He tilted his head in agreement. "But I have to say, I prefer the beautiful friends over the rich ones."

"Is that true?" I grinned behind my wineglass. "Then you and Cage should get along just fine."

The two men laughed too loudly, not caring who heard them, and I felt a pang of homesickness for the beautiful country I had fled. Though I loved Italy, it was France that had fostered my soul and turned me into a person I could be proud of.

My nostalgia got lodged in my throat when I dragged in a startlingly familiar smoky scent. I barely had time to swallow my mouthful of wine before I felt his presence behind me.

"It's good to know where I stand with you, Devereaux."

The newcomer's voice ran its fingers down the back of my neck, feathering along my spine like a light caress. I shuddered almost violently and nearly spilled my drink. Cage's heavily booted foot found my heeled one under the table, pushing against it lightly in a subtle show of support.

"Ah, but Sinclair, if it is any consolation, your date is both beautiful and rich, and for whatever reason, she chooses to associate herself with you so"—Dev shrugged charmingly—"that is something, uh?"

I looked up at them as everyone laughed, at least, everyone but Sinclair. He was standing beside his companion, a gorgeously dressed Elena, with his eyes on me, hot and overexposed. Simultaneously, I wanted to tell him to quit being so obvious and lay myself out on the table before him, naked in offering.

I shuddered again.

"Giselle." My sister obstructed our gaze as she leaned down to brush her lips against my cheek, eschewing the Italian custom of kissing both. "What a lovely surprise."

She spoke like that, my sister. It had taken her longer to master the English language than she cared to admit, and she was determined to put her vocabulary and etiquette to good use. No trace of her accent remained, and though her tones were smooth and dulcet, they were missing softness.

In fact, as she stepped away from the kiss, I noticed the lack of softness anywhere on Elena. Her limbs were taut, honed by hours spent running and swimming, and her features were harder than mine, pinched further by a discontent that had plagued her for years. She was only twenty-six years old, a whopping thirteen months older than me, but she carried herself like a woman who covered her gray hairs and wore pearls.

I almost snorted when her hand went to a beautiful string of them at her throat.

"Cage." Sinclair had shifted his focus to the singer lounging in his chair like a god. "I wasn't aware you knew Giselle."

He shrugged and brushed the end of his braid against the plush weight of his bottom lip. It was such a sensual gesture that both Elena and I shifted restlessly. "We met in Paris. We are friends for a while now."

"You never mentioned," Sinclair said, his teeth slightly bared.

Cage shrugged again. "I didn't make the connection between Giselle and your lovely Elena until just now."

The atmosphere between us, already fraught, vibrated with tension. Elena looked between us all with a small smile that was far from genuine. My sister didn't like to be left out of the loop.

"You two are dating, then?" Something like distaste flashed across her face as she looked at Cage and a high flush crept up her neck.

"No," Sinclair barked, at the same time that Cage grinned at me and winked.

"Would it be the end of the world if they were, Daniel?" Elena looked at him with disapproving concern, and I was surprised that we were getting away with the barely-concealed deception. It was so obvious to me that a secret was being—poorly—hidden right before her eyes, but for all her natural curiosity and brainpower, Elena was oblivious.

"Yes." Dev nodded solemnly. "You see, there is already a line."

"A line?"

He nodded again. "A waiting list for the honor of taking this lovely woman out to dinner."

I laughed at the flirtatious Frenchman, grateful to him for reasons he couldn't possibly understand. Playing along, I placed my hand on his arm and leaned in intimately. "Technically, you beat everyone to the punch. You've already fed me dinner."

We both looked at the empty plates littering the white-clothed dinner table and everyone, except for Sinclair, laughed.

"Cheater," Cage accused with playfully narrowed eyes, but I noticed them flick over to Sinclair and held my breath when he stirred restlessly next to me. "Although, if any woman is worth it, it's Giselle. Don't you agree, Elena?"

I kicked him hard under the table. That was taking his twisted game way too far, and I wasn't the only one who thought so. Sinclair glared at his best friend with such concentrated hatred that I thought his blood vessels might pop.

"Daniel." Elena tried to soothe him with a soft stroke down the arm.

If I had been in a position to offer comfort, I would have slid my hand into the back pocket of his slim-fitting trousers and squeezed his pert ass. It would have both turned him on and forced him to recognize my presence. My fingers twitched on the table to do just that, and I wasn't surprised when his eyes snapped to them. I extended my pinkie finger toward him, furious and ashamed that I could offer no more. A muscle in his jaw ticked once before his mask slid back into place.

"You are here for dinner?" Dev asked, standing up to flee

back to the kitchen and away from the awkwardness. "Let me show you to your table, *oui*?"

Elena's eyes flicked across our faces, her pink lips pursed. She was clever enough to sense the undercurrents swirling beneath the murky waters, and I wondered if her curiosity would get the better of her instinct to back away from the mess.

"Giselle, I have a favor to ask of you. Do you have a free moment tomorrow morning for coffee?"

I held my breath as my mind raced across excuses, leaping from one to another as if they were hot coals. Nothing seemed suitable, and besides, I had the stupid, crazy desire to see the apartment that my ex-lover and older sister shared.

"Sure."

I risked a glance at Sinclair and found him looking at me with guarded eyes. His lips moved slightly as if he wanted to say something, but Elena tugged him forward and broke our connection.

"Tomorrow then." She smiled slightly at me, the same tiny slice that Sinclair was prone to give out, but she ignored Cage, a snub that was notable if only because Elena prided herself on decorum.

As soon as they were out of hearing distance, my mouth fell open like a puncture mark on a heavy sigh. "That was horrible."

"Hell," Cage agreed. "But interesting."

I frowned at him from behind my wineglass as I downed the rest of the crimson liquid.

"Sinclair couldn't take his eyes off you, and Elena couldn't stand to look at you."

"She doesn't know if that's what you are trying to say. Elena hasn't been able to look me in the eye for years."

He nodded, but his dark eyes remained focused on the remains at the bottom of his wineglass. "I thought it was just me she hated the sight of."

His melancholy surprised me. "Are Mr. Rock Star's feelings hurt?"

My teasing tone had the effect I desired. He gulped back the rest of his wine and grinned at me. "Never. Now, I could use something a hell of a lot stronger than wine after that little situation." He wiggled his fingers over his shoulder at the departed couple. "I could also use a woman. And you could use a man, no?"

My heart clenched painfully, and for a second, I actually thought I was having a heart attack.

"Maybe."

He laughed beautifully. "Good enough. Let's go."

Chapter Six

I hadn't been to a club since the incident in Mexico, and at first, I had been nervous, especially when we entered Sinner's nightclub, and Cage was practically assaulted by a group of women. Most of them didn't know he was a rock star, but it didn't really matter. The French singer exuded sex and impossible magnetism. I tried to sidestep away, to give him space to entertain the scantily-clad women, but his hand had reached through the gaggle to snare me and tuck me against his side.

"Ladies," he rumbled in his low, accented voice. "I owe this gorgeous *chérie* a drink, so please, excuse us."

"So smooth." I laughed as he turned us toward the bar.

He shrugged and squeezed my waist. "You know how it is to be beautiful."

I didn't argue with him. As soon as we had left the restaurant, I decided to let Cage take the lead. A night in the life of a rock star had to be a thrilling experience, and I wanted to remember what I had felt like with Sinclair in Mexico, throbbing like a strobe light with sexuality.

"Four shots of tequila," Cage ordered, cutting to the front of the crowded bar without a fuss.

When I raised my brows at him, he lifted my hand and quickly licked my skin before shaking salt onto it. "For Mexico."

I sucked in a shaky breath, tucked a lime into one hand and the shot in my other. "For Mexico."

That had been four hours ago, I thought, or at least three. But I had lost all sense of time in the black space, punctuated only with flashing colors catching on glistening bare skin. My dress was damp with sweat, mine and those I had danced with, both men and women who had felt my body intimately as if being on a dance floor gave them the right.

My current partner, a handsome all-American kind of guy in the last pieces of the suit he had probably worn to his job on Wall Street, ran his hand up my knee to my thigh and hitched it over his leg to bring our pelvises closer. I closed my eyes and focused on the pulse of the bass-rich song and the swirl of alcohol tingling in my blood.

Cage was beside me, somehow dancing equally with three girls at the same time. His dark brow glittered with a crown of sweat that made him appear sexier, less civilized, and more heathen. He was keeping his eye on me, but it didn't feel obtrusive. He was my fun keeper, assuring that every moment I spent with him was filled to the brim with it.

My partner, Tim or Jim, pressed his nose into the damp hair above my ear and whispered, "You are so fucking sexy."

I pulled back, pressing one hand to his damp chest and smiled coyly as I bent at the knees, dragging my hand from his sternum to his hip as I descended. His groan vibrated against my hand.

He wanted me. The shape of his arousal through his slacks was obvious, and the heat in his eyes was blatant, almost pleading. I wondered hazily if it wouldn't be a good idea to go home with him. I'd never had a one-night stand, and Sinclair had awakened a neediness within me that I couldn't quench alone in the dark of my room with my fingers.

I was just opening my mouth, my lips grazing his dimpled chin, when he was jerked away. I lost my balance as I had been flush against him, and it took me a second to right myself and see what was unfolding. A man I had never seen before—massive and currently scowling—drew back one corded arm to pound it into Tim/Jim's nose. Blood erupted immediately and made it almost impossible to discern his curses as he crumpled in on himself.

I watched in a daze and reached behind me to find Cage. His hand snagged mine and threaded our fingers. Still distracted by the fight—it couldn't have been because of me, I didn't even know the guys—it took me a moment to recognize that the hand in mine was too lean to be Cage's, the fingers long and strong. My breath caught in my throat, and slowly, because I feared that he would fade away like an apparition as soon as I laid eyes on him, I looked over my shoulder.

Before I could turn fully, he was off, dragging me through the gathered bodies without issue. We passed close to Cage who was looking at me intently, the end of his braid in one hand brushing the tail against his lips.

Sinclair didn't break pace until we were off the main dance floor and climbing the steps to the open second level. The atmosphere was slower than the strobe light thrum of sexuality downstairs. Here, it was thick with sensuality. People spoke in low velvety voices, close together in semi-private booths obscured by glossy black curtains. A few people mingled on the dance floor, touching each other in slow motion with a deliberateness that spiked blood pressure.

I barely had time to observe the VIP lounge because Sinclair powered across the floor without speaking to any of the people who tried to stop him. Finally, we came to a stop at the far side of the second floor after shimmying through a small door in the bar. Without a word, he swiped a card and pushed me gently into the room. I whirled around to yell at him, but the door had already closed, and I could hear him speaking to someone through the barricade. I tried to yank open the door, but someone on the other side was holding it closed.

Furious, I spun back around to face my temporary prison. It was a medium-sized office, the front wall made entirely of glass in order to overlook the main dance floor below. The floor thrummed slightly with the force of the music, and the dark room flashed with colored lights. Suddenly cold, I rubbed my hands hard up and down my arms and decided to snoop a little. If Sinclair was going to shove me into a room like a freaking Neanderthal, then I was going to take advantage of it.

The large matte black desk was L-shaped, facing both the door and the windows, and it was clear of paraphernalia. Frustrated, I moved around to sit in the high-backed red leather chair in order to open a few drawers. I was just about to close the first one when I noticed the white edge of a Polaroid photograph sticking out between two black folders. My heart picked up speed as I carefully pulled it free and looked at a picture of me. In it, I lay on my back with my red hair a swirling mass around a sleepy, satiated face. My lids were low over slightly smiling eyes, and one hand rested against the creamy top of my breast. I barely remembered him taking the photo. Sometime after we returned to Sinclair's suite from the private beach on our last night together. I couldn't believe he had kept it, but somewhere beneath my shock, a sense of powerful calm was rising.

I didn't look up when the door opened and closed. Instead, I crossed my legs, aware of how high the hem of my dress rose over my thighs, and continued to look down at the picture.

"Pretty risky, having something like this lying around." I was grateful that the tremor in my heart wasn't echoed in my words.

"As I recall, it wasn't exactly 'lying around.'"

I leaned back in the chair, steeling myself to look up at him. "Why do you still have this, Daniel?"

He stood halfway between the door and the desk as if he was unsure about approaching. I had never seen him unsure about anything, and I wondered, hopefully, if I was making him *nervous*.

I sighed when he remained silent. "Fine. How about you tell me how you knew I was here? Or, better yet, what happened downstairs."

Amusement tipped the corner of his firm lips. "Don't feel like it."

"Excuse me?"

He shrugged and strode across the space confidently to take a seat in the chair across from the desk. "I don't feel like talking to you about that."

"Oh?" Indignation vibrated through me. "Well, I don't feel like being here."

Ha! How would he like that?

Again, he shrugged.

"Stop playing games with me, Sinclair. Why the hell am I here?"

His too blue eyes flamed, and he leaned forward, arms on the table so that he could move that gorgeous face closer to me.

"I love it when you say my name."

That caught me off guard. "Daniel?"

"Sinclair. You know, before you, I hated my family name."

"Why does everyone call you Sinclair then?"

"Cage always has, and he has a way of influencing people. It's his way of reminding me where I came from."

"Oh."

He smiled slightly at my lack of eloquence, his confident mask secured firmly over his face. "And you are here precisely because I don't want to play games with you. You're here because I saw you dancing in the pit with a dozen different men wearing my favorite dress and my favorite smile, and I couldn't stand it." Slowly, keeping eye contact with me the entire way, he got to his feet and stepped around the desk to stand in front of me, so tall that I had to tip the chair back to look into his eyes. "You are here, Giselle, simply and complicatedly, because I miss you."

My tongue was pasted to the roof of my mouth, stuck to the back of my teeth so that I could barely breathe, let alone respond. Tears pricked the backs of my eyes, and I realized with mortification that this was where the moisture had gone. But his gaze on me was tender and open, asking to receive whatever response I was able to give him.

A knock on the door jolted us both, and Sinclair chuckled softly as he called for them to come in. The young woman who entered was beautiful and all skin. The tiny crop top and black skirt she wore only covered the essentials. She licked her lips and beamed at Sinclair as she carried in a tray and placed it on the coffee table where he had directed her. They were speaking, polite small talk, but I was too focused on Sinclair's declaration to tune in.

He missed me.

My heart was too warm in my chest, like the sun over my tossing oceanic stomach. I was at once deathly ill and too alive, suspended on the rack of desire and pain with no sense of escape.

By the time the girl left, I was basically breathless.

Without a word, Sinclair reached down to take my hand and led me to the small lounge area toward the heavenly smell of... chocolate. I frowned down at the assortment of chocolates, mini cakes, and candies on the large gold lacquered tray and back up at Sinclair.

He grinned, one of his rare full and boyish smiles that hooked my heart and dragged it through the waters straight toward his net. "The club is called Sinner's for a reason. We cater to all the indulgences here, including gluttony. There is a dessert bar on the second floor."

I mouthed, *"Wow,"* and took a seat on the low red loveseat. Sinclair tugged one of the velvet chairs closer and sat down too.

"Drink." He nodded at the tall glass of water. "And eat."

I took a long drink of the cool liquid, grateful for its effect on my dry throat, and carefully bit into a chocolate-covered strawberry. My eyes fluttered closed at the explosion of bitter and sweet on my refreshed tongue.

When I opened them again, Sinclair was staring at me ravenously. I shivered, poised like a gong waiting for the hammer strike to bring me alive.

"You should be forbidden from eating in public." He shook his head and propped one ankle on his opposite knee. "I'd almost forgotten what a pleasure it is to watch you."

I swallowed hard and fought for purchase on the slippery surface of my morality. "You shouldn't be saying things like that."

"I would amend that statement. I *should* say things like that. Every. Single. Day. But you've assured me that you don't want to hear them so..." He opened his palms wide, at a loss.

"Are you..." I sighed. "What are you doing, Sinclair?"

"I'm renegotiating our agreement."

"We don't *have* an agreement."

He nodded, completely unfazed, and gestured to the tray of bite-sized sins. "Eat, please."

I looked between him and the sweets, both representing tempting threats to my body. I picked up the cocoa-dusted truffle, choosing the lesser of two evils.

"I didn't know you owned a club," I said because I felt impotent in our current line of conversation.

"It was my first asset, actually." He chuckled softly at my expression. "I was twenty-one years old, fresh out of university and still living with my controlling, conservative parents. It was a pretty cliché trope. I hoped, if they wouldn't let me leave, that I could get myself kicked out and owning a club seemed like the way to do it."

"I heard something about them. You didn't tell me they had adopted you."

"I didn't tell you a lot of things. That was part of our agreement. And the subject of my parents and my fruitless rebellions is not something I like to discuss." He glanced sidelong at me, a mischievous light in his eyes.

I found myself leaning forward, mouth slightly open like a fish hooked by the cheek. "So?"

"So what?" he said, a smug smile in his eyes.

"Did it work?"

"Not quite, but I did get a surprisingly profitable club out of it and my first million."

I leaned back with a huff. "So not exactly a classic teenage trope."

He laughed again, louder this time, and I realized this was the most I had ever heard the stirring sound. I wished my mind was clearer, unclouded by the copious amounts of liquor in my system, so that I could better absorb it.

"No, not exactly."

He stood with a grace that made my mouth water and moved to stand over me again. I kept my eyes on the confections but I wasn't sure if it was to ignore him or because the restless submissive was shifting and fighting for purchase inside me.

"Do you want to know what it taught me, Giselle?" His voice was deeper and his faintly accented words tingled like ice sliding down my spine.

He was so close that my cheek was almost pressed to his trouser-clad thigh. I wanted to take off those pants with my teeth and use my mouth, hands and throat on him.

"It taught me the art of patience. Have you ever heard the saying, good things come to those who wait?"

I shook my head slightly even though I had heard it before.

His breath was warm and whiskey scented over my crown as he leaned down to gently tip my chin up with one finger so that my neck was craned and my eyes rested on his.

"Patience is a virtue, virtue is a grace, Grace is a little girl who doesn't wash her face," I said.

I was close enough to see his features collapse, slowly at first like a loose domino tumbling a dozen more, into laughter.

When he was finished, he stared down at me with caged eyes filled with stars. "You always surprise me."

The cell phone on the desk vibrated angrily and he swiftly turned away from me to answer it, leaving me mid-shrug. He picked up and listened without saying a word of greeting.

"I don't care who his father is, get him *the fuck out of my club*."

My eyebrows shot up at his harsh tone and less than formal language. I was pretty sure Sinclair *never* raised his voice. Triggered by his sudden mood change, the air in the room stiffened and pressed against me until I was locked into place.

He placed the phone back on the cradle with a slow calm but when he looked over at me his face was implacable, his eyes just a color.

"As I was saying, you always surprise me. But tonight, I was not happy with your behavior. Drunkenly dancing with men like that." He shook his head. "I thought you would want to be more careful after the incident in Mexico."

I flinched as his dart landed with deadly accuracy in my breastbone. "Don't talk to me about Mexico. I was perfectly safe and aware tonight, Sinclair. And, if it appeals to your idiotic French misogyny, Cage was close by."

"Still, I did not like it." He wasn't speaking sternly now, in fact, his accent had thickened slightly and he seemed more disturbed than angry.

I shrugged beautifully, as if I wasn't affected by his concern, his potential jealousy. "You have no right to do anything about that."

"I have the right, Giselle, and I will always have that right. I am closer to you than any other man has ever been or will ever be."

"No."

"*Mais oui,*" he confirmed with that infernal, casual arrogance of the French. "I know things about you, the dark places and the deep, that even you do not like to explore. I know the things you hate about yourself, and I? I nurture them because I know them to be beautiful."

"Stop it," I breathed, suddenly aware of the slight tremor wracking my frame.

He lifted one shoulder insolently and tucked his hands in his pockets. "It is not something I can stop knowing."

"What do you want from me?" A scalding tear rolled over my lid and slid down my cheek.

Sinclair reached out to sweep the burning trail with his thumb. "We could be friends."

My laugh was soggy with my tears. "Don't be ridiculous."

"I can't say anyone has every accused me of being *ridicule* before."

"*Je ne le crois pas,*" I said wryly, *I don't believe that.*

"See, this is why we must be friends. You are the only person I have ever met who makes me feel like a boy."

I frowned, unsure if that was a compliment or not.

"You know *le Petit Prince*? There is a quote, it goes 'only children know what they are looking for.'"

I waited in silence for him to explain, but he only stared at me with those inscrutable eyes.

It didn't really matter what the motivation was behind his offer of friendship. I was desperate to grab it, to snare anything that represented time with him. Because he was right, of course. He knew me better than anyone. Even Cosima, who I loved devotedly yet knew so little about, even Brenna, who hadn't replied to my emails in over two weeks. A friendship with Sinclair meant that I could smile at him genuinely, that I could speak with him in front of our family like I knew him and spend time with him casually as if I had a right to.

"Okay."

"Okay?"

"Yes, I mean okay. I think we should be friends too."

We stared at each other without smiling because our joy was concentrated in the eyes. I wrapped myself in the warm blue hues and stopped breathing. He reached out slowly and wrapped his long fingers around my hand, gently pulling me to my feet.

His eyes creased slightly with the effort of holding back his smile. "I'm taking you home."

Desire plucked my strings like a puppet master, my mouth dropping open to gasp.

"Friends don't let drunk friends drive or get into cabs alone," he pointed out, stepping away to gather his wallet and keys from the desk.

I took the moment to suck in a deep, necessary breath. *Right*, friends. I had never needed to memorize and carry a piece of information so badly. I watched his lean form from the corner of my eye, the colored lights flashing against him like the light of a camera. I released the enormous breath and dragged in another to fill myself with my new mantra, *just friends.*

I knew the minute we opened the door that Cosima wasn't home. The air was cool and dark, unpunctuated by the habitual crackling fire and music crooning from the surround sound speakers. I wasn't sure if her absence was a blessing or a curse because the current of electricity that crackled constantly between Sinclair and me snapped with ferocity as soon as we understood our aloneness.

"Drink?" I murmured as we moved toward the kitchen at the back of the apartment.

Without waiting for an answer, I started to rifle through the fully stocked cupboards. I had no idea where Cosima kept the liquor, and I was too frazzled to properly guess at where she may have housed it.

"You sit," he demanded in that quiet, stern voice that made my bones shake with desire. "I'll fix us both a drink."

I nodded gratefully and slipped onto one of the stools at the large wooden island. I watched him maneuver about the kitchen gracefully, locating the ice, tumblers and whiskey as if he himself had placed them there.

"You come here a lot."

"Yes." He poured a perfect two fingers into each glass, one with ice and one without. "It is one of the reasons we can have a friendship. Cosima was my friend before I even met Elena."

An arrow of hatred painted with the name of my eldest sister found its home in the center of my heart. I cemented it there with guilt and shame and felt it throb.

"You know, I would say that I can't see you and Cosima being friends but," I laughed lightly, "she is infectious, isn't she?"

"Yes."

He handed me the glass with ice and watched me intently as I lifted it to my lips and touched the burning liquid to my tongue. I watched his eyes but he was either unaffected or being very careful.

"How did you meet her?" Talking about Cosima seemed as good a topic as any. In fact, it seemed to be one of the *only* topics I could even begin to feel comfortable talking about with Sinclair.

He stepped back to lean against the counter across from the island, giving me a full view of his beautiful suit-clad physique.

"Willa signed her." I recognized his adopted mother's name and noted that he didn't call her something affectionate like mom. "When she was nineteen. I was in Italy with Willa when she discovered her, standing in the rain wearing a long black dress. You couldn't tell where her hair ended and the dress began. She looked like something from Dante's *Inferno*."

He shook his head and stared into his glass as if divining a memory. I waited for him to continue but he remained silent. Cosima never spoke about her time away from home and honestly, I think the rest of us were too afraid to press her into confessing. What exactly did an eighteen-year-old girl have to do to pull her family out of destitution?

I shivered, pulling Sinclair from his reverie. His lips compressed into a flat line. "She was too young to have such sad eyes. I didn't want her living with my parents—she had obviously already been through a lot—so I offered to host her here in New York."

"Wow," I blinked a few times as I tried to process the picture of my vivacious sister inhabiting the same space as the fiercely private and enigmatic Frenchman.

A tiny smile twitched his lips. "It was an interesting experience to say the least. It was just for a short time; within the year, she had enough money to bring over Elena and Mama. Sebastian arrived from London soon after."

And you met her.

What would have happened if I had stayed in Italy? If I had moved to New York with my family and Sinclair had met both Elena and I at the same time?

The hypothetical made my teeth ache.

"You know," I said, to distract myself from that destructive line of thought, "I don't know very much about what happened to my family during the past five years. Cosima and Sebastian never talk about it, and as you know, I am not very close with Elena." I sighed and took a long sip of the burning whiskey. "We all used to be so close."

Sinclair crossed his arms and inclined his head, waiting for me to go on. I was surprised by his readiness to talk about my family when they were the cause of the mile-wide distance between us, but I was even more surprised by my relief at having someone to talk to who would understand.

"Have you been to Napoli?" He hesitated but shook his head. "Well, I can understand why not. Tourists go for the pizza and the history, but they never leave as enchanted as they were with Florence or Rome, Venice or Umbria. Naples is a deeply dirty place, especially if you are poor."

Sinclair nodded to convey that he was still listening before turning around to grab a few things from the fridge and cupboards. I watched him assemble the ingredients for crepes with a slight smile.

"You need to eat," he explained without facing me.

On cue, my alcohol-weighted stomach sloshed and turned over nauseously. "Okay."

"Continue."

I watched the ice in my glass swirl and tried to collect my thoughts.

"I'm sure you've heard about Seamus? He was an English professor at the university, but by the time the twins were born, he had basically been forced out due to his gambling and drinking problem. He loved Italy, every single thing about it, and it had been his goal growing up as an Irish Catholic in Boston to move to the country." My laugh was forced. "He was ridiculed by his family about it, and when he finally made the move, they basically disowned them. I don't even know their names."

"Would you like to?"

His question surprised me into answering honestly. "Yes, but only because I'd like to know how Seamus turned out the way he did. What made him decide to bury his family in debt to the mafia and disappear without a trace."

Sinclair nodded, and I paused for a minute to watch the surprisingly erotic sight of his strong wrist whisking the crepe batter.

"He disappeared after Cosima moved away. Sebastian moved to England a few months after that. We were almost destitute and so lonely." I could remember the dull vibration of too much silence in our small Neapolitan home and the collapsed look to Mama's handsome face, how her smile dragged and her soft hands trembled.

"It would be understandable if you resented them." He competently swirled the runny batter evenly over the surface of the pan while his eyes remained bolted to mine.

"I don't resent the twins. I never have, and I never could. They did everything to get us out of there, things that I don't know and probably never should." I hesitated, unsure if I should tell him the truth.

He flipped the completed crepe onto a waiting plate, moving with machine-like efficiency. His silence was a gift. I knew he wouldn't judge me because when it came down to the two of us, Sinclair was my musician, skillfully plucking and strumming until I produced just the right tune. I might make the sound, but how could he blame me when he had orchestrated it?

"I resent Elena and Mama sometimes."

Flip, slip, and the sizzle as butter landed in the pan.

"Mama for staying with Seamus for so long, for loving him when she should have left him. And Elena... We stopped being sisters when the twins left."

I wanted to tell him about Christopher, about what had happened between the three of us, and how Elena had never forgiven me. But it wasn't really my story to tell, at least not to Elena's present partner, whatever he might have meant to me.

Sinclair sprinkled brown sugar over a perfectly cooked crepe, folded it, and squeezed a sliced lemon easily in his fist over the top. He placed the plate in front of me but snagged my wrist before I could pick up the fork. With nimble fingers, he plucked the elastic off my wrist and moved behind me to gently gather my messy, still slightly damp hair between his hands. I shivered when cool fingers dragged over my heavy pulse. When my hair was secured in a ponytail, he lingered, and the only sound in the entire apartment was my heavy breathing. My head spun, and I realized I was still pretty intoxicated.

"Eat, Giselle."

I sighed but did as he told me, watching from the corner of my eye as he cleaned up the kitchen and ate his own rolled crepe standing up.

"How did you become interested in art? It doesn't seem like your childhood was conducive to frivolity or creativity," he asked after demolishing his crepe and starting to work rolling another. There was sugar stuck to his lemon juice slicked finger tips that I wished I could suck off with a curl of my tongue.

"No, but I did it anyway. I used sticks and dirt, made rock formations, and even got my hands on a canister of spray paint. We only had standard grade lead pencils and printer paper, sometimes something a little nicer if Seamus had done well at the tables. Cosima sent me my first paint set for my nineteenth birthday, this incredibly beautiful box of Sennelier oil paints. It was one of the only things I took with me to *L'École des Beaux-Arts*."

"That makes me unspeakably sad," he said simply.

I shrugged because it didn't matter to me anymore. I wouldn't let it. "It affected me a lot. I didn't know who I was or what I was allowed to do when opportunities eventually came my way. I felt unworthy, I think."

"You know better now."

"I do," I agreed. "Whatever else happened in Mexico, good or bad, you helped me lock that into place."

"That makes me unspeakably happy," he murmured as if my words weighed heavily in his chest and compressed his lungs.

His phone began to ring, but I wasn't startled or surprised. It only seemed right that our intimacy would be interrupted. I turned away before he could answer it and made my way to the bathroom.

"Elena." I heard him murmur her name before I was fully out of earshot.

I braced myself against the sink basin on wobbly arms and scowled at the mess of a redhead in the mirror. After so many years of staring at my reflection and seeing only how I didn't look like my gorgeous siblings, I was happy to find my own beauty lurking beneath the smudged mascara and sticky hair. It was impossible to view myself as ugly, as average, when a man like Sinclair found me so attractive.

I peeled off my clothes and turned the shower on to scalding hot. The pounding spray further sobered me, and I focused on the individual pricks of water against my skin instead of the gorgeous dilemma waiting for me somewhere in the apartment. After scrubbing myself from head to toe in a lavender-scented product, I stepped from the shower and into the steamy room.

Wiped clean, I felt raw and unprepared to face Sinclair. I desperately wanted to go to him as I was, naked and cooling like an un-iced cake. I wanted him to paint me in his sugary kisses and color me pink with desire.

As I stood in the middle of the bathroom, my hand found its way over my breast and down to my sex. I moved my hand through the downy curls and hissed as I found my clit. I braced one hand on the sink and stared at the slowly clearing mirror while I played with myself.

A reel of memories from our Mexican affair played in my mind; flashes of myself spread open and shockingly wet, the taste of his arousal on my tongue, the sharp string of a slap on the thin skin of my ass.

I was slick and throbbing, my breath fogging up the mirror again. I stretched two fingers past my entrance and moaned slightly, taking my lip between my teeth, biting it like Sinclair would do if he were kissing me, demanding me to come for him. My fingers were too small, too gentle on my skin, and I ached for the precision of his touch, the painful pinch and sexual pull of his hands on my body. I groaned again, loudly.

"Elle?"

His voice exploded against my skin, showering me with hot shards of desire. My fingers worked faster.

"Elle?" He was closer, just outside the slightly open door to the bathroom. "Is everything okay?"

My eyes drooped with the heaviness of my arousal, but I forced myself to keep them open and on the door in the mirror. I was rewarded with the sight of him coming into the room, the steam swirling around his legs and kissing his face with dew. I shuddered violently and pinched my clit hard between my fingers. I was so close.

He stood there, shocked, taking in the view of my pink sex peeking out from under my slightly bent bottom and the hand running over it eagerly. I saw his throat swell and bob as he swallowed hard.

I whimpered.

His burning eyes shot to mine in the mirror, and the fierce desire in them almost brought me to my knees.

"Stop." His voice lashed out across the room and hit me like a whip.

My hand increased its frenzied movements. I was too close to stop now.

"I said," he repeated in that glacial, exacting voice that never failed to make me wet, "stop."

My hand trembled as I took it away and placed it on the sink. I panted as I stared at him in the mirror, waiting for him to direct me.

His lips were pursed into a flat line, and his fists curled before he put them in his pockets. "Go to bed, Giselle."

My heart dropped to the wood floor with an audible splat as he turned and left. The steam had disappeared through the open door, and the cold apartment air grated goose bumps into my skin. I shivered and pulled a towel from the rack to wrap around my body.

Whatever hope I might have harbored that he would be waiting for me in my bedroom was crushed when I slunk into the dark room and found it cold and empty. Tears of humiliation stung my eyes and made my nose tickle.

I ditched the towel and lay on the duvet, letting the cold air bring my lava-filled body back down from its near eruption.

I was an idiot to be caught touching myself with Sinclair in the apartment. Whatever opportunity I might have had to be friends with him had obviously gone out the door with my inappropriate behavior. What had I expected? Did I really think he would suddenly succumb to nefarious desire and drag me into the bedroom like a Neanderthal and have his wicked way with me? This wasn't a romance novel, and Sinclair was certainly no caveman.

My eyes shot open at the clack of ice hitting ice in a glass.

Sinclair stood framed in the door and he maintained eye contact with me as he made his way to the high-backed chair across from my bed. He sat down, planted one foot atop the opposite knee, and took a sip of his whiskey.

I blinked.

He looked entirely comfortable sitting across from me, like a spectator at a movie or, more likely, a man waiting for the show at a strip club.

"By all means..." His voice was thicker than the steam from the bathroom and warmer than the cold air assaulting my bare skin. "Continue."

My breath streamed out through my slack mouth.

Could I do this?

Should I do this?

Touch myself in front of the man dating my sister?

But you have done this, the villainous voice inside me reminded, you've done this with Sinclair many, many times before. And besides, you want to.

Still, I hesitated, my mind whirring louder than my latent desire.

"Don't make me tell you again." Sinclair's voice wrapped firm fingers around my flailing thoughts and carefully bound them, gagged them. "Touch that pretty pussy for me, Giselle. I want to see you come."

A feathery moan escaped me, and my hand found my still damp sex without hesitation. I watched his stern face as I twirled one finger around my clit, not quite touching it, before moving down to my entrance to do the same thing. His jaw clenched, and I knew that teasing myself was teasing him even more. I feathered both hands over my inner thighs, tensing at the resulting tingle at my core, and sighed deeply.

"Spread your legs wider for me."

I pushed them farther with my palms and ran my fingers over my sex to open myself for him.

"Good girl," he crooned. "Do you remember the night I spanked you? Your ass was a beautiful shade of pink, and you begged me to take you, to ease the throbbing in your sweet little pussy."

His words sprinted like a brush fire across my skin, lighting the tiny hairs all over my body until I was scorched and completely bare. My eyes fell closed at the intensity.

"Open those eyes, siren. I want to watch my voice make you come."

I shuddered and pried my eyes open. His blue gaze still blazed, but his mouth was softened by a small smile that warmed my heart.

"Sinclair," I breathed restlessly, searching for the last component to trigger my release.

He stood, drained his whiskey, and made his way to my bedside. When he placed his cold glass over my bare navel, I shivered at its contrast to my feverish skin and held my breath as he leaned over me, bracing himself on one hand beside my left cheek.

"This is the last time, *ma petite voleuse*." He spoke just above my lips, the words slipping into my mouth on his warm breath. "So make it a good one."

I opened my mouth wider, maybe to protest or to beg, but his lips captured mine in a sweet open-mouth kiss. Two fingers trailed down my cheek and rested against my fluttering pulse.

"Come for me," he ordered softly as he pulled away.

And I did, in an explosion of sensation so deep that every muscle in my body contracted hard, so hard that I thought I was seizing. A scream ripped from my throat, and my legs scissored, trapping my hand between my thighs.

When I finally came down enough to open my eyes and release my hand, he was gone. The only sign of him was the empty tumbler on the bedside table and the feel of his control and desire lingering in my spent muscles. I squeezed my eyes shut and felt the tears come before I was even aware I was crying.

I'd wanted some kind of closure, fantasized about a sexual "farewell," and now that I'd had one, wrung from his voice and my hand, I felt despair deeper than any I had known before. Sinclair might have been in my life, a friend now, at least, but knowing I would never have his heart had never been so clear to me.

Chapter Seven

"**R**eally?"

I laughed loudly, but the lunch hour traffic on the busy terrace of the restaurant drowned out my lack of class. "Yes, really."

"I don't think I understand this." Mama's beautiful almond-shaped eyes squinted at me, a habit she had when English confounded her. "*Si vuole dipingere le persone aver fatto sesso?*"

You want to paint people having sex?

Cosima too was squinting, a thinner, younger look-alike. "No, Mama, it's Giselle."

I frowned at my family as they all nodded in agreement. They must be wrong, they thought, because sweet innocent Giselle would never do anything morally ambiguous and definitely not something so crude.

"I'm serious." I took a deep breath and slid my damp palms nervously over the soft jersey fabric of my dress. "I want to do a series depicting private sexual moments, a study of individual sexuality."

Elena blinked at me owlishly before laughing. I took a second to notice how light it was, tinkling like glass wind chimes. I almost winced at the comparison to my own brassy chuckle from a few minutes ago.

"You can't be serious? Who would even want to pose for you like that?"

I cleared my throat because this was part of the pitch that I really needed to nail. "I was hoping you would, for starters."

The second of shocked silence made me fidget. I reached out for my wineglass, almost tipped it over in my haste, and slipped my sweating palm back within the other.

"I can't believe you are asking your own family to pose nude for you." Elena's pretty features scrunched up in horror.

The shame I constantly felt in her presence threatened to overwhelm me, but I swallowed back the bile and forced myself to breathe.

"It's *art*, Elena, not porn, for fuck's sake," Sebastian chastized at her before turning to me with an arrogant grin. "How do you want me? I can give you a few phone numbers if you'd like a woman's opinion."

His wink made me snort, but Elena shook her head. "You are so crass."

"Which one of us is the more American, then, Elena? The crass one or the prude?"

He had a good point, but I covered my smile behind my hand.

"I'd be happy to do it," Cosima said softly, "but you might not like what you get."

I frowned at her. "You model swimsuits and lingerie, Cosi. Honestly, I didn't think this would be a tough sell for you."

She lifted one shoulder in an elegant shrug. "It is still enough clothing to cover secrets, no?"

"You don't want me. This body is old."

I turned sideways to face my beautiful mama. Caprice Lombardi was the kind of woman you dreamed up for an Italian centerfold; lushly curved under swathes of silky olive-toned skin gently creased like pleats at the corners of her light brown eyes, with hair too long for a woman her age in America but exactly right for an Italian, older but everlastingly sexy. She tugged at the end of her thick black braid now and stared at me with worried eyes as if she was letting me down for not being younger or prettier.

"You've been in America too long, Mama," Sebastian scolded, reaching across the table to take her hands. "A beautiful older woman is a delicacy."

Elena snorted softly and received a glare from both of the twins; otherwise, the remark went uncontested. It reminded me of what Elena had said when I had first arrived about Sebastian's affair with an older married woman. I resolved to ask him more about it, but he had been so busy since I'd arrived that I had barely seen him.

"He's right. You are gorgeous, Mama," I said and watched her beam at me.

She turned to Elena and pursed her lips, an indication that she was going to scold our eldest sister. Elena squirmed under the look.

"Of course, you will do this for Giselle too?"

It wasn't really a question, and I could see the darkness descend across Elena's features like a coming tempest.

"Really, Elena, if you don't want to do it—" I began.

"Of course she does!" Mama cried, her hands wildly punctuating the words. "We are a family; we do things, always, for each other, *si?*"

"*Si, Mama,*" we chorused diligently.

The twins shared a look, and Elena glared at me.

I sighed and played with the stem of my glass. Despite a few hiccoughs in our past, I still wasn't exactly sure why Elena hated me so much. It would have been awesome to have her on my side. We could have been a team of two like the twins, who were so close that it was easy to feel ostracized from them despite the wealth of their love for the rest of the family.

It had become impossible to think about Elena without Sinclair, and I wondered, in a growing series of what-ifs, whether I would still lust after, love after Sinclair if Elena and I were closer.

"I'm sorry I'm late." As if my thoughts had conjured him, Sinclair appeared beside Elena, bending down to place a kiss on her cheek.

He wore a perfectly tailored gray herringbone suit jacket with silvery gray flannel pants and a matching vest over a black button-up. His chestnut hair had been cut in the hours since I had last seen him, and it was now stylishly cropped short at the sides and longer at the top, softly waving back from his strong features. It softened and refined him, but I missed the length because it spoke of the slice of rebellion in his soul.

"It was my fault," Cage explained, coming up behind him with a wide grin. He took off his mirrored aviator sunglasses with a flourish and tossed them on the table. "The ladies couldn't get enough of me out front."

"I think it was Ryan Gosling they were after," Sinclair corrected dryly as he finished kissing Mama and Cosima's cheek, then shaking Sebastian's hand.

He was before me now, and I held my breath to see what he would do. Would he kiss me on both cheeks, or could we get away with a casual hello? He leaned down without hesitation, barely brushing his cool lips against my overheated skin.

"Hello, Giselle," he said, and I wondered if anyone else could hear the husky timbre in his voice.

"Ah, *ma belle chérie*." Cage swooped in to give me a slightly too long kiss on the mouth. His delicious scent, something like leather and pure masculine sex, wafted over me, and my lips softened under his firm pressure.

Sinclair cleared his throat loudly and thumped Cage on the back. "Sit down, Casanova."

Cage winked at me and sat down in the empty chair to my right, tugging my seat closer to his with a broad grin. He leaned over me to say to Mama, "You make gorgeous children, Caprice."

To my delight, Mama blushed. "You are very dangerous."

He barked with laughter, jutting his chin at Elena, the only person at the table not delighted with his presence. "Me? I wouldn't hurt a fly."

"Pfft, a fly, maybe no, but a woman's heart?" Mama shook her head somberly. "No chance."

We laughed at their banter, and everyone settled in to order their meals and catch up on small talk. I was glad for the reprieve. Being in Sinclair's presence after my embarrassing display of wantonness last night was awkward, to say the least, and I couldn't stop tugging anxiously on a lock of hair.

"Relax, Elle," Cage spoke with his head angled down at his menu, his full red lips unmoving. "You are acting like a thief in the police station."

I consciously slowed my darting gaze and looked over at him again to find his generous smile beaming back at me.

"I'm hopeless."

"Yes, but those in love normally are."

I sighed and rolled my shoulders back, determined to get over my own self-imposed discomfort.

"Much better," Cage murmured.

"You shouldn't have left me with him last night."

It wasn't his fault, not really. If Sinclair had wanted me, he would have succeeded with or without Cage's protests. In fact, I was about eighty-five percent sure that he had paid that guy to start a fight with my cute dance partner just to get him off me.

"*You* shouldn't have left him that last night."

My head jerked sharply over to him, my mouth slack.

Was he really bringing up Mexico in front of my entire family?

A quick look around the table confirmed that no one was listening and that Elena was affectionately fixing Sinclair's tie, but I still lowered my voice when I hissed, "You have no idea what you are talking about."

Cage ceased pretending to care about the menu and looked me straight in the eye. "It is you who has no idea what you could have had."

Before I could question him further, the waiter arrived to take our orders.

"Giselle wants to paint the family nude," Elena said before the server was even out of earshot.

My eyes were hot with embarrassment, but I tilted my chin up and tried to pretend she didn't make me feel like some kind of pervert.

"Oh?"

Oh? I glared at Sinclair. Really? All I get from the art connoisseur and ex-lover was a stupid, oh?

"Can I preorder those?" Cage asked innocently, speaking to me but looking at my older sister.

"Well, at least you know Cage will pose for you," Elena sneered.

"Yes, you might not believe it, but I look even better naked."

Sebastian leaned forward to pound fists with him, the movie star and the rock star bonding over their mutual self-love. It was almost adorable.

"I want to showcase sexuality," I tried to explain the idea that had come to me, fully formed, last night in the dirty wake of passion I had wallowed in after Sinclair left. "Those stolen, private moments that people are the most afraid to share."

"Interesting," Sinclair said. "Could you give us some examples?"

Elena frowned at him, but I continued, "Okay. An older woman propping her breasts up nostalgically, the press of a foot against an erection and the fetishism of it, or maybe a woman alone in a bathroom, staring at her reflection in the mirror as she masturbates."

Sinclair's eyes were on me. I could feel them roll off my face to the flushed skin of my chest like cold marbles.

"It will be tasteful, obviously," I hastened to add. "The point isn't the nudity or the sex; it's the vulnerability and the shame that stems from a person's most private desires."

I knew all too well the shame of desire. I could feel it like a punching glove to the heart every time I looked at Sinclair.

Everyone waited, looking at Sinclair, the man who owned a prestigious art gallery, a man whose opinion they would trust implicitly. I realized for the first time that I should have been anxious about impressing him because he was, in a sense, my *boss* in addition to my clandestine paramour.

I looked up, ready to face judgment, and our eyes locked with an audible *click*.

"Have you heard of Aleah Chapin? We hosted her at the gallery, and her work explores mature women in the nude. It's an interesting take, definitely a feminist one, and it has stirred a lot of interest in the art world." He paused, and a flicker of something like a smile teased the corners of his mouth. "I believe your show would stir a lot more than 'interest.' In fact, I believe you will have people lusting after your paintings faster than you can possibly produce them."

I smiled so hard that my cheeks hurt. "You really think so?"

He nodded curtly. "Without a doubt."

Cosima clapped her hands together. "Of course, they will! Our *bambina* is beautiful and talented."

Sebastian nodded thoughtfully. "You know, if you want to paint the family, would you be interested in including other famous people? I know a few actors who would be interested in posing for something like this."

My mouth dropped open in shock, and he laughed at me. "Close your mouth, *bambina*, it's not a sure thing."

"I think we need a bottle of Prosecco, *si*?" Mama smiled at the server and called him over. "We must have Prosecco, please."

"I'm afraid we only have champagne," he began to apologize, but Sinclair interrupted him.

"A bottle of Dom 2007, if you have it."

The young man nodded gratefully. "Excellent, sir. May I ask what the special occasion is?"

Mama beamed up at him. "My daughter is going to paint the naked people."

He blinked down owlishly at her before stuttering a nonsensical reply and scurrying off to get the champagne.

As soon as he was gone, we all dissolved into laughter. I giggled so hard that my belly ached, and Cosima was in tears. I caught Sinclair's eyes mid-laugh and saw him smiling at me, the rare soft and wide smile I loved so much. We stared at each other for what seemed like a long time, safe to indulge for a second amid the raucous laughter. I tried to convey my thanks for his approval, my guilty apology for my behavior the previous night, and the bittersweetness of sitting at my family table with him sharing a laugh with the people I loved most.

After a moment, he nodded at me as if he had understood every word in my gaze. Then he slowly dismantled the smile on his face so that when the others finally tuned back in, his features were once again perfect and impassive.

Cosima shed her clothes almost the moment we were in the door from lunch. Without a word, she had undone the knot at the back of her elaborately wrapped dress and let it fall to the ground.

"Where do you want me?"

My mouth opened and closed as I took in her scantily clad form, her breasts and lower half covered only in tiny scraps of web-like lace.

"You don't have to do this right now," I said even though my fingers itched to sketch her form, to imprint the beauty of her body and those tragic eyes Sinclair had spoken of onto canvas.

One slim shoulder rose and fell. "Why not?"

"It's just not really how it works, Cosi. I need to know more about your, well, your sexual history and what, well"—I blushed—"turns you on and stuff."

She stared at me with one eyebrow raised, amused and slightly condescending. "And stuff? My God, I hope you pitch this series better to the galleries."

I laughed and relaxed slightly. "You and me both."

"What shall I tell you, then?" She moved into the kitchen,

all grace and utter ease as she pulled out a chilled carafe of iced tea.

I took a seat at the island and watched her prepare me a drink, much like I had the night before with Sinclair. In a strange way, I wanted to ask Cosima many of the same questions I wished I could ask him.

"Do you have any sexual fetishes?"

Her nose wrinkled. "Sex is kinky by nature, no?"

"Well, sure, I guess. But I'm referring to specific things, terms maybe."

She was already shaking her head. "I've done a lot of things and rarely disliked any of them. American women might call me a slut."

I opened my mouth to protest, but her wink made me smile. "You're teasing me."

"A little."

I pouted.

"Alright, *bambina*, I will tell you a little something about sex." The word hissed out of her mouth and billowed into the air like steam from some fierce engine. "I've been nothing but this body for almost my entire life. It can be a powerful thing to be beautiful." She shrugged. "But if you don't have a reason to build strong bones beneath it, it is easy to become many very ugly things. Sad, used, dumb, or dead."

"You're strong."

Her slashing brows rose. "Maybe now, but let me tell you, I've also been sad, used, dumb, and very nearly dead."

We stared at each other. My heart was beating too fast, and I felt nauseous as my imagination went to work. What exactly had my little sister done to get us out of our poverty?

"The door was open."

Elena stood on the step below the kitchen, holding her pretty Prada purse in one hand and a bottle of wine in the other. She brandished it now and tried to smile. "I brought a peace offering. Daniel told me I was a bit... rude at lunch."

"You were a straight-up bitch, my darling Lena," Cosima corrected with a smile as she swooped down to hug her, uncaring of her unrobed state. "But I'm still glad you brought us wine."

I smiled slightly at Elena as she was ushered into the kitchen to the seat beside me, but I didn't acknowledge her quasi-apology because there was a much bigger one on the back of my tongue.

"Where are your clothes, Cosima?" Elena asked.

She grinned. "Giselle is going to paint me."

"What, now?"

"Yes," I said. "We were just getting started."

"Where would you like me?" Cosima asked.

I bit my lip as I contemplated what she had told me and gave her a brisk nod when an idea came to me. "I'll start with some sketches so you can keep your underwear on if you'd like. Stand over by the door."

She captured the pose I wanted in less than thirty seconds, her years of modeling experience making her the perfect visual muse. I had her standing astride, facing me like a proud warrior, naked and daring. Her body was lush in all the right places and defied gravity just as Cosima had defied the weight of poverty and then of expectation. I wanted her body in the sun, lit up under the brassy warmth like a trophy while her face, tucked slightly to the side, seeking the shadow, remained in the dark. I'd need to figure out how to catch the glimmer of gold in her eyes, the velvety softness of the color like worn cloth. The challenge excited me, and I trapped my tongue between my teeth as I littered the floor with page after page of sketches.

Every woman in the world wished they looked like that, unblemished golden skin glistening over long muscles and delicate bones. The midday sun was not kind to a body, but the harsh light shone like gilt on the inky waves rippling over her heavy breasts and tickling the bare skin above her pubis. Only three things disrupted her natural beauty; twin gold bars through her dark nipples, visible through the transparent lace bra, and a raised, bizarrely symmetrical scar three inches in diameter on her left butt cheek that she wouldn't really let me look at.

"I'm sorry about that," Cosima had said, dismissively gesturing at the nipple piercings. "Misspent youth and all that."

I wanted to see more of the brand, pepper her with questions until she couldn't help but sneeze out the answers.

Elena, for her part, kept curiously silent and empty of censure. I was pretty sure the nipple piercings had surprised her, and that Cosima's comfortable nudity offended her sensibilities. Still, she only sat perched on the stool with her legs crossed and her arms folded like a debutant at tea.

"You are so untroubled," she finally breathed after a long stretch of pencil scraping and silence.

"I've never had a hard time with nudity," Cosima said in a voice tinged with dark humor.

"How?"

I tried not to look at Elena, but I desperately wanted to see if her expression matched the quiet despair in her tone.

"We were all meant to be naked."

"Maybe women who look like you."

"No." Cosima's arched brows slammed down. "Every person is beautiful naked."

"Even without those curves?"

"Even with them?" I countered softly.

Elena and I looked at each other then and smiled over our shared sense of insecurity.

"You don't believe me because I look like this, but that is why I like Giselle's idea so much. Everyone is naked under his or her clothes, vulnerable under their masks, and a person's sexuality is an extension of their human need and their primitive desires. It is not a shameful thing."

"Who knew the swimsuit model was so wise?" I teased, my strokes on the thick paper looser now to accommodate Cosima's fluid expressions.

"You would be surprised by what standing in front of a camera every day will do to you." Cosima winked, but both Elena and I remained quiet because, I think, we had both wondered the exact same thing.

Elena sighed and propped her delicate face in her hands. "Listen, Giselle, I am sorry I was so negative earlier about your collection. I really would like to pose for you." She hesitated. "It will be hard for me, though, so maybe I could go last? By then, you might not even want me." She laughed awkwardly.

"I'll want you."

"Okay. I'd like to model then."

"Thank you, Elena." I smiled widely at her. "It means a lot to me."

"Well, I was hoping we could do a sort of trade? I'd love to commission you to do a painting of Daniel. His parents' anniversary is coming up, and I know it would make the perfect present."

"Um..." I tried desperately to analyze if it was a good idea or not. "I'm not sure if I'll have time with everything I have to do for the show."

"It would mean a lot to me," she echoed with a pretty smile, and I heard the trap catch around my ankle.

Cosima stifled a laugh at Elena's manipulation.

"Touché," I murmured.

"This is good. You should model for Giselle; you need to be more comfortable about sex. As the only one of us getting it regularly, Lena, I'm surprised you aren't more confident."

My heart stopped and stuttered at the restart.

Elena blushed, actually blushed. "He is insatiable."

A metallic taste flooded my mouth, and I realized that I had bitten clean through my lower lip.

Cosima laughed. "It's good to hear that you two are still going strong after so much time. Gives a girl some hope."

I swallowed back the nausea and focused on soothing my torn lip.

"Last night, he came home and practically accosted me," she admitted with that stupidly pretty blush. "He hasn't been like that for ages."

I stood before I could help it, the pencils in my lap clattering to the ground.

"Bathroom," I squawked before scurrying out of the room.

I pressed myself to the closed bathroom door and squeezed my eyes shut so tight they pulsed. I felt like a sickening swirl, circling the drain, full of dirt and debris.

Breathing heavily, I focused on reducing the thudding pace of my heart and tried to clear my mind.

Elena and Sinclair *lived* together. Of course, they were going to have sex. They belonged to each other; it was only natural.

A sob broke through my silence, and I clapped both hands over my wounded mouth.

Rational thought at the moment was definitely out of the question.

Before my thoughts could catch up to my actions, I had pulled out my cell phone and pressed his contact information.

"Faire Developments, Daniel Sinclair's office, Margot speaking."

Shit, I only had his office number.

"Hello, Margot." I cleared my throat. "This is Giselle Moore. I was hoping to speak with Mr. Sinclair about a recent development at DS Galleries."

There was a long pause as she digested both my name and

my stupid excuse to speak to her boss. "Any inquiries about the gallery can be made through Mrs. Rossi."

"I was told to speak to Mr. Sinclair specifically about this matter." *Bullshit, bullshit, bullshit.* Please buy it.

Another long hesitation ended in a sharp sigh. "Please hold."

My breath seemed grossly loud in the small bathroom, and I worried briefly about what my sisters would think I was doing. I thought about going out to tell them I was taking a call, or maybe just hanging up before I embarrassed myself further, when his voice came over the line.

"Miss Moore, how may I be of assistance?"

It was the businessman on the phone, not exactly what I wanted, yet his cool, perfectly formed words soothed me.

"Sinclair," I breathed because I didn't know what else to say.

There was a beat of silence. "Yes, I fully comprehend the seriousness of it. I'm in the middle of a meeting, though. I will call you back."

Click.

I stared at the home screen of my phone blankly for a second, absorbing the rush of disappointment that crashed over me. Of course, he was busy. I had no right to even call him in the first place. He was, at the most, my new friend and, at the worst, my ex-lover. You simply didn't call someone like that to vent, especially if it was about his or her goddamn partner.

"I'm going insane," I murmured to my wide-eyed reflection.

After a few deep breaths and chastisements, I washed my hands and went back to the kitchen where my sisters were chatting away amiably as if nothing had happened.

I guess nothing really had.

"I was just inviting Cosima to the annual Romani International charity gala next Friday," Elena said as I reclaimed my seat. "It's an organization that advocates for the rights of nomadic peoples across the world. I thought, maybe, and I know it is late notice"—she cleared her throat—"you might like to attend too?"

It was Sin's charity. My heart fluttered at the thought of discovering more about it and of seeing Candy Kay again.

"I would love to."

Elena and I smiled at each other for the second time that day, for the second time in over five years, and the tenderness I felt ached like a bruise.

My phone began to ring, and I looked down at the screen with surprise: *Faire Developments*.

"Excuse me." I slipped off my stool again and made my way to the balcony. "I should take this."

Cosima caught my eye as I moved past her, now clad in a robe, and I knew she was suspicious of my behavior. I ignored her and hustled outside.

"Hello?"

"Giselle." His voice was warmer. "I'm sorry about the delay. You sounded upset."

I sighed and leaned against the railing separating me from the nine-story drop. "I was, but that's no excuse. I'm sorry for bothering you."

"I'm flattered that you called me."

"Really?"

"Of course, it means I am the first person you think of when something bad happens. That's no mean status."

"No, I guess it isn't. Although, I was upset partially because of you."

"Ah, I suppose that makes sense." I could hear the humor in his voice. "What did I do this time?"

I smiled even though my words still hurt. "Elena was talking about your sex life. About, well, about how you went home last night and 'practically attacked her.'"

"I see."

I waited for him to elaborate or for me to somehow die of embarrassment, but neither happened.

"I told you it was silly. I'm sorry, I'll let you get back to work."

"Nothing you ever feel is silly, Elle." He sighed. "But what did you expect? Elena is my girlfriend."

"I know." God, I felt like a complete idiot.

"Don't feel stupid," he ordered, somehow reading my mind. "It's the fucking situation that is stupid, not you."

"I'm not making it any better," I admitted.

"And I am?"

We were both quiet for a moment. I stared down at the gorgeous chaos of early evening in New York, the yellow cabs and rivers of pedestrians. It seemed, at the moment, infinitely more organized than my life.

"Go fishing with me tomorrow."

"What?" Of all the things he could have said, I was least expecting that.

I told him so.

After he finished laughing, he said, "It won't compare to the Pacific, but autumn fishing in New York is the time to do it. I'll take you out to Manhattan Beach and introduce you to the Antonios of New York."

"There are more like him?" I couldn't imagine the eccentric Mexican fisherman being like anyone else.

"Not quite, but the regulars under the Verrazano Bridge are real urban fishermen. You'll like them. Better bring your camera."

I was grinning so widely it was difficult to speak. "I never go anywhere without it."

"It will be an early start," he warned. "On the water at five o'clock."

"Bring me a caramel latte, and I'm set."

"I'll be by at four thirty-five to pick you up."

"Okay."

"I'll see you then."

"Okay." My heart was beating fast; I didn't want to say good-bye. "I'll see you then."

"Just a thought before I sign off. Do you remember what you said when you discovered who I was? You weren't willing to hurt Elena. Admirable, Giselle, but maybe you should consider this; who else is hurting for your sacrifice?"

He hung up before I could respond, but I had nothing to say, so I guess it didn't really matter.

Chapter Eight

I woke up with a smile before dawn the next morning and sang loudly to Beatles music in the shower as I carefully washed every inch of my body. Though I usually let my hair dry naturally into thick waves, I applied curling product and blew it dry with a diffuser so that the red locks settled into large, messy curls around my flushed face. I knew it would be cold out on the water at the beginning of November, so I layered with care, rolling a gray turtleneck over my silk camisole and tugging thickly knit socks up to my knees over my blue jeans. The shades complemented my coloring beautifully, and when I put on the final touches, a dove gray knitted headband with matching gloves and scarf, I stared at my happy self in the mirror with quiet pride. This was the Giselle I wanted to be, happy and confident. It was hard to be like that under the current circumstances when I felt ugly and villainous with my family and desperate around Sinclair, but Cosima-level confidence took time, and I was happy with my progress.

I had been hoping to escape the apartment unobserved, but as soon as I left my room, I heard the swell of Italian music in the kitchen.

Cosima stood before the stove in thick socks and a pink cashmere robe, her inky hair swinging as she moved fluidly to the music, her voice raised in song.

"A bit early for Verdi, isn't it?"

She spun to face me with a wide smile, her quick eyes taking in my carefully coordinated outfit without expression.

"It is never too early for *il maestro*! Although, I would argue it is way too early to be looking so cute. Where are you off to?" she asked.

I poured myself a glass of water with ice from the fridge to buy myself some time. Sinclair hadn't said to lie about our outing, and was there really anything wrong with my sister's boyfriend taking me out? After all, I was new in town.

"Sinclair." I cleared my throat. "Daniel invited me fishing. I told him the other day at lunch that I had enjoyed it in Mexico, and he got pretty excited about taking me." I rolled my eyes. "Who would have guessed such a buttoned-up guy would be a fishing geek."

Cosima grinned as she stirred the fragrant concoction in her pan. "*Massive* fishing geek. He enters the Bassmaster Elite Series on Oneida lake every August, and I'm pretty sure he always takes his executives to Mexico just so he can get in some fishing."

I laughed, remembering how boyish and carefree he had been out on the water. "I'm looking forward to it."

"He's taken me out before." She scrunched her nose up. "Let's just say I'm more comfortable on land. I'd take horseback riding over fishing any day."

"Why are you up so early?" I accepted a plate of the stewed tomatoes and eggs with glee.

"A model dropped out of the Ralph Lauren shoot in England." She burned herself on the pan and cursed savagely in Italian. "I have to be in Cornwall by tomorrow."

"You don't seem too enthused, and that doesn't really explain the early start."

I had never been to England, but I did know Cosima had worked there after leaving Napoli.

"I hate England." She shrugged with one shoulder. "I leave later today, but I couldn't sleep thinking about it."

"That's a bit extreme, isn't it? I mean the entire country?" I grinned at her. "What did the Brits ever do to you?"

Her smile was uncharacteristically thin. "It's a smaller country than you'd think."

My phone lit up with a text from Sinclair. "I have to go."

I hopped out of my seat, shoveling another spoonful of tomato and eggy goodness into my mouth before pulling on my green gumboots. I spun around to give Cosima a hug, but she was already beside me, arms open.

Love bloomed in my chest like a prize-winning rose.

"If I don't see you before you leave, I'll miss you," I said, stepping into her spicy-scented embrace.

"I will be back in three days. If it was for any other brand, I wouldn't be going at all." She pressed a fragrant kiss to my cheek. "Now, be safe and enjoy your day. Sinclair can be a charming bastard when he wants to, so I'm sure you will have a grand adventure."

I smiled slightly, but her remark hit a little too close to home. She watched me with a curious smile as I collected my bag and slipped into an emerald green raincoat. Even after I had closed the door and descended into the lobby and out onto the street, I could still feel her eyes on me as if she had implanted a tracking device.

Happily, all thoughts of my sister fled when I saw Sinclair in a gorgeous blue Porsche idling at the curb. I squealed as I slid into the low two-seat car and swung to face him with a large grin. "This is *the* coolest car I have ever seen."

His small smile and sparkling eyes made me giddy. "It's a 964 series Singer Porsche 911."

At my blank look, he grinned boyishly as he gunned the throaty engine and pulled into the pre-dawn traffic. "I spent my early years in an orphanage in Nice, Giselle. I practically grew up watching beautiful cars drive by."

"Never close enough to touch," I murmured as I fingered the pale buttery leather seats.

He shrugged, but there was tightness around his eyes.

"I was not poor for long." He changed lanes and shot me a glance. "They found me when I was sixteen years old. Took me after two weeks of visitation."

"Love at first sight?"

His mouth twisted. "Willa was looking for the next big thing in Paris, and they took a vacation to the South, as if being in Paris wasn't vacation enough. She found Cage and me smoking in an alley and invited us for a drink. She was beautiful." He shrugged, but his muscles were too tense to pull it off. "I thought maybe she wanted to sleep with me. It happened sometimes."

"They didn't have to adopt you?"

"No, not really, and they didn't right away. You know they took both of us in, Cage and me, but I was the one they kept. Sometimes, I wonder if Cage hates me for it, but I'm the one who ended up with their bullshit."

"Wow." I blinked a few times as I digested the tide of information. "So you and Cage really have known each other forever. Did he go to America with you when you moved?"

"No, he stayed in Paris. They let him stay with their maid in their *pied-à-terre*. We visited every Christmas, but I haven't lived in France since I was seventeen."

"Do you miss it?" I asked.

I did every day, and I had only lived there for a handful of years.

"Yes and no. I think of myself as American now. It is this land that has sustained me. I will always love France; nearly everything is better there." I smiled at his typical French patriotism. "But I left many things there that are best left alone."

I bit my lip and stared out the window, debating whether to continue questioning him about his parents. I was so curious to know everything about him, but I didn't want to romanticize him further or make him uncomfortable.

But, as was always the case when I was around Sinclair, I couldn't help myself. "So, Willa represented you?"

His lids lowered. "Yes, but I only modeled for two years. When I turned eighteen, I demanded to be allowed to go to college. I was smart and well-mannered, the perfect young man in their eyes. I think they figured, why waste his potential? They already had Cage, the artistic prodigy and, to some extent, Cosima, who was the real talent in front of the camera and on the runway. Even better if their oldest son wanted to follow in his father's academic footsteps, maybe even follow him into politics."

"It's almost like a fairy tale. I mean, out of all the orphans in the world, they picked you. I would ask myself all the time how it happened. I mean, why you?"

His gaze snapped to mine, and I realized that I had touched a nerve. My hand reached out to brush through the thick reddish hair dangling in front of his face, and I pushed it back from his forehead.

"I know why I would have picked you," I amended softly.

He snorted. "You know, I didn't do anything to earn this face."

My heart twisted. How could he think he was only worth the value of his beauty? I had never met a more accomplished man in all my life, and I doubted I ever would.

"You're right. But you worked hard to develop into the sophisticated, intelligent, driven man you are today. And in my eyes, that's sexier than any six-pack."

He raised his eyebrows at me, and I giggled. "Okay, okay, I love your six-pack too."

There was a slight smile on his lips, and for a few moments, we drove in silence, listening to the deep rasp of Cage on the media system. He sang in English, his voice rising like the howl of the wind over the crashing drums and swooshing guitar. I had always loved *Caged,* and everyone in France seemed to quietly lust after at least one of the gorgeous band members, so I really hoped they could make it in America.

It was amazing to think about how inextricably linked we all were; Sinclair, Elena, Cosima, Cage, and I. They had been together for years, through the kind of experiences that I had only ever read about. Sure, I had known hunger and abuse, crime and drunkenness, but I had been young, shielded by the worst of it by my other siblings. I squirmed in my seat, feeling disgustingly naïve and fresh off the farm.

We finally pulled into a small packed lot beside the water, the lights of the city and Verrazano Bridge reflecting in the deep blue ocean. The combination of the urban and natural filled me with fizzy adrenaline and I quickly slipped out of the car with my camera to my eye in order to take a few pictures before the light picked up. But I was melancholy, sucked into the vortex of self-hatred and doubt that had plagued me throughout my younger years. It was a strange feeling to realize that I was extraordinarily lucky. I felt almost sick with it.

Sinclair was quiet too as he gathered our gear and briefly spoke to some other men going down to the rocky water's edge with their poles and coffee thermoses. I drifted away from him as he set up our stuff and politely asked to take some pictures of the beautifully weathered fishermen already sunk knee-deep in the icy waters. They consented without words, a grunt or nod or maybe a toothy grin was all I needed, and I was surprisingly grateful for their silence. The quiet felt good around me, like a warm blanket over my shivering sense of self.

When I finally made my way back carefully over the slippery rocks to our post, the sky was losing the last of its girlish blush, sinking into an eggshell blue. I stopped just to his left side and studied Sinclair through the lens, the way his hair rustled like liquid copper in the wind, and the slight flush that sat high on his pronounced cheekbones. I could understand why Willa had chosen him; his beauty was a strange thing, rare and almost inanimate, like a statue brought to life.

I don't know how long I stood there before he turned to me. We stared at each other, and I wished hopelessly that he could understand even one-tenth of the turmoil inside me.

He sighed, as if in answer to my unspoken desire, and placed his rod in a crevice between two large rocks. In three long, sure steps over slippery boulders, he was in front of me. I tipped my head to maintain eye contact. I was strangely breathless as his intensity exerted itself like the force of gravity on my lungs.

"Elle." His cool hands cupped my face. "Stop thinking."

I tried to articulate myself but could only shake my head.

"I didn't bring you out here to overthink, to stress or worry about if what we are doing is wrong. I brought you here because this is one of my favorite places in New York, and I wanted to share it with you. Can you please let it be as simple as that?"

I shook my head again, but this time, I found my voice. "Why me?"

His eyes darkened. "You won't like the answer to that."

My heart plummeted to the pit of my stomach so quickly

that I thought I would throw up. Somehow, I managed to smile thinly and step away from him instead.

"Fair enough," I said, moving past him to grab my smaller rod.

It was purple with a glittery grip, and I laughed wetly as I took it into my hand. When I looked over at him, he was shaking his head at me in irritation.

"Is this Elena's?" I asked because I was that masochistic.

"If you can't stop yourself from saying idiotic things, don't speak," he barked, striding back over to pick up his rod.

I blushed at his reprimand, but it was true. I was being petty and weak. Why couldn't I just enjoy this gorgeous morning with this gorgeous man? Don't look a gift horse in the mouth and all that. So—I took a deep breath and shoved all the grime in my soul under the rug—I wouldn't.

"You bought it for me, didn't you?" It was a rhetorical question because I knew he was too angry with me to answer. "Thank you, it's adorable."

He nodded curtly and adjusted his stance.

"*Je n'arrête pas de faire l'andouille,*" I murmured just loudly enough for Sinclair to hear me.

I snuck a glance over at him and saw his lips twitch reluctantly.

"I just can't stop making the sausage," I repeated, this time in English.

I beamed as he chuckled, shaking his head at my antics.

"You may be acting like a fool," he agreed, taking a side step to bump me with his hip. "But at least you are an adorable fool."

I laughed too, so relieved that the tension had dissipated that I felt almost giddy.

"I love French expressions." I sighed happily and leaned into him.

"They have to be the most nonsensical idioms in any

language," Sinclair noted, but his voice was warm, and I knew he was happy to have someone to speak to about France.

"Well, *les doigts dans le nez* happens to be my favorite, and it makes absolutely no sense. That's the beauty of them. I mean 'the fingers in the nose' does *not* translate well to 'with my eyes closed.'"

"Who do you think knows more?" Sinclair's eyes gleamed with challenge as he looked down at me.

"Me, hands down. You said yourself you haven't considered yourself French in a long time. At this point, I probably speak your language better than you do," I taunted.

He leaned down, so close to my face that I could smell his minty breath, and grinned boyishly.

"You're on."

We spent the entire morning in Brooklyn. After five hours in the water with three gorgeous striped bass in our cooler, we made our way to a small pizza shop that was already packed at eleven in the morning. The pie was cheesy, greasy, and loaded with fat speckled pepperoni, and we devoured it between sips of Sprite, which we both agreed wasn't nearly as refreshing as the French Schweppes.

He caught me up on the developments with the Mexican resort; Richard Denman was flying into town with the preliminary blueprints, and he was in the process of procuring a decrepit building near the Hudson, which he hoped to turn into high-end condos. I loved the passion in his eyes as he spoke about his work, and I knew that, despite his parents' wishes, he would never go into politics when he could be building things.

I told him about my years in Paris, how I had met Brenna and why my relationship with the Canadian boy had ended. Nothing serious passed our lips, and by the time the check came, my lips were rubbery from wearing a smile for so long.

As we slipped back into the Porsche, I thought about how easy it was to forget about everything else when I was with Sinclair. Our chemistry still sizzled in the air between us, but today had truly felt like a date between friends, our looks full of a different kind of intimacy.

The closer we got to Manhattan, the stiffer I became as reality began to encroach on my thoughts. In an hour, he would be home with Elena, and I would be back to pining for the unattainable Frenchman.

"Stop overthinking," Sinclair ordered, placing his hand on my thigh. "We just had an amazing morning. Let's not ruin it by thinking."

I sighed. "Am I that easy to read?"

"You forget how well I know your body."

His fingers splayed across my jean-clad thigh, and I could feel the heat of his touch through the thick material.

"I *should* forget," I said.

"No, don't ever."

I shifted out from under his hand and looked out the window. How could he so easily balance the morals of this situation? Was it because he really didn't care about me in any way other than as a friend, with only a lingering desire for my body? I knew he wasn't a bad person, that he wasn't hoping to use me for sex or manipulate me into falling further in love with him, but no matter his intentions, both outcomes were entirely possible.

"Why don't we swing by and pick up Cosima?" he suggested, his voice bright for my benefit. "When we first moved to New York, we went to a show on Broadway every Saturday."

"That's a good idea," I agreed, mostly because I knew he suggested it to put me at ease. If Cosima joined us, it wouldn't be so taboo. That he usually hung out with my sister suggested that our behavior was *fine*.

Sinclair waited in the car while I zipped up to our apartment to fetch her. I was pulling the keys out of my purse to open the door when I saw that it was already cracked open. The hairs on the back of my neck stood on end as I slowly pushed the door open.

I cautiously moved through to the back of the apartment and finally caught a glimpse of someone sitting at the island in the kitchen, someone I had never seen before. My gasp must have alerted him because the large, bare-chested man swiveled on the stool to face me.

His broad face was tight with pain, and my eyes quickly crossed the quilted breadth of his chest to latch onto the sight of his hand over a bloody towel pressed to his left side. Through my shock, I noted the thick, wavy dark hair falling into black eyes and bronzed skin. He was so gorgeous that he made my eyes water.

I was just opening my mouth to scream or question him when Cosima came sweeping into the room, her eyes focused on the medical kit in her hands.

"*Cazzo*, Dante, I don't know why you don't just –"

"Cosima," the man named Dante practically purred in a voice like none I had ever heard, thick and pulsating with sexual allure. "We have a visitor."

I was looking right at her when those golden eyes shot to me and widened. Her mouth formed a perfect 'O' of horror, and she dropped the tin box to the counter with a loud clang.

"What are you doing here?"

"Um, I live here. What is a man doing in our kitchen with a *bleeding wound*?"

Dante adjusted in the chair, leaning back as if he wasn't clutching what I was sure was a bullet wound.

"I..." Cosima sighed loudly and pushed her hair back with both hands. "Listen, Giselle, I need you to leave. Right now."

I looked between her and Dante, whose eyebrow was raised at her in curiosity.

"Are you kidding me right now? I'm not leaving you here like this!" I said, throwing an arm out to indicate the burly man in our kitchen.

"You are." Her voice was aflame with surety. "You are going to go out for the afternoon and enjoy the city, think about your show and see friends. You will *not* say anything about this to *anyone*, and I will text you when you can return to the apartment."

"Cosima," I started to yell, but her posture changed, arms crossed under her breasts and eyebrows drawn so low over her eyes I could only see dark pits of determination.

Dante stared at me impassively, but the moment his eyes flicked to my sister, they burned like hot coals. He seemed proud of her for showing me the door and not the least bit distressed that I had walked in on him or, more importantly, that blood was seeping through the towel and the firm press of his fingers, coating them a lacquered red.

"Cosima..." I tried again, my voice softer because I knew I would leave like she wanted me to.

She shook her head firmly but brushed her hand feather light down my cheek as she moved forward to tend to Dante.

"*Parta.* Go."

I backed away slowly, but they didn't notice or care. Cosima was bent over her wounded soldier whispering passionately in Italian while he closed his eyes and hissed with pain. They were a striking pair, and under other *normal* circumstances, I would have loved to stick around to get to know him better, to see what kind of relationship they had.

Instead, I tip-toed quietly to the front door, slipping past them without trouble, but I froze with my hand on the knob when I spotted the unfamiliar keys tossed on the small hallway table.

Beside them rested a small, strangely innocuous-looking black gun.

"Excuse me."

I turned around to see Dante looming over me, so tall that I had to crane my neck back uncomfortably to meet his black eyes. A shiver started at my ankles and coated every inch of my skin. He brought to mind the men I had known in Naples, the kind of men who took what they wanted regardless of the cost. They were the same ones Cosima had run away from when she left home.

Dante was a Mafia man.

"Uh, yes?" I asked, finally.

A smirk sliced the right side of his lips and gave his beautiful face an almost manic charisma. I held my breath as he stepped closer and slowly leaned toward me. I closed my eyes when his breath fanned across my face, although I wasn't sure what I was thinking in doing so.

His dark chuckle alerted me to the cool air now brushing my front, and I peeked through one eye to see him standing at a respectable distance again, this time with the gun in his large hand. I let out a sound somewhere between a yip and sigh. His grin stretched wider.

"Shouldn't leave this lying about now, should I?"

I frowned at his accent; somehow, I hadn't placed it before. "You're British."

A snarl tangled his features for just a second before he stared calmly at me. "And you are Giselle, the beloved sister of my Cosima. She wouldn't like it if she knew we were talking but, please, let me just say"—his blatantly sexy smile punched me in the gut with reluctant desire—"it is an absolute pleasure to finally meet you."

"I've never heard of you," I said as I moved closer to the door and twisted the knob.

Dante continued to smile at me. I had never seen a man with so many different kinds of smiles.

"You will," he promised.

I shut the door and fled down the hall to the elevators.

*W*e saw *Wicked*. I hadn't wanted to see it. After all, a play about a woman who descends the slippery slope into villainy was a little too close to home for my tastes, but Sinclair, with his slight smile—much preferable to Dante's sinister smirks—had insisted that it was not to be missed.

"Okay, okay," I admitted as we followed the crowd out of the theater. "That was absolutely amazing."

He shot me a sidelong look as we walked into the fading sunlight.

"Don't you dare tell me 'I told you so,'" I threatened, leveling a finger at his twitching lips.

He held his hands up in mock surrender, but his voice seriously lacked sincerity. "I don't even feel the need."

"And I don't want to hear anything about the bad witch being a sympathetic character or anything, okay?" I added with narrowed eyes. "Last time I checked, you didn't have a degree in English."

"No, you're right. Just psychology."

"You're kidding?"

His gorgeous eyes sparkled as his hand found my lower back to gently usher me through the throbbing crowds in Times Square. "And a Master's in Business Administration from Columbia."

I stared up at him, knowing that he would safely see me through the swarms of people. "I really don't know anything about you, do I?"

He shrugged, and I immediately regretted puncturing our beautiful bubble with the sharp edge of reality.

"You know considerably more than most people. The facts you are referring to can easily be looked up online."

"I thought about doing that, looking you up. But I was too nervous," I admitted as I stopped to root through the pocket of my parka for change.

The violinist who swayed to the sound of his own lilting tune nodded at me even though his eyes remained closed. He was so absorbed in his music, his passion, that he had transcended his body.

Art had always been the medium of my sublimity. My love for Sinclair was devastatingly similar, dangerous because it did not recognize right or wrong. It simply existed. I smiled at the violinist with my heart in my eyes before turning to look over at Sinclair, who viewed me with that inscrutable expression.

"I must admit I haven't read my own Wikipedia page. We have someone at the company to manage those sorts of things, but I am reasonably sure that there is no mention of me being a serial killer or something equally disturbing."

I snorted. "I wasn't worried about that. You tied me up and spanked me; if you had wanted to kill me, then you definitely had the opportunity to."

He grinned at me, shaking his head almost reluctantly as if he couldn't quite believe I was real. I beamed back at him and didn't notice the seriousness in his eyes until it was too late.

"You were worried about seeing pictures of me with Elena."

I swallowed painfully and nodded.

He sighed and brought us to a complete stop in the middle of Times Square. The darkness brought out the multicolored lights flashing against his features and reminded me of our strangely intimate time at his club.

"Giselle, I want you to listen to me when I say this because I know you will only let me tell you once." His hands fell heavily onto my shoulders so that he could bring me closer. "You have nothing to be ashamed of. At the risk of sounding callous, I do not regret the time I spent with you in Mexico and neither should you, not unless you truly did not enjoy it."

"Don't be ridiculous." My voice was fainter than I would have liked, but it was hard to speak past the gunk of volatile emotions clogging my throat. "It's not about me, though. It's about Elena."

"Is it?" His hands squeezed my shoulders. "Or could it just be about us?"

I was already shaking my head. "It doesn't work like that."

"We set the fucking rules, Giselle." He stepped back from me and glared, his eyes so cold they burned. I didn't know what he could have been thinking, staring at me with such furious intensity in the crowded space, the bodies bumping into us and the cacophony of downtown New York City completely forgotten.

"No, we don't." I laughed but there was a frenzied edge to it that made me realize I was close to having a panic attack. "I haven't set the rules for my own in life *ever*. And now? When I could ruin the life that my sister has so carefully constructed for herself? It's not the time to start."

Sinclair glared at me for another long minute before stuffing his hands in his pockets. He looked off into the crowd and shook his head.

"I would hate to call you a coward, Elle, but a person who does not pursue their own happiness is definitely that."

"I am happy." When his eyebrows rose coolly as I had known they would, I shrugged gracefully. "I really am. Right here, right now with you, I am happy."

"And when I go home to Elena?" he countered.

It was my turn to look off into the distance at the hundreds of people passing under the colored lights of Times Square.

Finally, I pursed my lips and faced him. "Will you be?"

"You've asked me before not to answer that question."

"You're right. You are still with her, though, so I guess I have my answer, don't I?"

He frowned at me, but I smiled softly at him and linked my arm through his to pull him through the crowd. I was done with heaviness and despair. The regret and the shame would surely visit me in the morning when I woke up heavy with my separation from him. For now, I was content to fool myself into a friendship with him, this man I loved.

"Want a pretzel?"

There was only a slight hesitation before he said, "Only if they have Dijon mustard."

I hid my sigh under a smile and fell just a little bit more in love with him for going along with my charade.

Chapter Nine

"You seem to be spending a lot of time with Daniel."

I paused, my hand hovering over the canvas precariously. I could see my hard heartbeat shake my hand.

"Huh?"

Cosima's gold eyes swiveled my way, but she didn't move a hair out of position. "I said, you seem to be spending a lot of time with Daniel."

I focused carefully on adding a dab of burnt umber to the mixture on my palette, darkening the shadow beneath Cosima's round breasts and between her proudly braced legs. The painted woman who stared out from the shadows of the canvas peered at me with the same expression as her real-life counterpart, unerringly direct and more than a little disconcerting.

I exhaled a breath I hadn't known I was holding when she shrugged and said, "It's nice that you get along. He has been part of my life, of the family, for so many years it is weird to think you two only just met."

Only just met... Well, we had only met two months ago almost to the day, but it felt like so much longer. And we had been spending a lot of time together, too much really if we wanted to fly under the radar. Sinclair had assured me that Elena worked too much to notice and that he often spent his free time with Cosima. Luckily, Cosima had been wrapped up in her own world for the past ten days, probably with the dangerous-eyed Dante.

"Yeah." I forced my voice to be casual. "He is a nice guy, if a little stuffy."

She ignored my attempt at criticism and broke her pose to open the door behind her. We were in her kitchen/dining area again, which had lately served more as my studio than anything else. Canvases were stacked against the island, and sketches were taped to the wall beside the door. In the last two weeks, I had finalized sketches of Cosima, Sebastian, Cage, and even one of Mama, hovering over the stove in a damp robe with the sheen of sweat on her soft skin. She hadn't blushed at all when I suggested the idea. I wanted to explore the tried and true roles of older women and exploit the sensuality they still retained despite the domestication. Mama had laughed joyfully at the suggestion.

"I have to admit, I'm a little surprised. You are one of my favorite humans on the planet." Her smile poured over me like sunshine. "But Daniel doesn't like change. I think the last friend he made was Elena."

My skin itched. I was always careful not to ask too many questions about their relationship, but this was just too good an opportunity to pass up.

"How did they meet?"

"Why don't you ask Elena? She should be here in ten minutes or so, and I have to get ready to leave."

She slipped on the translucent black robe laying on one of the stools, but something in my face made her hesitate on the way to her bedroom.

She sighed and came over to cup my face in her warm hands. "We have all been apart for a long time, Gigi, and we are all used to keeping ourselves to ourselves, yes? So, if you want to know something, you must not be afraid to *ask* it, or else you will never really know."

I nodded but didn't meet her eye as I moved away to clean my brushes before Elena arrived. Cosima's signature sigh punctuated her exit, and I was grateful for the few minutes alone I had before my older sister arrived.

I hadn't seen her since the day Sinclair had invited me fishing, but we had spoken over the phone about her appointment today. Though we hadn't talked yet about her sexual hang-ups, I was already picturing her standing tense and rigid before a background of wood planks, naked but for the magazines, something like *Playboy* or *Sports Illustrated*, held tight to her private areas. It wasn't an unusual feeling, the inferiority complex that could make a woman as stiff as a board, but I knew my sister had it in spades. I wasn't judging; before Sinclair, I had been very much like that too.

After washing my brushes gently in turpentine solution, I set them out to dry and moved my easel to face the wall so that it would remain private until its completion. I grabbed my large sketchbook and my tin of charcoal before settling on a stool at the counter to do some preliminary drawings.

My mind wandered as my hand swooped across the thick page, inevitably settling on my situation with Sinclair. In just over two weeks, we had lunched together twice, gone to see Cage play a solo set at a new bar in Soho, and attended an art show in Brooklyn. We had been careful, though, not to be anywhere private. After what had happened at Cosima's apartment, I think we were both wary of our control. It was also the reason I hadn't asked him to sit for me even though Elena wanted his portrait done in less than a month. Instead, I chose to work from picture and memory. There were enough photos of him on the boats in Mexico and online that I felt confident enough to produce his likeness.

I would see him tonight at the Romani International gala, but I knew it wouldn't be the same. He would be there with my sister, his girlfriend, on his arm. They made a beautiful couple, as immaculate as wedding cake toppers.

Even though we hadn't touched inappropriately since I had stroked myself at his behest after the club that night, the electric current between us was constantly charged, and I wondered if we would be able to mask it well enough to fool our families tonight.

"Giselle."

I looked up at Elena and tried not to sigh in defeat. She stood before me in a gorgeous gray cashmere coat that perfectly complemented her shoulder-length artfully curled red hair. Her heart-shaped face was exactly the same as mine, but her features were more refined, and perfectly symmeterical like a China doll. Only her eyes, a deep gray under slightly heavy lids, could have been anything but classically stunning, maybe even sexy if she let them be.

I shook myself as I stood to give her a kiss on each cheek. "You look lovely. Would you like a cup of tea?"

She shook her head and swallowed. "It's after four, isn't it? I'd love some whiskey."

My eyebrows shot up before I could help it. "Uh, sure. Why don't you make yourself comfortable, and I'll get us some glasses."

We were quiet as I puttered about the kitchen, looking for

the alcohol and tumblers, but she was thinking so loudly it rivaled the buzz of the refrigerator.

I smiled gently at her as I sat down and handed over her drink. "I know you might be uncomfortable, but we should talk about your, um, sexual preferences before we get started."

"I don't like it," she blurted out, her eyes enormous with horror. Her hand clamped over her mouth as she shook her head.

I watched her mutely as she took a long sip of the burning whiskey and straightened her shoulders. "I apologize. I meant to say, I don't really enjoy sex."

What!? How could she not enjoy sex with Sinclair? Of all the things she could have divulged, I never would have guessed it was this.

"I understand that men need it," Elena explained calmly as if we were talking about the weather. "But I've never really understood the appeal."

"Have you never orgasmed?" Again, I couldn't fathom that Sinclair, the man who had unraveled me so thoroughly in Mexico, could have failed to bring any woman the ultimate pleasure.

I felt a little sick talking to Elena about Sinclair like that, but I had trapped myself in a corner and could only pray we ended the conversation quickly.

She stared into her nearly empty glass and swirled the contents. Her face was slack with unspeakable sadness.

"Do you remember Christopher?"

A shudder wracked my body. Why was she bringing him into this? I nodded.

"When you left, he came back for me. He still wanted to marry me." Her accent had slipped back into her words, a silk ribbon strangling her speech. "Mama approved. She didn't know about what had happened between you and him." She shot me a look, not accusatory—I could have dealt with that—just sad. "She let me stay with him a lot because we were going to be married. He took advantage of it, keeping me for days at a time."

"What did he do?" I whispered.

I knew what Christopher was capable of.

She shrugged soggy shoulders. "A lot of things. Things that I don't have words for. One day, he went too far. Luckily, Cosima was in town. She came to take us to America." She laughed wetly, her sloe-eyes glistening. "I still don't know how she found me, but that was the last time I ever saw him."

We were silent. My hand trembled as I poured her more whiskey.

"Anyway, I can enjoy sex and, trust me, with Daniel, I do. But the desire for it?" She shrugged. "It's just not really there."

I stared down at my sketchpad for a few minutes as I tried to digest our conversation. The silence wasn't awkward, though, and when I looked back up at my older sister, she was biting her thumbnail like she had done as a child.

"Hey, Elena?" I murmured, waiting until her low-lidded eyes met mine. "Do you want to go out for a drink?"

"Well, what about the painting?"

I stood and winked at her. "I'd rather get drunk."

"Oh, thank God." Elena grinned too. "Let's do it."

We didn't get drunk. After all, I was drinking with Elena, a notorious stick in the mud, and we were only a few hours away from a highly publicized charity gala. But we had a few glasses of delicious Italian wine at a ridiculously chic bar Elena had chosen not far from the apartment. We talked about work mostly because it was one of the only things on the very short list of acceptable topics to talk about with each other. Her passion for the law came through in her suddenly expressive hands and the way her speech slipped and swayed into broken English in her haste to explain the legal profession to me.

When she tried to deviate, I choked a little.

"Excuse me?"

She shrugged elegantly. "You seem to be very close with him. I was just curious, are you sleeping with him?"

"Elena!" I laughed nervously and watched as she took it the wrong way, thinking it was true, that I must be sleeping with the sexy French singer.

I didn't know what to do. How could I tell her it was because I was sleeping with the sexy French businessman instead?

"You've been spending too much time with Cosima. Her

dramatics are rubbing off on you," she teased, only slightly awkward.

"Oh, calm down. I was just shocked that my conservative older sister wants to discuss my sex life. Sebastian would be in hysterics if he heard you now."

She frowned, and I took a moment to notice how the expression barely creased the skin across her forehead beside her eyes. She was so perfectly modulated that it was like interacting with a robot, one dressed very tastefully in a silk sheath dress.

I sighed. "I am not sleeping with Cage. He's just a good friend."

"A very handsome one."

"Are you saying handsome boys and girls can't be friends, Elena? That seems like pretty simple thinking." I couldn't help the little barb. Insulting her intelligence was the weakest chink in her armor.

"I don't believe they can." She sniffed. "And anyway, I don't know why you would want to spend time with such a barbarian."

I laughed. "Cage is hardly a barbarian. Now, who's being dramatic?"

"Who's being defensive?"

I glared at her. "Listen, Elena. I'm not comfortable talking about my sex life with you, but that doesn't mean I'd lie about being with Cage. I'm not."

She pursed her lips and stared at me intently as I swung my coat over my shoulders and collected my bag.

"Please don't tell me I'm the only one in our family without some weirdo fetish."

My head snapped back so quickly it hurt, but I masked the pain and my horror so that I could look at her unaffected. I wondered briefly if Sinclair was rubbing off on me.

"Weirdo?" I echoed.

When she remained unfazed, her eyes wide and filled with insecurity-infested waters, I realized that my older sister, a pillar of strength, was terrified of being found wanting.

I sighed and leaned over into her personal space to press a warm kiss to her cheek. It was something Cosima or Seb would have done, but I was beginning to understand how much more eloquent touch could be than the spoken word.

"You're perfect, Elena. No comparisons necessary."

She smiled and patted my hand where it rested on the table. I watched her awkward movements with a raised brow, and she sighed lightly before entwining our fingers. A lock of beautifully curled hair fell across her pale forehead like a wine stain on a fancy tablecloth. She was so lovely in her timidity that it took my breath away.

"I'm not very good at this communicating thing," she said, waving a hand through the air to illustrate her lack of eloquence. "To be perfectly frank, you make me uncomfortable. I know you don't mean to, but that's how I've always felt."

"Um, okay," I said, because while I appreciated her attempt to open up, what else was I supposed to say to that?

She squeezed my hand before releasing it. Our increased physical distance seemed to calm her skittishness. "What I mean to say is, family is important to me, and I would appreciate it if we could both make a greater effort to get to know each other again."

The portion of my soul that was supposed to house my moral compass was achingly empty and hollow against the knock her words had rung upon it. My hand shook slightly with the reverberations as I reached for my glass and swallowed the last of my wine.

"I'd like that, Elena. Very much."

She smiled, a slight but genuine tilt of her closed lips. "Good. As an olive branch, I would love to set you up with a wonderful friend of mine. His name is Ulrich Wick. He works in finance, and he has the loveliest head of hair."

I bit my lip against my protest because as far as olive branches went, it was relatively harmless, and honestly, it would probably do me good to go out with someone new.

"That sounds lovely." I leaned in to give her a hug and smiled slightly when she gave me her customary pat on the back.

"Does Wednesday work for you?"

"Sounds great," I said. I donned my coat and began to walk toward the door. "I'll see you tonight."

"Excellent. Oh and Giselle?" she called after me. "Try to wear something more appropriate for daytime when you see Ulrich, he's a tad old fashioned."

I waved my consent at her over my shoulder and pushed through the door into the welcome city bustle.

Despite the awkwardness, I was glad we had spent some quality time alone. It didn't change how I felt about Sinclair. It hadn't lessened or intensified my guilt, and honestly, it hadn't made me feel any closer to Elena.

It was strange how indifference could cripple a relationship just as assuredly as animosity.

Still, I hadn't spent quality time with my eldest sister in years, and it was interesting to catalog her growth and sameness. She went for a manicure every month but still picked at her hangnails when she was nervous, and she spoke with a perfect English accent, but the wrinkle between her brow when people spoke too quickly belied her aptitude with the language. She was such a writhing mass of contradictions I wasn't sure how to read her, let alone get along with her. And I was okay with that.

Did it make me a terrible person that I found my time spent with Elena most lent itself to my relationship, or lack of one, with Sinclair?

Because I could understand now how he could love her, how very compatible they were even if it was artificially. The superficiality of their likeness was exactly the point of their relationship; they both liked to live life behind a meticulously honed mask of respectability and elegance.

*L*ater that night, I looked in the mirror as I carefully applied the last of my lipstick, a deep reddish-pink that complemented the dark gray, silver threaded dress Cosima had helped me choose earlier that week. The silk flowed down my curves like rainwater over steel, binding my waist and baring a deep square of flesh between my breasts. My auburn hair, lighter than it had been since my sun-kissed summers in Napoli, spiraled softly around my lightly freckled shoulders.

"It's good," I murmured to myself in the mirror, sucking in a deep breath and adjusting my full breasts in the tight panels to show them off to their best advantage.

But I didn't feel good. My heart was fragile and dry in my chest, something that had been set aflame and with each beat turned slowly to ash. I wished Cosima was here to press a fragrant kiss to my cheek and tell me I was beautiful or Brenna, who would have already popped the champagne and made our preparation into a party. I wasn't used to dressing up, but it felt sad and a little wrong to do it alone, especially when I was already wretched with the thought of facing Éclair (my couple name for Elena and Sinclair).

I grabbed my jeweled clutch and slipped my feet into delicately strapped black shoes before opening the door to leave.

"Mind a tag-along?"

My head whipped up, a lock of my hair sticking to my eyelashes, to see Sebastian decked out in a gorgeous black tuxedo. He held a box of sweets from Dylan's Candy Bar and a small silver flask.

"This is to get us through the night." He indicated the flask and then held up the candies. "And this is your reward for afterward."

"A handsome man comes to my door bearing gifts? I'd be a fool not to take him." I slipped into his arms for a spicy scented hug and closed my eyes for a second to absorb how good it felt to be with my brother again.

We stood like that for a moment before I murmured, "How did you know I'd need you?"

He hesitated and pressed a kiss to the top of my hair. "Cosima might have suggested it."

My heart stuttered. I knew Cosima was perceptive, but how much had she surmised about my relationship with Sinclair? Could she possibly know?

"Come on, Cinderella, you'll be late for the ball."

Sebastian gently pulled me from his arms, placed the candy on the side table, and locked up the apartment with his spare key.

We traveled in Sebastian's luxurious Bentley, whose cream leather interior retained its new car smell. His driver, a short, stocky man with vibrant orange hair, greeted me in a thick Scottish accent before Sebastian put up the privacy screen.

He opened the flask, took a long swig, and passed it to me, watching me with narrowed eyes as I swallowed a burning mouthful.

"You are so different, *bambina*." His voice held only the faintest trace of Italy, a whisper that suggested he was foreign but gave no indication of his nationality unless you were familiar with the sounds of Naples.

"So are you."

He leaned back in his seat, slinging an arm over the ledge above the in-car bar. His thick black hair waved across his bronze forehead and accentuated the pure gold of his eyes. He was so handsome, but the way he held his mouth, even to smile, was off. Crooked in a way that might have been sexy to some but just seemed sad to me. There were so many secrets between my family members that it seemed impossible we could ever regain our childhood closeness.

"I had an affair in Mexico."

It was a huge admission for me, but Seb, the seasoned movie star, only raised one brow, so I barreled on.

"He was amazing." I couldn't keep my voice from turning dreamy. "No one has ever made me feel so safe and so inspired to push past my comfort zone. He was handsome and intelligent and just remote enough to make him seem mysterious." I laughed at myself and shrugged. "So, obviously, I fell in love with him."

"But?" I raised my eyebrows at him, and he sighed dramatically before explaining himself. "As a man, I know there is always a 'but' with women, and it is almost always justifiable."

"Well, you're right. The 'but' is that he is taken."

"Ah, that is a significant 'but.'" His eyes sparkled as he took another sip from the flask. "Is it just me, or have you forgotten what type of butts we are talking about?"

I laughed and hit him lightly in the shoulder. "You are such a goofball."

"Self-proclaimed and proud of it." He winked.

My giggle ended on a sigh as I looked out the window and spotted the Four Seasons Hotel looming ahead of us. I startled when Sebastian reached over to take my hand in his, but I didn't look over at him when he started to speak.

"For whatever reasons, tonight is going to be difficult for both of us. I want you to know that I'm here with you, *bambina*. We are going into this hive of bees together unified. If you want to leave at any time, say the Italian word."

The Italian word was a precaution we had established as children when Seamus would return home twitchy and bloated after days of drinking and gambling. When the fights grew too loud between our parents, and mostly, when the Camorra came to collect their payments from Seamus, whether he had the money or not, Elena would call out *insieme*. We each had our own hiding places; the twins were tucked into the closet behind the water heater while I was placed under the back porch. Elena had taken the worst haven, under the sink in the kitchen, a place that was kept empty by Mama specifically for that reason. I had always wondered how much my older sister had witnessed from her cramped hideaway, how much the violence and conflict had affected her. I knew the hours spent cold and alone outside had led me to detest the feeling of both.

"*Insieme*," I murmured. "Together."

Sebastian nodded and placed a kiss on my knuckles as we came to a stop in front of the gorgeous hotel, an elegant pale stone façade surrounded by modern glass architecture. I was in awe as Seb ushered me from the car into the tasteful lobby and up the sweeping marble staircase to the main event room.

I blinked rapidly when we entered the formal space, blinded momentarily by the wealth of marble and crystal, silk-clad ladies and tuxedoed gentlemen. There couldn't have been more than two hundred people in attendance, but they were some of the richest individuals in Manhattan, and it wasn't hard to feel awed by their hard-won or inherited wealth and grace.

Sebastian chuckled at my déclassé expression and tugged me farther into the room.

"Beautifully dressed sharks in a pretty tank, *cara*. Nothing more," he reminded me as we pulled up at the bar to grab retro champagne glasses.

"Yeah, and I'm Nemo," I muttered, smoothing the front of my dress with a clammy palm.

"Sebastian."

His laughter cut off abruptly at the breathy sound of his name, his shoulders hunching slightly and his knuckles white against the edge of the bar. He let out a deep exhale before turning around to face the woman who had said his name.

She was absolutely lovely, like a movie star out of the 1960s. Her large blue eyes were wreathed in a tasteful ring of kohl, and her tiny mouth was red and full like a rosebud. She was petite in a way I had always desired to be, with fine bones and slim hips emphasized by the fluidity of her gown. Despite her youthful features, the grace of her posture and the fine lines across her pale forehead denoted her age. She put on a good show in the filmy black dress with the long white opera gloves, but she couldn't fool the artist in me. I would have been surprised if she was a day under forty.

I knew who she was even before Sebastian cleared his throat, and said, "Savannah."

They stared at each other for a long, heated moment, completely ignorant of everyone else around them. I was surprised by their chemistry even though Elena had made it apparent in her insults that Seb had had an affair with an older woman. The proper Savannah Richardson did not seem at all like my fun-loving brother's type.

I cleared my throat and stepped forward with a genuine smile. "Hello, I'm Giselle. It's very nice to meet you. I've heard such wonderful things."

One icy blond brow rose slowly as she looked back and forth between my brother and me, but she did deign to take my offered hand.

"The pleasure is mine. I wasn't aware you were in town." Her eyes darted briefly to Sebastian, who remained standing stiffly at my side. "I very much hope you are enjoying being reunited with your family."

"I am, thank you." I continued to smile at her even though the situation was strangely grave. "Sebastian decided to be my white knight and accompany me here tonight." I leaned in conspiratorially. "I've never been to such an opulent event before."

She laughed lightly, and I caught a glimpse of something younger in her, something almost childlike and delicate. Her wide blue eyes slid to Sebastian again, inexorably drawn to him, and I felt a pang of empathy for the older lady. I knew all too well what it was like to love an unattainable man.

"You are in good hands with Sebastian then. I've dragged him to enough of these over the years to make him a hardened veteran, isn't that right?"

Seb grunted noncommittally and shot me a glare when I dug my elbow in his side. I was opening my mouth to appease Savannah, maybe even apologize for my thuggish brother, when an older gentleman stepped up beside her and placed a heavy hand on her birdlike shoulder.

"Savannah, darling, I've been looking for you." He spoke in a loud, gruff voice; a radio announcer from the 50s accompanied by the static rasp of an old stereo. It added to his old-school tails, the cummerbund, and slicked silver hair. He was a handsome man, robust and virile despite his age, and I immediately liked him.

"Seb, my boy." He beamed when he noticed my brother and stepped forward to grab him in a rough hug. "How the hell are you?"

"Fine as ever, Tate." Sebastian's lips twisted in a reluctant grin. "I was just introducing your *lovely wife* to my sister, Giselle Moore."

Savannah flinched slightly at Sebastian's casually spoken truth, and I realized then why Sebastian had said tonight held its own hardship. They were obviously in love, or, at least, they had been, and it had ended on less than auspicious terms.

"Giselle, the artistic one, right?" Tate grabbed my hand between his two mitts and squeezed it gently. "Tate Richardson. Media mogul, producer, director, and the lucky bastard married to this beautiful lady."

Savannah straightened, and any softness I had seen before vanished. She was suddenly the kind of New York matron I expected, haughty and beautifully aloof as if nothing could touch her. Sebastian scowled at the change, and something flickered in her eyes. It was pretty obvious to me that *he* was the only one who could touch her.

"You haven't been by in far too long, son." Tate had turned back to Sebastian. "What ever happened to our family Sunday dinners?"

Sebastian shifted slightly away from me as if the slight distance would make it harder for me to hear this conversation.

"I didn't know you two were in New York, and I've been busy working on a new project." He finished his flute of champagne in one long drink and reached behind the bar to grab something stronger, an expensive brand of whiskey that he poured into a short glass. The bartender eyed him warily, but after a quick wink, she let him be. She was only human, after all.

"Well, I'm sorry to take my brother away from you, but I see our sister over by the windows, and she will kill us if we don't check in," I said with a huge smile.

Tate nodded his head and said something in his booming voice to Sebastian so I took the opportunity to lean in close to Savannah and pressed my hand to her arm. She looked at me sharply but softened when she saw my slight smile.

"He's okay?" she whispered.

I hesitated before responding. "I think you're better equipped to answer that question."

She sucked in a quick breath before looking away. I knew I was dismissed, but I forgave her sudden coldness because it was obvious she wasn't dealing well with her separation from Sebastian.

I badly wanted to ply him with alcohol and attack him with questions about their relationship, but as we left the older couple and Sebastian became more and more relaxed with each step away from the mature blonde, I knew I couldn't. Not only would it be awkward and painful for him but it was also hypocritical of me to question his apparently sketchy relationship when I couldn't even face my own.

"Where did you say they are?"

"I didn't actually see them." I shrugged when he shot me a sidelong look. "*Insieme*, Sebastian. We needed to get out of there."

He looked at me for a long second before nodding curtly. "We did. Should we find our table then?"

We headed over to the table displays and found ours in the middle of the vast venue, far enough away from the live band not to have to shout over the music but essentially front and center given the layout of the room.

"Why would we be at such an important table?" I murmured as Sebastian weaved between the round tables and future diners.

He shot a look over his shoulder. "A movie star, a business

tycoon, a lawyer from one of the best New York City law firms, an up-and-coming artist, and a politician? I think that group warrants a good table."

"A politician?" I asked, but we were already at our table, and the sight of the people sitting around it made me forget my question.

Before I could even digest the sight of Elena or Sinclair, someone was in my arms, wrapping me in an embrace that made my heart ache for an earlier time.

"Candy," I breathed as she squeezed me tighter.

"Candy," she agreed, releasing me only enough to smile her buck-toothed smile into my face. "I can see you're shocked I'm here, so I'll give you a second to get over it and be excited to see me again. Although I'm not going to give you too long because I'm furious with you for not getting in touch with me after three long months of separation."

"Two months," I corrected automatically.

She blinked before tossing her head back and laughing. "Okay, the fury lasted for a much shorter time than I anticipated. You are officially forgiven. But you've got to make it up to me by sitting beside me."

She took my hand and finally had the wherewithal to see Sebastian standing beside us, staring bemusedly down at her. She stopped mid-step and gaped openly at him before turning back to play-whisper, "And introduce me to this guy."

It was my turn to laugh, and the distraction of their introduction was a welcome one as the three of us took our seats. I felt warm and safe with the two of them beside me so when I finally looked up at the rest of the table, I did so with a faux confidence I didn't really feel.

My eyes landed immediately on Sinclair, which wasn't surprising given the fact that I had known where he sat at the table as soon as we were in its vicinity. He was already staring at me, those blue eyes electric with intensity as they swept over my body, taking careful inventory of everything about my person. When they reached mine, his mouth softened into something close to a smile.

God, he was gorgeous.

"Giselle." Elena's voice brought my attention to her seat beside him, and I noticed that they matched—his ice blue tie and her velvet dress. She looked like a modern-day Audrey Hepburn, and my hands found my bodice self-consciously before I could help it.

"Elena, you look absolutely lovely. Thank you so much for inviting me tonight."

"Thank you, but I wasn't the one to extend the invitation. Willa and Mortimer wanted to meet the last addition to my family." She beamed at the older couple I had yet to notice who sat to her right.

"We've heard a great deal about you," Willa Percy said with a close-lipped smile as her brown eyes scraped over my body with the precision of a scalpel, searching for flaws with the gravitas of a surgeon.

Logically, I knew that Willa was a beautiful woman; African American with a light brown complexion smoother than silk and thick wavy hair she wore cut into a chic shoulder-length bob. But I found nothing warm in her expression or any charisma in the way she carried herself. She seemed almost like a doll, perfectly turned out in every way except for the lack of vitality in her eyes.

On the other hand, Mortimer Percy struck me as the kind of man to play Santa at a charity event or roll around in the mud with his sons. He was a broad-shouldered, All-American kind of man with a square jaw and a full head of golden-brown hair streaked with silver. With looks like that, it was no wonder he was a popular politician.

"No one told us you would be so pretty, though." Mortimer

smiled broadly. "We just heard some nonsense about you being a fantastic artist or something of the sort."

I laughed because he wanted me to, and his good humor was infectious. "What did I do to deserve such flattery?"

"Don't lay that at my son's doorstep. I'm afraid he's not the effusive type. Is he, Elena?" Mortimer guffawed.

Elena laughed too, but I was uncomfortable with the assertion, and when my eyes found Sinclair, the muscle in his jaw was ticking as it did when he was trying to control himself. Sensing my gaze, he looked up at me. I held his stare, opening myself to any thoughts he needed to purge himself of. I willed him to trust me with the emotions he normally carved up and shoved into the furthest recesses of his mind. His mouth opened slightly on a long exhale, and he shook his head slightly.

"*Later*," he mouthed.

My heart clenched in anticipation of seeing him again.

"It was Mama," Elena admitted. "She never could shut up about you."

"Elena," Sebastian warned under his breath, but she didn't take heed.

"Giselle was always Mama's special girl. She's thrilled to have her back, of course. The entire Lombardi clan together again. Although Giselle still goes by our father's last name."

I watched as Sinclair surreptitiously moved Elena's wineglass over to his side of the place setting.

"Names are so important." Willa stepped in, boredom laced throughout her words. "Daniel never did consent to take the Percy name."

"You never offered it to Cage," Sinclair said quietly. "And it was easier to keep Sinclair."

Willa sniffed, but Mortimer put his hand over hers to quell her. "We understand, Daniel, of course. Names are unimportant in the grand scheme of things. We are a family of choice, not circumstance."

His words set fire to my chest. I wanted a relationship of choice; I wanted Sinclair to choose me.

"There are no reporters at the table, Mortimer. You can stop the politicking," Willa said.

"Mom," Sinclair chastised, and I was surprised to see it had a positive effect on Willa, who straightened in her chair and applied a smile to her smooth cheeks.

"Very well. Elena, darling, how is the adoption process going?"

I almost choked on the sip of delicate white wine I was drinking. Could this evening get any more excruciating?

"Slowly, unfortunately."

"You must use our connections. Why forge relationships if you can't use them to your advantage, hmm?"

"We're in no rush," Sinclair reminded them. "Elena is only twenty-six. We have time enough to start a family."

"He's just nervous." Margot appeared at the table, a sharp smile on her face as she slipped into one of two empty chairs beside Candy. By the way she stared right at me, I knew Sin had warned her of my presence. "As long as I've known him, Daniel has always wanted to be a father."

Candy's hand found mine under the table and squeezed.

Sebastian snorted and muttered under this breath, "This is going to be one long fucking dinner."

I couldn't have agreed more.

Chapter Ten

It was better when the music started in earnest, and people began to dance. Elena was occupied with Mortimer, so Sinclair took Margot for a spin while my charming brother guided Willa—who actually laughed in delight—around the floor.

It had been a long and stifling dinner, and the sudden absence of tension made the air taste like ambrosia.

Candy gave me a solid thirty seconds of peace before descending on me.

"Okay, I have no idea how you are dealing with this." She stared at me incredulously, but when I didn't respond, she huffed. "That wasn't a rhetorical statement, Elle. How the hell are you dealing with this, this weirdness?"

"I'm not. I mean, I'm not dealing with it well."

"Sinclair briefed me, but you know him."

I smiled because I did. "What did he say?"

"Oh, *pfft*." She blew the bangs out of her face, and I loved her for her artlessness. "Something like 'Candace, Elle is in Manhattan. She also happens to be Elena's sister. You'll come to the gala tonight and see her. I would appreciate your discretion.'"

"Typical." I nodded with mock sincerity.

"Totally," she agreed.

We beamed at each other.

"This is a mess."

"Totally," I agreed.

"What are you going to do about it?"

I shrugged, and the heaviness of my guilt and desire broke the filter I had kept so far over my thoughts.

"Come on, Elle, you *love* him. Don't tell me you're okay with the status quo?"

"Of course not. But what would you have me do? Ruin my sister's life?"

Candy waved her hand dismissively. "That's a bit dramatic. She'd be heart broken, sure, but she would get over it. Anyone can see those two aren't soul mates."

"Soul mates? Honestly, Candy, who can say such a thing even exists?"

"You can!"

I slumped back in my chair even though I shouldn't have been shocked by her words. Was Sinclair my soul mate? I had never really thought about the term or what it could mean. I only knew how I felt about the enigmatic Frenchman I had met in Mexico and the gravitational pull between us. I craved him in a way that was more elemental than addiction but still dangerous, more respectful than reverential but still sacred. I wanted to be with him more than I wanted nearly anything else in the world even though I hardly knew him.

The question fell so easily into my lap that I was surprised I hadn't seen it all along. It really came down to this; did I want him more than I wanted my sister's happiness? Did I want him enough to live with the guilt? And I guess, most importantly, did he love me enough to take those on too?

"Richard said it in Mexico, and I'll say it again; I've never seen Sinclair lighter or happier than I have when he was with you. I didn't know you before, so I can't track the same changes, but I know you love him, and the girl I came to admire the hell out of in Mexico would not let something so precious go so easily."

"She's my sister," I said for what felt like the billionth time.

"Excuses."

"A good one," I amended, but I wasn't sure she was so wrong.

"You don't seem to be behaving yourself, Candace."

I looked up and over my shoulder to see Sinclair. He wore a deep navy, nearly black suit that fit his lean body perfectly and emphasized the crazy blue of his eyes. I was still getting used to his new haircut, but the lock of mahogany hair that fell over his forehead made him almost shockingly gorgeous.

"Do I ever?" Candy asked, baring her prominent teeth in a full smile.

I was happy she had abandoned her effort to keep them hidden, and I wondered what had prompted the change. I made a note to ask her later, feeling a little guilty that I had dominated our conversation.

"Touché." His lips twitched with humor, but when he shifted to look down at me, his eyes blazed with stark hunger. "Giselle, accompany me outside for some air."

It was that question that wasn't a question; the dominance I had come to crave from him. My body was primed and ready, and he hadn't even touched me yet.

I nodded, not trusting my voice, and took his hand to help

me up from the chair. A subtle glance confirmed that Elena was still busy, near the bar now and surrounded by a large group of lovely, wealthy people. She was laughing and carefree as she bantered with like-minded elites, and I realized how much she fit into this scene, how much she loved it.

We didn't speak as he ushered me outside, but the light touch of his hand on my lower back radiated like a beacon across my skin. The cool air felt amazing against my overheated skin, and I was immediately seduced by the murmur of traffic and the pulsing thrum of city life.

"New York is louder than Paris, crowded and coarser, but I absolutely adore it." I shook my head and leaned over the balustrade to peer at the darkened garden below. "I didn't expect to love it like this."

"For all its glamour and beauty, there is a certain artlessness to the city that is its most appealing quality."

I beamed over my shoulder at him. "Exactly."

"You are happy here, then?"

I turned back to the shadowed gardens to hide my frown. It was a harder question than it should have been, and the reason for that stood just behind me, exuding a cool sexuality that sent tingles over my skin.

"I am. Despite the occasional awkwardness of being reunited with my sisters and brother after years apart, it's good to feel at home again."

He stepped up to the stone railing beside me and braced his arms against it. His knuckles were white even in the darkness. I could feel his tension as if it were my own, the line he had hooked through my heart pulled taut by the strain.

"I'm jeopardizing that."

"A bit."

He smiled slightly at my honesty. "Before you, I never knew how selfish a person could truly be."

"Because you want both Elena and me?" I ripped the question off my heart quickly like a Band-Aid, but the pain still radiated through me and made my jaw ache.

He was silent for a lot longer than I was comfortable with, but I tried to remain patient and still. This was hardly the place or time for such a conversation, but I wasn't willing to end it, not after weeks of wondering.

"It's more complicated than that," he said finally.

"How?"

His jaw tensed, the muscle skipping in his cheek.

"How?" I pressed.

"I have," he hesitated, "a responsibility to Elena. I owe her happiness."

My throat was being stitched closed inch by inch. "You can't stay with someone because you feel beholden to them."

"You can," he argued firmly, turning to face me with eyes like chips of dry ice. "In fact, I would argue that most relationships are based on exactly that."

"Those relationships fail," I whispered.

I felt like an egg leaning too far over the balustrade, waiting with bone-chilling apprehension for the right breeze to tumble me over the edge.

"What are you saying, Elle?" His hands were suddenly on my arms, grasping them so firmly that I gasped. "You said yourself, you were not willing to sacrifice your sister's happiness, and now this? What the fuck do you want from me? Because when you ask me these infernal questions and when you look at me with those gray eyes, what do you expect me to do? I am no saint, and I won't pretend for one second longer that I'm anything close to a gentleman."

His lips crashed onto mine, and the feel of them went off like a bomb through my body. He tugged my shaking form closer until we were flush against each other, pressed so tightly I could feel him everywhere. His tongue swept between my teeth and took exactly want he wanted; my pleasure, my surrender.

I gasped into his mouth when his hands slid down my curves and grabbed my butt to lift me onto the ledge. As soon as I was settled, he stepped close, pushing my dress up and spreading my legs open to make room for him against my center. I tipped my head back to moan, my eyes absorbed by the sight of the moon as Sinclair's lips found the sensitive skin under my ear.

"You want this," he rasped, pressing even closer so that I could feel his erection against my heat. "Why can't you admit that you want this?"

My head was dizzy with sensation, but the conscious part of me hated his question. Why couldn't I admit I wanted this? More, that I *needed* it. I bit back a sob at the idea of never having him like this again and tightened my hands in his hair.

His hand lowered, finding my heeled foot and running his fingers gently around my anklebone before moving up, cool and fluid as rainwater, to my inner thigh. I panted when he pulled away to look into my eyes, his fingertips lazily swirling across the heated skin just beside my sex.

"Admit you want this."

I moaned because I could still see the people inside, splashes of rich color behind the slightly mottled glass doors.

Elena was in there.

"Even with all those people mere steps away and your sister just inside, you want this, Elle."

I leaned forward, pressing my lips to his neck to lick at his delicious salty skin. But he wouldn't let me escape into the fantasy. Instead, he pulled me back and grasped my chin firmly between his thumb and forefinger.

"Tell me."

"Yes," I breathed.

"Yes to what?" Sinclair's eyes sparkled in the starlight, and I knew he was enjoying this. "You know how much I like it when you use your words."

"Yes," I said, louder this time. "I want you. I *need* this."

I watched my words ignite him, the way goose bumps raced across his skin like a lit fuse toward his fiery gaze.

"*Elle*," he groaned, before simultaneously claiming my mouth and plunging two fingers deep inside me.

He caught my moan between his teeth and echoed it with one of his own. Combined with the roar of my blood rushing through my veins, it took me a moment to realize someone was clearing their throat behind Sinclair. I thought quickly, pulling him to me instead of pushing him away, placing my hands over his hair as I tucked his face into the side of my neck. That way, someone might not notice who I was kissing. Sinclair tensed but allowed me to hide him.

I sighed heavily when I saw Cage standing there with his hands in the pockets of his all-black ensemble.

"You scared me."

"I can't imagine why, *chérie*, when you chose such an excellent place for a clandestine *rendezvous*."

I frowned at him as Sinclair extricated himself from my embrace and smoothed down my long skirt before turning to Cage.

"You're late."

Cage laughed, but it was a hollow sound. "That is the least of our transgressions."

Sinclair's lips thinned, and he stepped forward, barring me partially from Cage's cold look. "Are you judging me, rock star?"

"Are you implying I don't have a right to, gypsy?"

I blinked as the acidity of the atmosphere stung my eyes. I could understand why Cage would be disappointed in us for falling into each other's arms yet again. Still, he had been there in Mexico, and more than that, he had encouraged me to pursue Sinclair again, even knowing Elena was my sister. Why the hell was he being so antagonistic?

"Cage," I began, but he held up a hand.

"No, Giselle, I think I will tell you some things, hmm?" He tugged at the end of his braid and sighed roughly. "I care for you two, and I do not care much for your woman or your sister, Elena. But I just came from talking with her about a baby, a baby she hopes to have with you, Sin. She was smiling, you see, in a way I did not think she was capable of. The idea of family made her smile like that. And you are both her family."

He shrugged with the tired wisdom of someone eternal. "I want you to be together. I'm, as you say, Team Giselle. But you both need to take your heads out of your asses and figure this out before you all get fucked."

I don't know when I started to cry, but by the time he was finished, I couldn't see through the tears, and a thin trail of snot was seeping from my nose. It wasn't because of Cage's cruelty. It was because he had no choice but to speak so harshly; the truth of our clandestine relationship *was* cruel.

"Jesus, Cage," Sinclair said.

His rage was palpable, but instead of ripping into his friend, he stepped back to me and took my face in his hands so that I was forced to look up at him. He pulled out a handkerchief from the inside pocket of his blazer and tenderly wiped my tear-streaked face. Cage was watching us, and people inside were waiting for us, but I realized with growing warmth that Sinclair wouldn't leave without making sure I was okay.

"I'll take you home."

"No." He flinched at my rejection, so I placed a soothing hand against his on my cheek. "No, you need to go inside to Elena. Cage is"—I sniffed grossly, but he didn't recoil—"right. This isn't fair to anyone. We agreed to be friends, and it needs to stay that way."

Sinclair closed his eyes and breathed deeply before

touching his forehead to mine and admitting in a soft, quiet voice that mended my heart as quickly as it was broken, "I can't leave it like this. I thought I could but ..." His sigh feathered against my lips. "I need more time with you. Give me more time with you."

It wasn't quite a question, but it didn't matter. I pressed my lips to his nose and whispered, "Okay."

His full smile took my breath away, and I laughed when his lips crashed inelegantly against mine. Pushing a lock of hair gently behind my ear, he bent his knees so that our eyes were level, and when he spoke, his voice was pure smoke.

"Tuesday night, my siren. That's when I'll have you."

"*Y*ou look flushed."

I was startled out of my daydreaming by Sebastian, who had joined me at the bar where I waited for a glass of wine.

"Hmm?"

"I said you look flushed."

His eyes were sharp, so I straightened up self-consciously. It was dangerous to have one's head in the clouds around one of the twins; they saw things most people shouldn't.

"It's warm in here."

"But you were just outside," he countered, too casually. "With Cage?"

"Yes, the poor guy can't keep his hands off me." I giggled nervously.

He didn't buy it.

"Interesting, he can't seem to keep his hands off that one either." He tilted his head to indicate Cage, who was kissing a beautiful woman's neck on the dance floor.

"My heart," I joked, clutching at it dramatically.

Sebastian bit down on his smirk, which made me realize how serious he was about seeing this line of questioning through to the end. I didn't know if it was because I was still high on Sinclair's kisses or if it was because I was so tired of lying and feeling guilty, but either way, I crossed my arms and gave Sebastian my best no-nonsense glare.

"Seems like another poor guy can't keep his eyes off you."

Ah. I knew who he was referring to without following his gaze behind me. I had felt his eyes on me as soon as he and Cage had followed me inside after a short private conversation. I wore that gaze with pride as an invisible mantle across my shoulders, infusing me with a cheeky confidence and power.

"I don't know what you're talking about, Seb," I demurred. "But I may have been distracted by Savannah Richardson's multiple attempts to catch your eye."

We stared at each other for a long moment, and I wondered if yet another of my familial relationships would be reduced to this—acridity and defensiveness.

But Sebastian mocked me for my pessimism by dissolving into full-throated laughter. Still chuckling, he leaned forward to swing his arms around me and tug me closer.

"*Ti amo, bambina.*"

"I love you too," I said as I pressed my smile into the soft fabric of his blazer.

A slight cough alerted us to the arrival of Elena, who stood with her fingers clutched tightly in front of her gorgeous Grecian-inspired velvet gown. Despite her dark coloring and slumberous sexy eyes, Elena conducted herself like an ice queen. I wondered idly if she had ever seen *Frozen*.

"What's so funny?"

"Nothing." I waved away her question and nodded at the older man behind her. "Who is this?"

Elena's eyes narrowed even though her lips automatically formed a genteel smile as she stepped backward to introduce him. "Mr. Paulson, please let me introduce my siblings, Sebastian and Giselle."

Mr. Paulson wore a light metallic silver suit that perfectly matched his coiffed helmet of hair and stern expression. Despite his austerity, deep brackets around his broad mouth indicated he smiled often, and his orange pocket square meant he couldn't take himself too seriously.

"Wonderful to meet you." He clasped my hand in both of his, and even though I understood he wanted the gesture to be warm and welcoming, the feel of his eyes cataloging every inch of me negated the effect.

"Mr. Paulson is the CEO of Dogwood International Hotels," Elena explained with a significant eyebrow raise, trying to convey the importance of this fact. "Daniel and I invited him tonight to meet the family. Unfortunately, my youngest sister Cosima is away at the moment on a photo shoot, but she sends her regrets."

"Ah, Cosima." Mr. Paulson had a surprisingly soft voice, his words carefully spoken. "She is a delightful young woman. I thought for certain she would be married by now."

I frowned and opened my mouth to question his odd comment, but Elena shot me a glare before I could.

She laughed lightly and placed a gentle hand on his arm. "She receives proposals by the dozens, but my younger sister believes in the sanctity of marriage and doesn't take entering into it lightly."

While they smiled at each other, I nudged Sebastian in the ribs, and he shrugged, rolling his eyes.

"You and Sinclair have been engaged for ages now. When are you lovebirds going to tie the knot?" Mr. Paulson asked Elena, but his eyes veered toward me.

It was a smart move. It took me at least three seconds to rearrange my shocked features into some semblance of normalcy. Engaged?

Sebastian's hand pressed between my shoulders comfortingly, and I watched him jerk his head slightly from side to side.

Aware of Mr. Paulson's eyes, I swallowed my relieved sigh.

"We are happy as we are," Elena was saying, but she fiddled with the long string of pink pearls at her neck nervously. "In fact, I've never been happier. My entire family is living in the same city for the first time in years."

Seamus wasn't here, but he had long ago ceased to exist for us, so I guess our father's absence didn't really matter. Still, Elena's increasing insincerity made me uncomfortable, and my fidgeting brought Mr. Paulson's attention to me.

"Family is the most important thing in a person's life, I've come to realize. My wife is the most important person in my life. Are you married, young woman?"

I bristled slightly at his condescension but hid it behind a flashy smile. "I am not."

"And you?"

Sebastian laughed. "Happily single."

Mr. Paulson's disapproving frown was nowhere near the magnitude of Elena's glare. A sharp prickle of foreboding lanced my spine.

"Companionship is the greatest treasure in life," he said.

Sebastian's answering grin was glorious. "I assure you, Mr. Paulson, I do not lack for companionship."

The older man's face twisted with disgust. "*True* companionship is about loyalty and commitment. It does not come and go as the changing of the tide."

"Not the best analogy," Seb winced theatrically. "The waves always kiss the shore."

The two men stared at each other, but I couldn't take my eyes off Elena, whose lips were so pursed that I wondered if they would produce a diamond if I put coal between them.

"Paulson, I see you've met Giselle and Sebastian," Sinclair said as he stepped slightly in front of Sebastian to shake the businessman's hand.

I hid my smile behind my hand as my brother glowered at the back of Sin's head.

"Yes, yes, it's good of you to bring your fiancée's family to an event like this. It's important to have your support system beside you," Paulson said with a broad smile that brought out surprisingly charming dimples in his cheeks.

He was definitely a man stuck in the 1950s, but he did seem to genuinely like Sinclair.

"Fiancée," Sinclair murmured softly.

Elena fidgeted nervously, and it was obvious that I wasn't the only one who knew he spoke quietly when he was upset.

Paulson was pleasantly oblivious. "Yes, yes, though I have to say you're making it an awfully long engagement. I had my wife at the altar before she could change her mind, let me tell you." He guffawed.

Sinclair smiled slightly, but when Elena placed a hand on his arm, his entire body stiffened.

"Pauly, please don't tell me you are embarrassing me again," a surprisingly young woman protested in a brassy Brooklyn accent.

Mrs. Paulson was maybe forty, at least fifteen years younger than her husband, with long dark permed hair and acrylic nails painted a vivid red that matched her lipstick. Though her dress was the same demure silver as her husband's suit, it was obvious that she was rough around the edges and not born into the same blue blood stock as most of the other guests in the room. I instantly liked her.

"Never," Paulson assured her with a dramatic wink before introducing Teresa to the rest of us.

I watched him tuck her firmly into his side, how she placed her hand over his heart as if it was meant to be there. I sighed, long and gustily, before I could help it. Seb elbowed me gently, and I realized that she was saying something to me.

"Excuse me?"

"You're Giselle Moore, the artist," she repeated, her brown eyes wide with excitement. "Sinclair told me how wonderful you were, and I just had to look you up. I would be over the moon if you'd do a commission for Pauly and me."

I really didn't have the time with the showcase coming up, but I understood how much it would mean to Sinclair to make the couple happy, and I was delighted he had taken the time to mention me to them.

"I would be honored. Thank you, Mrs. Paulson."

Her laugh was brassy, and I thought, awesome. "Terry, please. We must be on familiar terms if you are going to paint me."

Elena hid her smile behind her hand, and even though it was studied to look like a subtle gesture, it drew the eye of everyone in our little group.

"Is something funny?" Terry asked.

My sister waved her hand airily. "It's nothing really."

But I recognized the sharp edges in that lady-like smile, and my stomach cramped because I knew what was coming.

"No really, what is it?"

Elena sighed. "If you really want to know, I just thought it was funny because Giselle's upcoming collection is a series of nudes."

The Paulsons both turned their heads to me in tandem. If I hadn't been about to vomit, it might have been kind of funny.

The men—Sebastian, Cage, and Sinclair—were all frowning at Elena with varying degrees of condemnation, but it was the latter who wrapped a strong hand around her wrist in warning.

She didn't heed it.

"Yes, I know, that was exactly my reaction at first. It might make more sense if you understand the theme. It's about sexual perversions," she explained as if *a* plus *b* equaled *c*.

"Elena," Sebastian gasped.

Cage just shook his head in disgust.

Mr. Paulson looked at me with unmitigated horror.

I had never seen Sinclair so still, his entire body as hard as marble with restraint. One more wrong word, one breath released the wrong way, and he would shatter into a terrifying fury.

Terry looked at me for a long time. I waited without breathing for her to berate me, to laugh, or even turn on her heel in disgust. But she just looked at me until I felt dizzy.

Then she did the most interesting thing.

She tilted her head to the side, squinted her eyes, and threw back her head in raucous, completely genuine laughter. No one moved an inch as she laughed and laughed and clapped her red-tipped hands.

"How wonderful! How does one paint sexual perversions? I imagine it's something like *Fifty Shades of Gray* but done in paint?" she said, laughter still bouncing through her speech. "I have to admit that I usually find art kind of"—her nose wrinkled adorably—"stodgy, but I could definitely sink my teeth into something like that, couldn't I, Pauly?"

To my shock and mild horror, Mr. Paulson blushed like a

schoolboy and patted his wife on the arm. "I'm sure you could, darling."

"Tell me..." She leaned forward to stage whisper, "Would you be willing to paint me like that?"

It took me a few seconds to find my voice again, but I could feel Cage and Seb at my back like the warmth from a fire, and it filled me with confidence.

"I would be absolutely delighted. And to tell you the honest truth"—I leaned forward with my hand over my mouth, imitating her dramatics—"I think art can be pretty boring too."

Terry laughed. "My God, you are a treasure. I'm going to give you my card, and you, you amazing girl, are going to promise to call me no later than tomorrow to make an appointment with me."

"I promise," I said solemnly though my eyes sparkled back at her.

She nodded decisively and patted Mr. Paulson over the heart. "Good. Well, I'm sorry to pull my handsome husband away, but I fancy a dance before we get dragged into another business discussion, so if you don't mind?"

"Not at all," Sinclair said, inclining his head.

Terry laughed at him and actually reached up to pat his cheek. "So polite, Mr. Sinclair, but I see the trouble buttoned up under your coat."

She winked at me as Mr. Paulson said his goodbyes.

We were all quiet for a moment after they left before we turned on each other.

"Are you fucking kidding me, Elena?" Sebastian said, rounding on her with clenched fists.

"Me?" she asked, her eyes wide with faux sincerity. "What did I do wrong? In fact, I think Giselle should thank me. I just secured her a commission."

Even I gasped at that.

Sinclair dropped her arm as if it were a poisonous thing

and looked down at her with cool censure. "Giselle's grace just secured her the commission, as well you know. You tried to make her feel little, *non*?"

Elena opened her mouth to protest, but Cage cut in, "Karma's a bitch, uh, Elena?"

Her lips pursed with delicate displeasure, but her eyes flashed as they swept over me, striking me with the force of a tiger's paw. I stepped back as pain radiated through my chest.

"Daniel, I really didn't mean anything by it." She looked up at him from under her lashes. It wasn't until that moment that fury took root in my heart. Was she really going to try to bamboozle him out of his anger?

I vibrated.

Cage put a hand on my arm to calm me. I was surprised when it helped a little.

"I don't care what you intended," I said before Sinclair could completely lose what little resolve he had left to keep calm. "Either way, it was a thoughtless thing to say. I am not painting sexual perversions, and if you feel that way about my work, please keep it to yourself or, at the very least, don't speak about it with potential patrons."

She stared at me with storm cloud eyes just a few shades darker than my own, and I stared right back. It was the first time I had really stood up to her passive-aggressiveness, and it felt scary but really good.

Finally, she gave a little nod and said, "I misspoke, I shouldn't have called them perversions, but I don't know the language of these things. Of course, Giselle, if you don't want me to speak about you, I won't."

It wasn't really an apology, but I nodded anyway before turning to Cage and Sebastian. "Well, I think we've had enough of tonight, don't you?"

Sebastian laughed softly and slung an arm over my shoulder. "Hell yeah."

"We'll see you Thursday for Thanksgiving, though," Elena reminded us sharply as we began to walk away.

"Oh goody," Sebastian murmured drolly, and we walked out laughing even though we had both left our hearts in the Four Seasons ballroom.

M y heart was beating like a mad thing in my chest, hammering against the ribbed walls almost painfully.

It was finally Tuesday.

Sure, it would probably be the last night I would ever spend with him, but I was grateful for the closure and maybe just the teeniest bit hopeful that it wouldn't be the end.

I smiled at my reflection, pleased to find the Giselle I had unearthed in Mexico smiling back at me. My entire day had been decadent, mostly thanks to Candy, who insisted on a girls' day at the spa. I had been steamed, plucked, manicured, pedicured and, for the first time in my life, waxed bare. I'd run my hands over the ultra-sensitive flesh as I pulled on my carefully selected lingerie—art nouveau-inspired high-waisted satin panties and a balconette that barely contained my breasts. My waves were brushed out until they gleamed, the usual mascara and blush was applied, and I had anointed my pulse points with lavender oil, knowing how much Sinclair enjoyed the scent on me.

It was fun to take a day to pamper myself, and it wasn't something I would have done even six months ago. So, I made a promise to myself that even if this was my last night with Sinclair, I wouldn't let it impact the positive changes his presence had made on me.

But I also promised myself that I wouldn't ruin the night with heaviness and questions, and even though I was so incandescently happy that I felt like I could float into space like a rising star, there was no accounting for how the night would evolve, and I wanted to be prepared.

I was just putting on some music after finally deciding between John Legend and Nora Jones when my phone vibrated violently and fell off the kitchen counter.

"Hello?"

"I'm sorry, I was so nervous I had to call! Is he there yet?" Candy's voice chirped through the phone as if she was yelling in my ear.

"Obviously not, or I wouldn't have answered."

"Right." She paused sagely. "So, what's up?"

"Candy!" I laughed. "Why are you bothering me?"

"Oh come on, it's not like you don't need the distraction. He isn't due for another fifteen minutes, and don't you dare tell me you haven't already fluffed the pillows, plumped up the girls, and turned on some sultry tunes. I bet you're practically itching with restless anticipation."

She wasn't wrong, so I sighed and flopped down on the mahogany leather loveseat in the living room with a clear view of the door.

"I fluffed the pillows twice actually."

She snorted. "I don't doubt it. This is your big chance to show him that you're the right choice. It's a pretty big deal."

I hummed into the phone, but a niggling question kept popping into my head. "Candy? How do *you* know I'm the right choice? I don't even know if I believe that."

"Oh, Elle, I know your naïvety is part of your wonderful charm, but I do wish you could see yourself the way other people do. You are, I don't know," she huffed, "lovely. Just natural and kind and charming. Everything that Sinclair has a hard time emulating."

It was my turn to snort. "I've completely fucked up his life."

"Well, yeah, that too," she agreed cheerfully. "But in a good way."

"This conversation is giving me a headache."

"Really? I think it will be the highlight of my night."

"Maybe we should spend more time talking about your love life then." I paused. "I saw you dancing with Cage at the gala."

There was a long stretch of silence. I stared at my pale lavender manicure while I waited.

"That's an entirely different can of worms," she said finally. "Don't get me wrong, I'm fantastic. But Cage is going to be an American rock star, and he will never think of me as anything besides Candy Kay, Sinclair's trusty sidekick."

I wanted to argue with her, but the thing was, I didn't want to lie either, and I wasn't sure if Cage ever *would* see Candy in a romantic light. Truthfully, I had seen him look at Elena with more passion than he had ever expressed with Candy.

"Wow, now that I've finished being a Debbie Downer, tell me what you're wearing."

I almost choked on my laughter. "You helped me pick them out this afternoon!"

"Right, damn. Okay, you are officially no fun. I'm going to get back to my riveting night of Netflix binge-watching and rabid popcorn eating."

"What show is it tonight?" I asked through my chuckle.

"The new season of *Succession*. Is it wrong that I think Logan Roy is a total hunk?"

"Cage *and* Logan Roy? You have eclectic taste. I'll give you that."

She snorted. "Yours is better."

A brisk knock on the door struck my heart into a staccato beat. I jumped up from the couch and was halfway to the door before I realized I was still on with Candy.

"It is," I agreed, already beaming as I hung up and swung open the red door.

Sinclair was smiling too. My favorite smile, the one that curved his cheeks and broke the ice in his blue eyes so that they flooded with warmth. We stood staring at each other like that for a long time, and even though I felt stupid just standing there staring at the too-good-to-be-true man in front of me, I was too giddy to care because he was doing the exact same thing.

"Hi," I finally said, a little breathlessly.

"Hi." His grin deepened. "Are you going to invite me in?"

"Yes, of course." I blushed, which made him chuckle, which, of course, made me flush even further.

We had been alone together for thirty seconds, and it was already the best night of my life.

I stepped to the side as he moved into the apartment and inhaled deeply when he leaned forward to press a chaste kiss to my cheek. I pressed my hand to his chest, felt the beat beneath my splayed fingers, and grinned up into his face.

"Can I say that I'm so happy you're here?"

Sinclair's face was neutral again, perfectly held in repose more beautiful than Michelangelo's *David,* but his eyes gleamed with contentment.

"Only if I can say it back."

I tipped my head back and laughed. "God, that was cheesy."

One of his dark brows arched. "Oh, really?"

His hand slipped between my breasts, down my belly, and around to the base of my spine, where he flattened it and pulled me against his groin. I groaned when I felt the hard ridge of his erection against my belly.

"Is this cheesy?" he taunted before capturing my mouth in a deep kiss, his tongue sweeping past my lips in a way that made my knees buckle.

I didn't worry, though, because a second later, his hands were under my butt, lifting me into his arms. I wrapped my legs around his waist as he pushed me against the door, gasping against his lips when he ground his hips into me.

It took me a moment to reorient myself when he suddenly pulled away, setting me gently on my feet as he stepped back. I blinked at him, my swollen lips open over my panting breath.

His chuckle was deep, a frequency that made me shiver compulsively. "Don't fret, my siren." He brushed his cool thumb over my bottom lip. "We have time. We have all night."

"What?"

"We have all night," he repeated casually, but his lips twitched.

"Elena's out of town?"

His thumb dipped between my teeth and rested on my tongue. Automatically, I closed my lips over it and sucked. I watched his eyes darken and felt myself throb.

"We have all night," he said again.

My cheeks ached with the force of my grin, and even though I was desperate to touch him after weeks of careful avoidance, I didn't. There was still so much between us that if I pressed my hand to the gap stuck between us, I knew it would push fruitlessly against the clotted air. There were ways to cut through it, but most were so dangerous, so scary in ways both good and bad, that I didn't know how to take action.

So, I just stared at him with a dumb smile while I cataloged the fall of his dark hair over his forehead, barely red in the low light of the entryway, and the way his tailored Oxford blue button-down conformed to the honed muscles underneath. He stood with both hands in his pockets, fists clenched, and even though his face was as implacable as always, I knew that tell. He wanted to claim me just as badly as I needed to be taken by him. He could have been hesitating for so many reasons, but I hoped it was because he feared that he'd lose his eternal control.

I looked at the floor, happy that my hair fell forward to cover my suddenly shy smile. "Can I take your coat?"

He slipped out of the heavy black coat and handed it to me without letting our fingers brush. My heart was beating strangely, sliding and skipping over beats in my chest. I was breathing erratically, too, in anticipation.

Sinclair toed off his beautiful leather loafers, and on some strange impulse, I ducked down to grab them, thinking to put them in the closet with the rest of the shoes, but Sinclair's hand on the top of my head froze me in a crouch. My body hummed under his touch.

"What are you doing?" His voice was liquid, and when I looked up into his face, it was taut with desire.

I swallowed convulsively. "I thought I would put your shoes away." I laughed nervously. "I actually don't have a clue."

"I have to disagree with you on that. You seem to know exactly what you're doing."

My heart clipped briskly against my ribs, and I licked my lips, wondering if maybe I did know what I was doing. If I had subconsciously known how being on my knees before him would affect him. I shifted from my crouch to my knees and sat down on my heels, spreading my legs slightly and placing my hands demurely before me. My heart beat so quickly it fluttered, a hummingbird knocking on my pulse points. My hair fell in a soft curtain around my face as I tilted my gaze to the floor. I knew how I looked sitting like that because I had practiced the traditional submissive pose in the mirror in preparation for tonight.

It was astonishing to me that I could enjoy being so bold, taunting him as I just had, yet so deeply crave my submission to him. Six months ago, I hadn't known anything beyond the bounds of sexual abuse and timid sexuality. Now, I felt like a live wire, still beneath the plastic coating but always thrumming with a vibrant sensuality.

His sharp intake of breath filled me with triumph.

"Yes, siren, I think you know exactly what you are doing."

His hand slipped from the top of my head, down the side of my cheek to grasp my chin and raise it gently to meet his gaze. "I am in a shockingly good mood, so I am going to give you a choice. You can get up, hang up my coat, and lead me into the kitchen where we can continue the night as if we were on our first real date, with all the sweetness and awkwardness that accompanies that..." He paused, and his eyes glittered as his hand sank deep into my hair to tilt my head back almost brutally. "Or you can take me between those sweet lips like you've been wanting to do for weeks. I think you missed pleasing me almost more than I missed the feel of your wet mouth around my cock."

I moaned, both shocked and overwhelmed by his words. My body was already changing, my muscles melting into pliability, ready to mold themselves into whatever position he desired. Saliva flooded my mouth, moisture pooled between my legs, and my nipples furled atop my heavy breasts. In two sentences, Sinclair had turned me on more than anything else ever had.

"Tell me what you want."

I wanted to moan again, but I knew he loved the words. "I want you in my mouth."

"Who do you want me to be?"

I opened my mouth to ask what he meant, but one look in his eyes showed me the dominant caged there, yearning for release even as he gave me the keys to the lock.

I hadn't planned on starting the evening this way, but I should have known we wouldn't be able to resist. It had been too long since our last night together, and even though we had only ever been together sexually for one week, my body was trained to respond to his like this. More than that, I wanted his dominance and control because they were intrinsically married to *my* power and pleasure.

"You," I said firmly. "My Sinclair."

His hand clenched in my hair, and his nostrils flared as the Dom was unleashed. "Very well. Clasp your hands behind your back. You may only use your mouth."

I threaded my fingers together at the base of my spine obediently while he undid the buckle of his leather belt and lowered his zipper. I was already panting. The rough sound of the zipper was like a physical caress against my overheated flesh, and I shuddered when his hand disappeared within his loosened slacks to reappear with my prize.

He was already magnificently hard. The sight of his swollen flesh within his fist, slowly stroking, made me whimper.

"So eager," he murmured. "I've dreamed of you, Elle, exactly like this. I love knowing that I put that flush on your creamy skin, that you're wet just sitting like that for me, waiting for me to touch you. I love knowing that even this"—his fingers trailed from the edge of my jaw to the hollow of my collarbone —"turns you on. You want me with every breath you take."

He stepped closer until he was almost brushing my lips. A bead of moisture adorned his crown, and I licked my lips unconsciously. My tongue caught the edge of his flesh, the salty taste of his skin making me moan. He brushed the tip of his erection against my open lips, painting them with his arousal like lipstick. When I tried to take him into my mouth, he pulled back, stroking himself faster but still in control.

"Please," I breathed, embarrassed by my supplication until I saw his hand stutter mid-movement.

He stopped stroking, letting his hands fall to his sides so that I could take control of his pleasure. I let out a breathy little sigh and nuzzled the hot flesh with my cheek. I drew my nose down his long length before taking one of his silky balls into my mouth. I rolled my tongue around it, humming with pleasure as I did so.

My sex was dripping down my open thighs to the cold floor beneath my knees, and the front door to my apartment was still slightly open two feet behind me. Someone could catch me like that, wanton and exposed.

"Anyone could come in and find you like this," Sinclair rasped, reading my mind as only he could. His hands threaded through my hair, pulling slightly but not manipulating the movement of my lips across his shaft. "But you wouldn't stop, would you?"

I groaned deeply, taking him between my lips to the very back of my throat in answer.

His hands tightened in my hair, forcibly pulling me off his cock with a popping sound so that I had no choice but to look up at him from a painful angle. He was so tall, towering over me with a dark gleam in his eyes that thrilled me.

"I want you to get up and go into the kitchen. Take off all of your clothes and wait for me in front of the balcony doors," he directed, his clipped, cool words trailing across my skin like ice.

I hesitated, old habits overriding my instinctive desire to obey.

"You wanted *your* Sinclair, Elle," he reminded me. "You only have to say stop to make it all end."

My gut clenched at the thought of it ending, of him leaving.

I needed this, his dominance, almost as much as I needed his love.

"Yes, sir," I murmured, lowering my gaze respectfully.

His hands pulsed in my hair at my submissive gesture before he let go.

Without another word, I scrambled to my feet and headed into the kitchen. I quickly shucked my clothes, leaving them in a messy pile, and positioned myself before the doors with my head lowered and my hands lightly clasped, my bare back to the kitchen behind me.

I became absorbed in the soft colors of the setting sun melting like candle wax between the iron spikes of the city skyline. The contrast reminded me of Sinclair and me, the soft with the hard, the warm and the cold. So opposite but so perfectly matched.

I didn't know how long I was zoned out for, standing nearly pressed to the cool glass, but I startled when Sinclair's hands skimmed down my arms.

"Trust me."

He wasn't asking, but I had the power to say no, and it was a heady realization.

"Always."

"If you want me to stop, you need a safe word."

I'd thought about that while I had been researching the ins and outs of submissive life. I wasn't sure I liked the idea of a safe word. It seemed almost like a prenuptial agreement; it took the edge out of the scene and created a different sort of tension. Would he go far enough for me to have to use it? Would I break his trust by uttering it in a moment of knee-jerk panic before I could adjust to the boundaries he pushed me past? But I knew the serious necessity of it, and I was ready with an answer I hoped would please him.

"Heartbeat."

There was a question in the way he stilled behind me.

"Because even if I need you to stop, you'll still own me. When we're like this, you own every beat of my heart."

"My siren," he breathed, planting a delicate kiss on my neck to express his pleasure with me. "You are a constant delight to me but..." He shifted behind me, firm and tall once again. "I am in the mood to punish you."

I shivered as he raised my arms in front of me and stepped flush against my back, reaching around with a long red scarf to competently bind my hands together. Once I was secured, he looped the end of the fabric over the curtain rod above the doors, jerking it twice to check its stability, before securing it once more to my tied hands. He stepped back, giving me room to test the bonds. I found that even though I couldn't lower my arms, I could move side to side.

"Legs apart," he said even as his knee slipped between my thighs and forced them open.

I sighed when his hands came around to cup my breasts, pressing the nipples firmly between his fingers until they burned. Too quickly, he moved on, smoothing his palms over my soft belly, around to the firm flare of my hips, and to the inside of my thighs. His chin rested on my shoulder, his lips against my pulse.

"You've tortured me. Having this body so close but unable to touch you"—his lips parted, and his tongue swept over my skin—"has been agony."

He pushed on the inside of my thighs until I spread them even wider, my muscles burning with the effort. I could feel my arousal trickle down one thigh and shivered.

"Did you mean to do that to me, siren? Did you wear those short skirts and lick your pouty mouth knowing how hard it would make me?"

He trailed his fingers in my wetness, running them back and forth like laps in a swimming pool. I throbbed for him, greedily sucking at his finger as he dipped one inside me. He circled my opening and then thrust to his first knuckle, repeating the movement over and over again until I was a panting mess, writhing in my bonds.

"Hush," he demanded. "Stay completely still and do not make a sound."

One hand continued its excruciating rhythm on my sex while the other disappeared beyond my vision. Two seconds later, both hands were on my breasts, smearing my wetness across my nipples and rolling them brutally between his fingers.

"You have gorgeous breasts," he said. "So responsive to the simplest touch."

He flicked one nipple and then the other, making me gasp despite my vow of silence. His dark chuckle stirred my hair. "Don't make a sound."

My body screamed when he snapped two clothespins over my already aching nipples. I wanted to buck and moan wildly at the intense sensation, but I wanted to please Sinclair even more. I bit my lip until it pulsed with pain. I needed to be in control of myself just as much as Sinclair was if I wanted to be his sub. This was my audition; this was what I had been planning for since the gala. There was no way in hell I was going to be anything less than perfect.

"Good girl," he murmured. "Do you like being displayed like this for me and for anyone with the good fortune to look out the window across from us?"

I focused on the buildings across the way, on the sliver of sunlight fading slowly over the horizon, and I shivered. The idea of someone watching us made me flush with pleasure.

"You have to be punished for being such a tease, and I can make your body sing in so many sweet ways." His hand lifted and came slapping down over my core, the other arm already wrapped around my belly to hold me up when my knees wobbled.

He circled my opening and then entered me to his first knuckle, repeating the movement over and over again until I was a panting mess, writhing in my bonds.

"Hush," he demanded.

He swatted my heat again, harder this time, jiggling my clamped breasts. I bit off a whimper.

"I said, quiet," he warned.

He slapped me again, and the force radiated through me. I was so close to the edge, my toes on its very precipice, but I had nothing to rub against, no voice to beg with, no power to do anything but accept the pleasure Sinclair doled out to me.

His hands left me for only a second, but I immediately missed the contact, my body bowing uncomfortably in an effort to follow his touch.

"I'm going to taste you now, but remember you are being punished. You are not permitted to come, and if you do so without my permission..." He trailed off, and I knew enough to fill in the blanks.

If I hadn't wanted to impress him so much, I might have orgasmed on purpose just to see what kind of punishment I would get.

His cool lips fluttered over the inside of my damp thighs, traveling gentle as a breeze to my center and over to the other thigh, where he bit down firmly on the flesh. I groaned loudly and was rewarded with a slap on the ass.

"Quiet," Sin said and then blew cool air across my sex.

His tongue lapped at me carefully, following my folds like a cartographer, and when my knees grew weak, he placed them over his shoulders so that I was practically sitting on him. The sensation of being suspended, reliant on Sinclair for my balance and my ultimate release, was so arousing that I was sweating and grinding my teeth after only thirty seconds to keep from orgasming without his consent.

"Please," I panted finally, as pins and needles of painful pleasure assaulted my body.

Instead of answering me, he grasped my bottom tightly in both hands and pressed me closer to his mouth. My legs started to shake as I was wracked with pleasure and a scream gathered speed, collecting in my gut and surging through my lungs.

"That's right, siren," Sinclair said against the inside of my thigh. "Let go. Show me how much you missed me."

I was so grateful for his permission that I could have kissed him. But my body reacted before my brain, seizing my pleasure and ripping it from the seams of my body until I spilled open, achingly exposed. I only noticed that I was sobbing when Sinclair stole my breath with a demanding kiss and entered me in one fluid motion. He caught my gasp between his lips, biting my lip and angling his hips as he pumped into me. I tried to lock my legs around his waist, but he held them up and out, stretching me until I could feel the delicious burn between my legs.

"The world is watching, Elle," he panted against my damp neck. My aching sex clenched hard in another brutal orgasm, or maybe the first one had never stopped.

He growled and bit firmly into the base of my neck as he came inside me. I couldn't see his face, but I could sense the impression of it on my closed lids like the imprint of sunlight, glowing so brilliantly it left a scar on my retinas.

Chapter Twelve

I was glad I had planned a cold supper because it was after midnight before we dragged ourselves from bed—where we ended up after the kitchen—to refuel. Sinclair carried me to one of the barstools and retrieved a blanket from the living room to wrap around my naked shoulders so that I wouldn't be cold. I watched him silently as he moved through the kitchen in only his black boxer briefs, collecting the gazpacho I had made that afternoon, the skewers of prosciutto-wrapped melon, a bundle of deep red grapes, a baguette, and a gorgeous round of Camembert cheese. His brow was wrinkled in concentration as he arranged everything on two large platters, and he frowned further when I laughed at him.

"Yes?"

I covered my mouth with a hand and said, "I won't judge you on presentation, Sin."

He shrugged, but I caught the sparkles in his eyes before he lowered them back to the work at hand. "You are an artist. Of course you will judge me on presentation."

I tucked my tongue into my cheek and gave his half-nude form a lascivious once-over. "Trust me, baby, it's an A plus every time."

He blinked at me before laughing freely, tipping his golden throat back to bark at the ceiling. I smiled, too, and leaned forward to watch him.

"You make a man feel like a god."

"You are one."

His eyebrows slammed down, and he leaned against the counter to cross his arms and stare at me disapprovingly. I knew it shouldn't have, but that look always made me wet.

"Don't put me on a pedestal. I don't belong up there."

"I didn't say you were a god to everyone, Sinclair. Just to me," I amended.

"After what I just did to you, I'm surprised you would equate me with anything so holy."

My body tingled with the imprints of his lips, teeth, hands, and cock. Even against the softness of the bed our second time around, the sex had been rough, two animals locked in heat and only conquered by the eventual need to sustain themselves on something other than flesh.

He took the plates in hand and placed them at the small table beside the little balcony. I followed with a nearly empty bottle of crisp Pinot Grigio.

"I don't think there is anything really dirty about what we do together," I admitted as I popped a grape between my lips. "It's honest and sometimes a bit brutal, but I think that is what makes it special."

"You are very poetic."

I frowned and leaned forward over the table to accept a grape from Sinclair's fingers. "It doesn't make what I'm saying any less true."

"No, I suppose you're right. It's been a long time since I heard anyone speak about BDSM like that." He looked out into the brightly lit nightscape; the glimmer of red and white lights highlighted his puckered forehead and soured mouth.

"When did you start experimenting with it?" I asked, unsure if I was phrasing the question in an insulting way.

His lips twisted, and for a moment, I wasn't sure if he was going to say anything.

"I've always had the desire to control. A number of therapists have surmised that it has everything to do with being powerless as an orphan and then under the thumb of very authoritarian foster parents." He rolled his eyes, illustrating how little he thought of their theory. "The truth is much simpler, and it might offend you. I have always had the desire to control, to manipulate and weld the will of others into forms of my own making. BDSM is the physical manifestation of those desires."

"That sounds very super villainy," I admitted.

His small smile surprised me. "On the contrary, I believe it to be soothing. As the Dom, it's my responsibility to provide exactly what my sub needs, even if they are unconscious of those desires. It is about finding the balance, that golden edge between pain and pleasure, reluctance and desire. Love and hate. It is on that fine line between those extremes that I might find the true you, the one that no one but me will ever see."

"You already have that."

"No, I don't." He smiled that small, warped smile that I hated so much. "Only when you really belong to me can I know you like that."

Silence descended, but it wasn't uncomfortable. These moments were inevitable between us, I thought, because there were so many dead ends in a conversation where the future was not to be discussed or changed. If I was a different person, better maybe or worse, I would have used the moment to tell him that I wanted to belong to him more than I wanted my next breath.

Instead, I slid my hand over his lightly, pulling his attention back to me. "Tell me what it would be like if we were in an actual relationship type thing."

Despite myself, I blushed at the thought of discussing such things, and despite the dark, Sinclair could see that.

"You can beg me to make you come, but you can't actually say the words Dominant and submissive?" he asked.

I shrugged and spooned a helping of gazpacho into my mouth so that I wouldn't really have to answer.

His eyes crinkled with suppressed mirth, but he sat back in his chair and studied me thoughtfully. I loved that about him— how he took everything I gave him and mulled over it as if I was special, important, and worth consideration.

"Alright, Elle, why don't we start with the basics? There are different D/s relationships with varying degrees of control. On one end of the spectrum, there are the slaves and Masters. A slave is expected to obey commands at all times, to be controlled in all aspects of his or her life by the Master."

"That sounds horrible," I said. The honesty burst from my lips like the grape between my teeth.

Sinclair chuckled easily, and I loved that I could coax that from him. "I think we can safely rule out that kind of relationship. I have no desire to control your life." He reached across the table to run two calloused fingers along my jaw. "Not when you live so beautifully."

"Now who's poetic?" I said softly.

His eyes darkened to wet blue velvet, and I gasped when his fingers tightened on my chin. "Submission is poetic too. Get on your knees, siren."

I was sliding out of my chair before I had even fully absorbed his words.

"Come closer."

I hesitated. My inclination was to stand and walk over, but I knew what a real submissive would do, and the idea of crawling to him lit a fire in my belly. I kept my eyes on the ground as I moved forward on my hands and knees, ass swaying.

When I settled at his side, he spoke again. "This is something we might do in a real relationship. I might have you eat at my feet, only by my hand."

His fingers appeared in my lowered line of sight with a purple grape in his grasp. I immediately parted my lips and tilted my head back to receive the morsel, taking care to swipe my tongue against his skin as he fed me.

"Behave," he warned mildly before continuing in an almost bored tone. "There would be rules, of course."

He waited, but I had the feeling I wasn't supposed to respond.

I could hear the smile in his voice when he finally said, "Exactly. You would not speak unless expressly ordered to, and when you did, how do you think you would address me?"

"With appropriate respect, sir," I said.

My voice was breathy, and he hadn't even touched me.

"Very good. I cannot count the things I want to do to you, not least of all because you would blush to your toes to hear me give voice to them."

I could feel that full-bodied blush, how my blood ricocheted through my veins and my heart knocked brutally against my ribs. Idly, I worried about heart failure.

"Please, tell me," I whispered hoarsely because I was so filled with desire that even my throat was swollen with it.

He studied me dispassionately for what felt like a long time. The more his gaze cooled, the warmer I grew. I couldn't think when he looked at me like that, not of Elena or the stress of my upcoming showcase, not of my lifelong insecurities or even my own name. When Sinclair looked at me with those aloof and commanding eyes the color of lightning, my very soul felt electrified.

Finally, he stood, so close to me that my nose was pressed into the inside of his lower thigh. I breathed deeply, so intoxicated by his smoky, masculine scent that I almost felt high.

His hand lowered heavily to the top of my head, and he said, "I would rather show you."

I let out a breathy little sigh before I could help myself. His hand slid over my crown and threaded through my hair, pulling firmly at the roots until pain prickled deliciously down my spine. My back arched to release some of the tension. Slowly, he tugged my head back until I was looking up at him. With his other hand, he placed his thumb on my bottom lip, rubbing back and forth until my mouth blossomed open under his touch.

He was so masterfully made, his features so perfectly chiseled that they were almost brutal to look upon, especially now when he loomed over me like the statue of a god.

My God. Oh, how I wanted to devote myself to him, venerate him with everything I had.

I swept my tongue along the ridge of his thumb, staring into his eyes through my eyelashes as I daringly took him into my mouth and scraped my teeth across the pad of his digit. His eyes flared.

"This lifestyle is not always about pain and restraint," he explained. "It is about worship."

His ability to read my mind no longer surprised me.

"I worship you," I breathed.

He pulled his thumb from my mouth and drew two fingers tenderly down my cheek before saying, "And I you."

Without another word, he reached down to pull me into his arms. Cradled securely against his chest, I let myself listen to the beat of his heart as he led me into the bedroom and gently laid me on the bed. Languidly, I watched as he went into the bathroom, re-emerging with a bottle of lavender-scented massage oil and the same red scarf he had bound me with earlier. Warmth pooled between my legs just at the sight of it.

I studied him silently as he straddled my prone body on the bed and blindfolded me by gently secured the fabric around my head. I gasped in disappointment when his body left mine once more, but he returned to me quickly after plugging his phone into the music system. Glass Animal's "Toes" beat sexily from the speakers.

"This is about you, my siren. I control you to discover you, to unlock the secrets of your heart and the hidden desires in that brilliant mind of yours." His voice was as smooth and warm as the massage oil he heated between his palms and applied to my shoulders.

I hummed with pleasure as he began to knead my neck and chest, my mind empty of everything but the exquisite pressure of his hands against my skin. His fingers moved down my arms to my very fingertips, where he released an uncanny amount of tension just by pinching the pads of each digit. After working his way from my stomach to the bottom of my feet, he tenderly rolled me onto my stomach and began to caress my back.

A moan built deep in my gut. It was in no way a sexual massage, but I felt restless with desire nonetheless. Each press of his strong fingers into my muscles molded me further and further into a creature of his own making, as supple and easily manipulated as clay beneath his touch.

I was mindless, made only of sensation by the time his thumb found the pronounced curve of my bottom. He pressed hard into the muscles there, almost painfully so that I sucked air between my teeth. I wasn't sure where the massage oil ended and my own wetness began.

"On your knees."

His voice slithered into my subconscious. I raised my heavy body as quickly as I could, tucking my knees underneath me, arching my back so that my ass was raised with my hands grasping my ankles and my face pressed into the sheets. Cool air drifted deliciously over my overheated flesh.

The slow, arousing massage continued, but this time, it was punctuated by the sound of his cool voice washing over me. "I remember the first time you displayed your pussy like this for me. You were so wet." His thumbs dipped down the crease and pulled apart my lips to expose my wet, pink core. "I could smell you from across the room."

I groaned softly into the bed and wriggled, desperate for more stimulation.

He punished me with a swift, brutal spank that left my skin singing out for mercy. His hand squeezed the smarting skin, clenching it under his strong grip until I whimpered.

"I wanted to punish you just like this for bewitching me."

Another painful slap, my skin even more sensitive under the sheen of oil.

"I wanted to take this perfectly plump ass in my hands, warm these cheeks, and spread them open for my tongue."

I tensed in anticipation as he spanked me twice more, harder than before, and slowly spread my burning cheeks so that my most forbidden place was exposed to his gaze. His thumbs commenced their massage over my abused flesh.

I shuddered when his hot breath wafted over my center. "I'm going to take your ass, Elle. Would you like that?"

My answer was the bestial groan he wrought from me as his hot, velvet tongue stroked heavily over my asshole. I shuddered at the depth of pleasure, the heat of my embarrassment only providing further kindling for the fire raging inside me.

He slapped my ass again. "Use your words, siren."

"Yes, sir," I breathed.

"Yes, sir, what?"

"Yes, sir, I want you to take my ass."

Saying the words out loud set my oiled skin aflame. I wasn't mortified. I was desperate. Desperate to show him how much I could take, how eager I was to be physically and emotionally splayed open before him, used by him.

His finger slowly followed the track of my wetness from the inside of my knee to its source at my center.

"So wet for me."

"Yes," I hissed, locking my knees to keep from rocking back against his gently questing fingers.

I needed more. My tender flesh missed the pain; my mind craved debasement.

"Please, sir," I begged.

His tongue was back at the tightly furled entrance between my cheeks. He circled my opening languidly, his hands roughly suppressing the undulation of my hips.

I wanted to buck back at him like a bitch in heat, howl at the sky, force Sinclair to break his control and take me like an animal. Instead, he enforced my stillness, my silence, and caged the sensations roiling through me, heightening them until I was a churning mess of incoherent need.

"You've done this before," he reminded me, and I was momentarily surprised he remembered that. "But you've never had me here." His thumb firmly circled my anus before plunging inside. "No one will ever own this ass but me."

The tightly knotted mass of shame that had lain at the core of my psyche since the moment Christopher had initiated contact with me began to unravel. With the mental release came a flash of gut-wrenching memories; Christopher's pale hands as they coaxed me onto the bed, his casual suggestions that I might please him as payment for his kindness to my family and his sincere promise to keep my "virginity" intact. He was never physically forceful, but his emotional manipulation of my teenage self had been perfectly calculated.

Goose flesh rippled across my skin, and I pressed my teary eyes harder into the bedsheets until the scent of Sinclair and me, of our intimacy, killed the images like mustard gas.

I gasped as Sinclair pushed forward with two fingers, pumping and twisting them firmly inside me. It was so decadent, these dual feelings of fullness and taboo, that I was drunk from it.

Sin's hand pressed hard on the base of my spine so that my bottom was steeply arched into the air.

"What are you thinking of, siren?"

His fingers inside me, stretching. His smoky scent braided with the smell of lavender, the smell of me. His words saturated every conscious thought so that they fell into a heavy sleep, and I was only my body.

"You," I said.

"Yes, me. When we are together, you only think of me."

"Even when we aren't."

He swatted me again.

"Who is in this room? Only you and me, Sinclair and Elle. A Dom and his sub." His voice lowered dangerously, and his touch left me. I felt his absence more painfully than any spanking. "I will ask you again. What are you thinking of?"

"You, only you." I jerked my hips back at him. "Always you."

His hands were back on my ass, powerfully clenching and pulling them apart to make way for his cock. He nudged my slicked opening and paused.

"I could own you, all of you."

"Yes."

The head of his cock slid slowly, only an inch, inside me.

"Do you know how I know that?" he asked, his voice softer now, smoother than the hand that stroked down my back as he pushed farther inside me. "I know because you own *me*, my siren."

I buried my face in the blanket and groaned raggedly as he

seated himself fully inside me. The pain was like a heated blade cutting through me, and my bottom was raw from the spanking. I was surprised by how much I liked the pain, loved how it unlocked my mind and sent it reeling into velvety darkness. Loved that it was Sinclair in this most private part of me. The feeling was so intense that I wanted to wriggle away from it, but each undulation of my ass only pressed him further against me.

"Ah," I said, chasing after each elusive breath.

"Hush."

His hands were all over my skin, soothing away my restlessness by lighting fire to my nipples with firm twists and tugs, dipping into my drenched sex to pinch my clit. After endless minutes, he rooted one hand in my hair and tugged until my neck was craned back, and he was hunched over me with his tongue on my ear.

"I'm going to fuck you now. I expect you to ask permission before you come."

I didn't know if I could orgasm like that, but I held back my concern.

His hands rubbed roughly over my ass, reawakening the ache there. "You can, and you will come for me like this."

The first sinuous glide of his cock leaving my body was strange and wonderful, and as he began to saw in and out of me at an infuriatingly slow pace, my clit began to throb like a strobe light.

The calloused fingers of one hand plucked at my nipples while the other flattened across my stomach and urged me to sit back against his thighs. I whimpered and moaned, ugly little animal sounds as I churned up and down, grinding and bucking in any way I could to relieve the ache swelling uncomfortably inside me.

"Ah, Sinclair," I begged, unable to speak but desperate to convey how much I needed more, more, more.

He turned my head, fusing his mouth over mine to absorb my cries into himself as his fingers grew cruel against my breasts and his hips jutted punishingly against mine. I screamed against his lips as his hand slid lower and rhythmically pinched my clit to the beat of his savage strokes.

I tore my lips from his, the separation painful as if Velcro secured us. "Please, let me come."

He hummed but continued the torment.

"Please, please."

His mouth found my ear, nibbling at the lobe before his tongue slid down my salty neck. His voice filled me like a second cock. "What are you thinking about, siren?"

The feel of his sweat-slicked skin against mine, the powerful clench of his hands on my hips, the sound of our bodies slapping and panting... Him, him, *him*.

"You."

"Yes," he hissed, and three of his fingers plunged into my sex. "Come for me."

I had never been so happy to obey anyone in my life.

Chapter Thirteen

I'd never had a vision of the kind of man I might fall in love with.

My sisters always had. Cosima imagined herself with an Italian, someone who worked with their hands and came home smelling of earth and wine. They would love passionately and fight passionately and have a brood of gorgeous children who constantly got underfoot. I had yet to see her with such a man, but I knew she kept that dream sewn into the lining of her soul.

Elena's prince was a little more typical and a whole lot more modern. She didn't want to be treated like the timeless woman the way Cosima did, like a sexual creature and a domestic goddess. Elena wanted a relationship of equals, a partnership that afforded her individual power and independence. Her man was eloquent, elegantly opinionated, and urbane.

And technically, that man stood before me right now, his lean back gold and black in the acidic sunlight streaming in through the windows of Cosima's kitchen. He was Elena's ideal; smart, classy, and eternally composed. Hell, he even wore three-piece suits on a daily basis. They were practically made for each other.

Yet I was watching a completely different man cook me breakfast. There was boyishness in the chestnut hair flopping over his forehead and gentle humor in the way he rolled his shoulders to the beat of Meghan Trainor's "All About That Bass." He had laughed when I blasted it from the speakers, shaking my booty so that the bare skin winked at him from under the tail of his dress shirt. I could count the number of times I had heard Sinclair laugh on my fingers, but this was the best yet because he kept laughing as he reached out to tug me into his arms. I smiled into my coffee at the memory.

This man, the kind that only laughed at the really good stuff and looked at me with a heady mixture of authority and awe, was *my* kind of man.

"I better be the reason behind that gorgeous smile, siren."

I looked up to see him looking at me, his electric eyes sparking with mirth even though his lips remained smooth and impassive.

I shrugged one shoulder as he slid a plate laden with bacon and avocado studded scrambled eggs in front of me. "I wouldn't say that exactly."

His eyes narrowed. In less than a second, the soft Sinclair, the one with the boyish curl and the wide, almost awkward smile, was gone, and in his place was Sinclair the Dom. He wore his icy control like a king's mantle across his shoulders, and when he moved around the island to stand before me, the liquidity of his gait froze the air in my lungs.

He didn't touch me, but he might as well have. The thin

slice of space between our bodies vibrated with palpable tension and set my body's rhythm to his like a tuning fork.

"What would you say then?" he said in that quiet voice that echoed through my entire body.

I swallowed hard before answering. "You're more than the reason behind one smile. You hold the lease on my happiness."

The tic in his jaw was the only sign of his shock. He stared at me for a long time, caging me against the island with his arms braced on either side of me.

"I want to *own* your happiness," he said, finally.

I sucked in so much air my lungs expanded to the point of pain.

"I want you to own me," I whispered.

We had never been this forthright, and even though it felt good, scary and good, *scary good*, I wasn't sure it was a good idea.

Sinclair shook his head, and a piece of his newly shorn hair fell across his forehead. My fingers itched to smooth it back, but I resisted because, despite our sexual proclivities, we didn't have the casual kind of intimacy that came from dating.

So instead, I watched the battle in his eyes as he fought between taking me right there on the stool and storming out of the apartment, never to return. Maybe it was overdramatic, but in a situation like ours, nothing was understated.

"I do," he said in a tight voice because there wasn't enough air in his lungs.

Hope—the scrappy kind that you fight for with every pounding beat of your heart—could leave you breathless like that.

I shook my head, mute with emotion, but he pressed a finger to my lips.

"I own you in the dark. The moment you turn off the lights, I own your thoughts and your body. I dictate your touch." His hand skimmed too lightly down the exposed skin between the panels of my shirt. "When you touch yourself, it is because I want you to. You're only echoing my thoughts in the dark, reading my will from across the city. So perfectly obedient. And after you come, my name on your sweet lips like a prayer, you'll dream of me because the entire night is ours, and I won't give you up for one second of it."

I was hot and cold with arousal, but tears still pressed at my eyes. "I'll still wake up alone."

His eyes softened, and the hand that had been tickling the upper swell of my breasts moved up to take a firm hold at the base of my neck. It was almost scary how both actions brought me utter calm.

"Greedy girl," he teased, but when I didn't smile, his grip flexed tight. "There isn't much more of me to take."

Only the part of you in Elena's grip, I thought. But even that poignant reminder didn't hold the same weight as it had as little as two weeks ago. I was turning into a different kind of person, one who didn't care about the consequences of my desires. I couldn't tell if it was a devolution or not. Only the fittest survive, and only those with the selfishness to go after their ambitions succeed.

"Your eggs are cold." He ducked down to press a kiss above his grip on my neck, right on my jumping pulse, before releasing me.

I stared down at the yellow curds without thinking while he cleaned up in the kitchen and came around to sit beside me with his own breakfast. His hand fell heavily onto my thigh, jerking me out of my trance, but when I looked up, he was focused on his tablet, rapidly reading and responding to a deluge of emails. The hand was a reminder of his authority, his presence lest I forget it, and it released me from my worries the way nothing else could.

Happily, I dug into my cold eggs.

We ate silently, and even when I squirmed to relieve the tension at my pleasantly raw core, he only had to squeeze my leg to relay his satisfaction with my discomfort and his will for me to sit still. It was the intimacy of our secret tryst merging seamlessly, beautifully like a watercolor sunset, into something more mundane but just as meaningful. It felt really, really good.

When I was done with the eggs, I made us both another coffee and retrieved my sketchbook before sitting down again. My mind was beautifully vacant, the kind of mental state artists strive for, but only the best are capable of achieving on a regular basis, and I wanted to take advantage of it. My pencil twisted over the paper in loose, languid strokes.

I wasn't surprised when something distinctly sexual emerged from the gray mass of swirls, but the dark taint of the image, the stark disobedience of it did bewilder me. A woman with shadowy hair wrapping around her arousal swollen flesh like bindings yelled across the page, her mouth invitingly wide but dangerous, temperamental.

I realized as I stared at her that she was me. This woman who dared you to fuck her, dominate her, and then dared those who would condemn her to resist her charms. It was so ironic that the more sexually powerful I became, the more I wanted someone to leash me.

"What are your plans for the day?" Sinclair asked.

He had been watching me. I knew because I had harnessed that scorching gaze and locked it around the fierce woman in my drawing.

"I need to paint."

"Of course, your exhibition is coming quickly. January is not so far off."

I stared at him for a second. "I didn't think you knew."

He frowned at me. "Elle, not only is it my business to know about the goings-on at *my* gallery but it is also your first show in America. I assure you, the date has been noted on my calendar since it was decided upon."

I smudged the shadowy lock of hair falling over my drawn woman's face with my thumb and mumbled, "I just remember you saying that you didn't want anything to do with it."

He sighed, and a second later, my stool was tugged toward him so that I was between his spread legs. His fingers threaded through my hair and tilted my head until I was looking up into his eyes. Instantly, I relaxed as my ricocheting thoughts bounced against his palms and slunk back into my skull like chastised dogs.

"How can you be so confident under my hands and otherwise so unsure? Giselle, I said that because you had upset me. You came into my office looking gorgeous and unflappable, and then this soft-spoken woman told me to *go to hell*."

I blushed because that *had* been a little unfair. "I didn't mean it."

"We both said a lot of things we didn't mean that day."

I felt the hook that connected my heart to his sink deeper into my left aorta.

"I do not want to stop seeing you."

My eyes fluttered close to better savor those edible words. When I opened them, his lips were ever so slightly tilted in a bemused smile.

"We see each other all the time," I reminded him.

Just because his admission made me ecstatic didn't mean I was going to be an easy catch.

His gaze narrowed. "It's difficult to play hard to get when you've already told me that you are in love with me."

I bristled, but he did have a point. Instead of answering, I gathered our dirty dishes and put them in the dishwasher, taking my time to completely avoid his burning stare. I was just walking past him to get my sketchbook when he grabbed me around the waist and tugged me between his legs, wrapping his limbs around me so that I was trapped.

"Get off me," I ordered in my haughtiest voice.

"Don't feel like it."

"Sinclair," I said, laughter seeping into my tone. "*Tu es con*, let me go!"

"Nope, maybe if I keep you captive long enough, you will remember that time you said you loved me. In fact, I think you said it *multiple* times."

I rolled my eyes, and even though he couldn't see me do it, he gave me a tight squeeze.

"I have no idea to what you are referring."

His fingers dug into my sides and began to tickle me. I writhed in his grip as laughter exploded from my lips, huge unfeminine guffaws that made my entire body shake.

"Stop... please... Sin," I begged breathlessly, tears streaming down my face.

He spun me around in his arms, smiling that boyish smile that made my heart forget to function.

"I want you to tell me again," he explained, pouting adorably.

A part of me was floating near the ceiling, buoyed by his good humor and obvious affection, while the other part, smaller than a sandbag, kept me tethered to the earth. I cupped his achingly handsome face in my hands because it made me feel better about what I had to say.

"Daniel." He flinched slightly, but I tightened my hands on his cheeks. "I haven't asked you to leave Elena, and I'm not going to. I have no right to ask you, and I can promise you right now, I will never ask you that. But in return, I need you to promise me that you will never ask me if I love you again. I can deal with this." I rolled my head around to indicate our fucked-up situation in the most eloquent way I knew how. "With Elena keeping you, but only if you let me keep a part of myself to myself.”

With a heavy sigh, I took a moment to collect my thoughts and project them clearly through my gaze when I met his eyes again.

“You could take it.” I thumped my chest. “You could take everything I am. And you know what? A part of me wants that like crazy.”

His hands found my hips and rested there, just gently on the curve. I was grateful for it because he was letting me know that he understood what I was trying to say.

“But I have to be realistic, even if I don’t want to be. You aren’t going to leave Elena, and I refuse to put my heart in a cage I don’t have the key to open.”

His lips were screwed tight like a lid over the emotions bubbling up at his center. I could see some of it rise to the surface of his gaze, but he was looking over my shoulder, shielding most of it from me.

I swallowed hard and decided to throw in the last of my grenades. “Also, I have a lunch date today.”

His eyes snapped to me, flashing like neon lights. “Excuse me?”

“You heard me.”

His hands flexed painfully on my waist, but the silence was worse than the physical discomfort. It stretched long and torturous before us like a road littered with mines.

“You’re going to sit across from another man when your ass is still sore from my hand?”

I raised my eyebrows. “You’re going to go home to my sister when your hand is still sore from my ass?”

Fury emanated from him like dry ice, and I instantly regretted my barb.

I sighed. “Sin, it’s just a lunch date. Elena basically insisted on setting us up, and I wanted to seem like a normal girl, one who was interested in other men." I laughed a little. "We both know who I would rather be with."

"Do we?"

"You're kidding, right?"

But he wasn't. He sat utterly rigid on the stool, and his eyes had been reduced to icy shields.

"I want to be with you," I said slowly and maybe a little condescending because I thought it was blindingly obvious.

His jaw clenched, and he stared at me hard for a long moment before standing up and stalking away to the balcony doors.

"Sin?" I stayed where I was because I wasn't sure how to deal with an angry Frenchman even after all my time in Paris.

He continued to stare broodingly out the window. In only his low-slung jeans with the sunlight kissing his skin, he looked like stolen artwork, something far too glorious to ever belong to me.

"You cut a dashing figure standing there, but maybe you could talk to me?" I asked as I scooted onto a stool to make myself comfortable while I waited.

He looked over his shoulder at me, but his face was cast in shadow. "Come here."

I slid off the stool before I could even process his request, and I hesitated when I realized how easily my body revealed his dominion over me. He was in front of me before I could make a decision one way or another, his fingers sinking into the hair over my ears while his thumbs tilted my chin up.

"I have done nothing in my life to deserve you, Elle. Absolutely nothing. I've fought to be a good person when it is not in my nature to be kind or good, not like you." He shook his head, and his thumb brushed against my lower lip. "I do not deserve to hold something so precious in my hands."

I turned my head, dislodging one of his hands so I could kiss his palm, leaving the imprint of my love for him like a lucky coin. I closed his fist over it and held it with both my hands. There was no way to articulate the toxic cocktail of emotions rolling churlishly through my veins, and I knew if I couldn't, my enigmatic Frenchman probably couldn't either.

Besides, we hadn't really spoken about where we would go from here, but as it stood, this was my last morning as Daniel Sinclair's lover, and I wanted to make the most of it.

"Can I show you something?" I asked, my girlish excitement making me bounce on my toes.

Without waiting for his answer, I turned around to grab the large canvas tilted to the left of the French doors. My heart trilled with nerves as I turned to prop it on the easel. I avoided looking back at Sinclair as I stepped back into line with him so he could see the painting unobstructed. It was the one I had been slaving over between my projects for the art gallery opening, but I had only finished it yesterday.

It was based on the sketch I had started in Mexico, the one with the two contrasting lovers a breath away from a kiss. It was my favorite piece in my growing collection because it was so clearly Sinclair and me, lost in the murky shadows but burning so brightly our features were nearly obscured in the blaze.

I looked up at him, bouncing maniacally now, but his gorgeous face betrayed no emotions.

"Well?"

His lips twitched, and he crossed his arms. "Well what, siren?" His grin broke free when I hip-checked him. "It's simply remarkable."

"You think?"

He turned to face me, taking my hands in his so that he could stare down at them. My nails were industriously short, and charcoal was smudged across the thumb and forefinger on my right hand from sketching earlier, but Sinclair gazed down at them as if they were precious gems. He brushed each finger with his lips, slowly and reverently, before looking down into my eyes.

"I know. You are extraordinarily gifted, Giselle, and beyond that, you are brave. Exploring the hidden side of lust and longing is not for the faint of heart."

"No," I agreed, thinking of us. "It isn't. But I'm hoping that it's worth it in the end."

Chapter Fourteen

Other than Mama's, Prune was my favorite restaurant in New York, particularly for the insanely busy Sunday brunches, so I was pleased when my blind date suggested the restaurant for our outing. I decided to walk there even though it was on the opposite side of Manhattan, which meant I had to say goodbye to Sinclair earlier than I wanted to. He had stayed over longer and ended up heading into the office over three hours later than usual. His tardiness delighted me.

The Indian summer was finally ending, and the breeze was cool between the tightly packed buildings, but I welcomed it. Since Sinclair had left, my heart had stopped racing, but my body was still flushed with the memory of his touch. My nipples scraped against the lacy material of my bra, sensitive from his mouth and the clothespins. In the aftermath of last night, my skin was so responsive that it was hard to resist the urge to touch the swell of my tastefully exposed breasts or the delicate inside of my wrists where Sinclair had nibbled just that morning.

The only thing that intruded on my memories—apart from the occasional New Yorker's elbow—was the prickly feeling at the base of my neck. At first, I thought it was a stray itch, one that I scratched until the skin was raw, but as I neared the restaurant, the feeling grew until I was almost certain someone was following me. Looking over my shoulder and finding unfamiliar faces every time didn't alleviate my growing anxiety.

I pulled out my phone and dialed the first number on my speed dial.

"Hello?" Cosima's throaty voice was breathless. "*Bambina*, what's the matter?"

"Would you think I was crazy if I said someone was following me?"

There was a long pause and a vague cacophony on the other end of the line.

"How long?"

I exhaled loudly, grateful but unsurprised that she believed me. Cosima had always had a suspicious mind, and given her close association with the Camorra in Napoli and the black-eyed Dante, I knew she had experience with this kind of thing.

"About fifteen minutes," I guessed, walking a little more quickly as the heat of paranoia lit me on fire.

"Okay." Cosima spoke calmly, but I could still hear the mess of her movements in the background and the low register of a male voice. "Stay on a busy street. Where are you going?" I told her, and she thought about it for a second before continuing, "I hope you are wearing something cute, *bambina*. You have been too lonely since your mystery lover in Mexico."

"Shouldn't I cancel if someone really is following me?"

"No, it's best if you keep to your normal schedule and go to lunch. You should be fine once you get into the restaurant, but call me before you leave."

There was more noise as she spoke with someone in the room with her. It could have been my imagination, but I thought I heard a British accent.

"I can't be home for a while more, and I don't want you to be at the apartment alone," she said. "So, I just texted Elena, and you are going to stay there tonight."

"No," I blurted out before I could stop myself.

"Gigi, now isn't the time to pull the sibling rivalry card. Mama is working tonight, and Sebastian is in Toronto. Until we figure out what is going on, it is safer for you to stay with family." She hesitated before adding, "There have been a few strange phone calls to the apartment. A man asked for you the first time, but otherwise, it is always silent on the other line. Please, stay with Elena tonight and let me take care of this."

I chewed on my bottom lip as I focused on the pink awning of Prune in the distance. I really didn't want to stay with Elena and her Daniel after I had just spent a remarkable night with *my* Sinclair. But I didn't want to worry Cosima or be one of those stupid girls in horror films who went against common logic and got murdered.

So I promised Cosima I would and hung up just as my phone buzzed with an incoming text.

Elena: Guest bedroom is made up. Left a key with the receptionist, please let yourself in.

I sighed and was about to put my phone away when another text came in.

The Frenchman: *Please don't worry about tonight. And, more importantly, please think of me during your 'date.'*

I grinned, shook my head, and tucked my phone in my bag just as I reached the long line leading into Prune.

$\mathcal{U}$lrich Wick was an incredibly nice guy.

He was also incredibly dull.

"I tried to explain how important the discrepancies were to the overall dynamic of the company's infrastructure," he continued, "but of course, it was beyond comprehension for someone with such a pea-sized intellect."

"Of course," I murmured, looking down at the salad he had ordered for me without my consent. Prune had so many delicious things on the menu that I had felt robbed when I arrived to see him already seated and our orders in place. I had spent the past twenty minutes watching him daintily consume a plate of *spaghetti alla carbonara,* and it was torture.

Not to mention the endless conversation about corporate accounting.

"You wouldn't know either, though, I suppose, being a painter." He smiled at me, and the worst thing was that it was a pretty smile, a truly kind one despite his patronizing words.

"Oh, excuse me for a moment, but I believe that is Willa Percy coming this way." Ulrich pushed ungracefully out of his chair, exhibiting more passion in the single movement than in our entire hour-long brunch. I couldn't understand his enthusiasm. I had met Willa Percy, and she was not passion-inducing.

"Mrs. Percy, it is lovely to see you again," Ulrich gushed, reaching out with both hands.

Willa's eyes weren't on my date, though. Her stare pinned me in place so that she could get a really good look at every inch of me, finding fault with my freckled skin, overdramatic curves, and harlot red hair.

But instead of burning shame, of comparing myself to my flawless sisters, I thought about Sinclair, the only person in the Percy family I cared about. I thought about the map his hands, lips, and body had drawn over my skin in the past twenty-four hours, and suddenly, Willa's scrutiny didn't matter anymore.

Ulrich was still talking, and Willa was indulging him with minuscule facial tics, but eventually, he noticed the tension and petered off.

"Giselle," Willa began, her voice cool as silk wrapping around my throat. "You will wait with me while they bring my car around."

It wasn't a question, and normally, I would have protested, but Ulrich looked ready to swoon at the privilege I was being bestowed. I didn't have the heart to tell him that Willa Percy was a self-serving heartless bitch, so I grabbed my purse and followed her outside.

She didn't speak for a moment, opting to fix her lipstick in the mirror of a Chanel compact instead. Her elegance was absolute, from the tips of her pale pink painted nails to the bottoms of her low-heeled cream pumps, and I felt worse than bohemian next to her. I wondered if she had ever known poverty, how she would have judged my perfect older sister or me if she had witnessed the desperation of our childhood.

"You think I don't like you," she began in a cool voice like poured cream, "and you are mostly correct. It is obvious that you lack elevated social graces, a sense of fashion, and the common sense not to get involved with a taken man, let alone a man pledged to your very sibling."

A thin smile punctured her cheek, cutting off my protest before I could even open my mouth.

"I know my son very well, Miss Moore, and it does not escape my notice that he seems to be very much in lust with you. You do not need to protest because I do not blame either of you. My son is quite simply an incredible man, and you have your..." She hesitated and gestured vaguely to my body. "Obvious charms. So, I do not blame you for your initial bad judgment, but I am encouraging you as civilly as possible to cease and desist."

My lips twisted into something like a sneer, but she only laughed softly. "Abandon your pride and think for a moment. If you love my son, as I'm certain you think that you do, then you know that Elena is the best choice for him. Her elegance, intelligence, and stature are perfectly suited to Daniel's pursuits. You know, one day he wants to run for office, just like his father."

My insecurity vibrated as Willa hammered her point home. I didn't want to listen to her, but it was hard to ignore the truth of her statement, especially when she spoke so calmly, so rationally. It was tricky to argue against a lack of passion.

"Daniel had a rough beginning, and I, for one, believe that he deserves happiness now. You may believe that you are the one to bring him that happiness, but you're mistaken." Her eyes swept over me dismissively. "You do not have what it takes to stand by my son."

A beige Town Car rolled up to the curb, and a handsomely dressed young man with skin like roasted coffee beans came around to open the door for the governor's wife.

"Go back inside, enjoy the rest of your meal with Mr. Wick, then go home and call my son. End it. I'm asking nicely, my dear, but the Lord knows I have other ways at my disposal."

I stood silently, stupidly, while she slid into the car, closed the door, and rolled down the window so she could stare at me as they pulled into traffic. I stayed there for a long moment after she was gone, my eyes closed and my senses open to the riotous noises of a New York City afternoon. The cacophony calmed the turmoil churning through me, and when I opened my eyes again, I started off down the street toward my next destination with renewed confidence.

*D*espite my earlier determination to see him, I was nervous giving my name to the receptionist. The young ginger-haired man smiled warmly at me and complimented my choice of dress, but his recognition of my discomfort only heightened my nervousness. If it was that apparent, I wondered if the entire office might know about our secret affair?

I was obviously being paranoid, but not without reason. Sebastian and Cosima already suspected, and I wouldn't be surprised at all if they'd figured it out for themselves. It seemed almost ridiculous that anyone could remain oblivious to the sultry, heavy air between Sinclair and me when we're together, but the mind was a powerful thing. It was easy to believe what you wanted to believe.

I was still dwelling on it when I was ushered into the office, so it took me a moment to recognize the slick dark-haired man grinning at me with his arms outstretched. Of course, the outrageously loud burnt umber blazer helped.

"Santiago!"

He laughed richly as I stepped into his arms. "Beautiful Elle, the New York smog does wonders for your complexion."

I laughed with him. "You're just being kind."

He nodded solemnly. "I am. But this is easy with such a beautiful woman before me. Isn't it, Sinclair?"

We both turned to smile at the Frenchman who was staring at us with his arms crossed and his feet braced. He looked every inch the successful property developer behind his glass and chrome desk, his hair perfectly smoothed away from his broad forehead. I wanted desperately to tousle it with my fingers.

"She is lovely, though I don't believe that gives you the right to fawn all over her, Iago."

Santiago's laughter was a series of quick, high yips that made me grin. I allowed him to usher me to the seat beside his across from Sinclair's desk.

"I have to say I am pleasantly surprised to see you. Last time I spoke with Sinclair, he was cursing the fact you had abandoned him in Mexico. There must be a good story here," Santiago said.

I bit my lip and looked at Sinclair to answer his friend. I was surprised that my decision to flee had perturbed him, but the longer I thought about it, the more it made sense. Sinclair was a man who appreciated closure and neatly tied-up ends. Even more, he was a man of power, and I had unwittingly stripped him of that power by leaving before he could say anything.

God, was it outrageous to think that he might have wanted

to stop me? That he might have wanted to solidify the bond between us with facts and figures, the where and who of it all so that we might have really been together?

My head pulsed painfully in time with my heart.

"...so I would appreciate your discretion on the matter. You know how much I dislike mixing business with pleasure," Sinclair was saying when I tuned back into the conversation.

Santiago was frowning, though, his thick brows knotting together in one long black smear. "This is ridiculous."

I laughed weakly. "You can't make stuff like this up."

"No, no, you cannot. The situation is ridiculous, but what I really meant was that you, Sinclair, are ridiculous. The only reason Elle isn't Mrs. Santiago Herrera right now is because you were there first, but if you insist on being ridiculous about it, then..." He petered off with a shrug as if he couldn't be held accountable for what happened next.

Something like a growl emanated from Sinclair's direction, but before he could calmly slice his friend into ribbons with a steely retort, I said, "Let me assure you, that is not the only reason I'm not your wife, Iago." I sniffed dramatically. "Now if you bought me a ring bigger than your second wife's... then we could talk."

He laughed again, and even Sinclair's lips twitched, which effectively defused the atmosphere.

"Anyway, I hate to interrupt business," I said with wide, innocent eyes as I waited for them to protest.

Santiago opened his mouth to do so, but Sin's chuckle caught him off guard.

"She's just fishing for compliments. You weren't interrupting. Iago has been here for much longer than his allotted appointment, and if I'm not mistaken, he is keeping a lovely woman waiting in his hotel suite uptown."

The Mexican magnate shrugged. "She may be my fourth wife if Elle won't have me."

"Is Katarina with you?" I asked, jumping slightly in my seat at the thought of seeing his wonderful sister.

"Alas, she is back home. Had I known you would be here, I couldn't have stopped her from joining me. She has remarked a number of times with sadness that you did not exchange information."

"Give her my card," I said, pushing one of my newly minted business cards toward him. "I'm actually having a showing the second week of January at DS Galleries. I don't suppose you'll still be here for it?"

His large obsidian eyes lit up, and his smile was overlarge, goofy, like a kid with a candy bar. "I wouldn't miss it."

"If you are in town, you have to come to our family Thanksgiving tomorrow."

"If you insist," he agreed easily.

We beamed at each other until Sinclair cleared his throat, and then we both laughed before turning to look at him.

"Yes, sir?" I asked mildly.

He raised one haughty brow at my innuendo, and the simple gesture was enough to send an arrow of desire straight to my core. God, but that man could imply a lot with a simple look. It probably helped that he was already sinfully attractive.

"If you'll excuse us, Iago, I have plans to show Elle around the office."

It was my turn to raise my brows, but Santiago leaned forward to take both my hands in his for lingering kisses.

"Of course, but allow me to request Giselle's company on my walk to the elevator. One does get lonely in a foreign city," he added sagely.

Sinclair would have snorted, I think, if it wasn't such an undignified thing to do.

I linked my arm through Santiago's and smiled over my shoulder at Sin as we exited. "Be back in a moment."

Margot was at her desk outside his office when we passed

by, but happily, Santiago blocked her view of me, and we escaped unscathed. He must have sensed my relaxation as soon as we were out of hearing distance because it was only then that he patted my hand where it rested on his arm and leaned in close to say, "Are you a religious woman, Elle?"

I startled a bit at the randomness of the question. "Um, no, not particularly. My parents used to be Roman and Irish Catholics, but we all kind of abandoned religion when we felt God had abandoned us to poverty and abuse during my childhood."

He frowned down at me, not in sympathy as I might have expected, but appraisingly. "I sensed poverty in you. It gives a person a certain quality, a greedy ruthlessness."

I tried to step away from him, but his clutch on my arm only tightened, and he tutted me like an old matron. "Now, now, don't shy away from the truth. I didn't mean it as an insult. Only when you've known true hunger and desperation are you willing to go after what you want, consequences be damned. It is, if not an admirable quality, then certainly a successful one."

He gave me a moment of silence in order to digest his words while we waited for the elevators. The unpalatable thing was, I agreed with what he was saying. Only the ruthless succeeded. I truly believed that. The only thing I remained unsure of was if I had the balls to submit to my brutal instinct to steal happiness away from my own sister.

Santiago was watching me as if he was asking himself the same question. "You are no longer the person you thought we were before you met him, Giselle. That woman, one whom you undoubtedly thought was good and moral? She has already been murdered by the new you, the one who went after a taken man knowingly, even if it wasn't without qualms." He held up a single finger to hush my protest. "There was strength in making that decision. Do not be weak and unkind now by not going after what you want. In my experience, it only leads to misery for everyone."

My throat was swollen and aching as if I was responding to his words with anaphylactic shock.

"Besides"—he cast me a sidelong glance—"wickedness looks good on you."

I was mute as he leaned forward to press a kiss against my cheek, smelling like heat and expensive cologne. He stepped into the elevator without breaking eye contact, and we watched each other as the doors slid close.

Just before he winked out of sight behind the metal partition, he lifted his hand to his throat and said, "You would look even better in a collar."

Chapter Fifteen

I didn't go back to Sinclair's office.

He would come looking for me, I knew, but I still needed a moment to digest Santiago's words. Besides, I reasoned as I fled the sixtieth floor in an elevator of people dressed in impeccable business attire, I had business to conduct in the gallery, and I might as well take care of it while I was in the building.

I made my way to the storeroom where my completed paintings were housed, too preoccupied to notice the woman following in my wake. It was only when the door closed with a slam that I twirled around to see Margot Silver standing against it with her thin arms crossed over her chest.

I sighed. "I don't suppose you came down to help me move these?"

"Don't be cute with me, Giselle. We both know it's just an act."

I crossed my arms to mimic her pose and raised my eyebrows Sinclair-style.

She rolled her eyes at my demonstration. "I'll get to the point because spending any amount of time with you rubs me the wrong way. Stop fucking around with Sinclair."

"I hate to break it to you when you've been so nice to me, but I don't care what you think. You don't know anything about the situation."

"I know that Daniel Sinclair is the best man I know, yet he's acting like a moronic dickhead chasing after your nice pair of tits."

"Aw, thank you, Margot," I said with faux delight.

"If you think I'm the only one who has noticed you two, you're an idiot."

That gave me pause. I had wondered about the twins knowing, but the people Sin worked with? I didn't want them to think less of him.

She practically snarled at me. "I'm not being a bitch because I enjoy it. I'm doing this, whether you choose to believe it or not, because what you two are doing is going to hurt everyone involved. Are you really willing to tank your career and lose your family over what God only knows has to be admittedly pretty damn good sex?"

I gritted my teeth. Those words were my own, the ones that echoed in my head every goddamn day since I'd discovered Sin's Darling was Elena. Yet hearing them voiced with such vitriol made me defensive. Her darkness brought to light all the wonderful things I had experienced with him. We were so much more than the (admittedly damn good) sex.

"I'm not willing to lose anything, including Sinclair. If you're his guard dog, shouldn't you consider the fact I make him happy?"

"Are you so sure that you do?"

Okay, that arrow found its mark.

She grinned like a viper, her small teeth like shiny, poison-slicked weapons. "I'm asking you as nicely as I know how. Back *the fuck* off. You don't have the balls to see this through to the end. If you don't care about ruining your own life, what about his?"

I shivered at her icy tone. She didn't understand that it wasn't just my choice not to follow through on my attraction to Sinclair. He was just as reluctant to fuck up his life as she was.

"If you talked to him, you'd realize he doesn't want anything more. It's over now, anyway," I said.

She snorted. "If you knew him, you would realize that Sin is about the things he doesn't say."

My brow tangled before I could mask the expression from her. She was right, but it didn't sit well with me. Had I been focusing too much on his uttered protests and not enough on the sweet touches and longing kisses? The fact that he still couldn't get enough of me.

My heart fluttered like a hummingbird between one extreme and the next. I broke out in a confused sweat and blinked up at Margot without malice.

She sighed heavily and dropped her arms. "You're a nice girl, Elle. So do the right thing."

I turned away from her as she left. My paintings lay carefully propped and concealed against the wall. I ran my fingers over them lovingly, taking comfort from my art while my emotions rolled on ten-foot waves of indecision within my gut.

"Giselle?"

I startled at the sound of his voice even though I caught a whiff of his smoky scent seconds before he spoke. When I didn't respond, he came to stand behind me. Goose bumps broke out over my skin as he gathered my hair and moved it over one shoulder. He wasn't touching me, but his lips hovered close to my neck, his hot breath like a kiss.

"I thought you'd run away."

I huffed. "Apparently, I can't stay away."

"I don't want you to."

"Sinclair..."

"Giselle..." I could hear his amusement. "Stop worrying, stop hiding. Come out and let me introduce you to some of my team upstairs. I have at least another hour of work to do before we go back to my place, but I'll leave you with Candy. She would love the distraction."

I turned around, tipping my head back to look up at his phenomenal face. "Okay."

"Okay? I was expecting you to protest."

I shrugged. "I want to meet the people you work with. I don't know much about what you do."

"I'm a property developer, and you have actually met most of my core team. Duncan Wright is my CFO, Richard Denman is one of our chief architects, Candy is my right-hand woman, and Robert Corbett is head of our construction division."

"Do they all work in the building?"

"No, most of the time, they are out on location working on projects, but Duncan should be here. Would you like to say hello?"

"Would that be okay?" I asked, unsure about the etiquette.

He shook his head and took my hand to lead me out of the back room. "Haven't you realized by now that I can't deny you anything?"

I was tempted for a moment to test his words by asking him to leave Elena for me. Happily, Rossi found us a moment later, and the opportunity was lost.

*É*clair's apartment suited them. Tucked into a beautifully maintained Greek revival townhouse in Gramercy Park, it was luxurious without being ostentatious, and stylish and classy without being too cold. I recognized the art on the walls as pieces that Sinclair would have chosen himself, and the large pearly grand piano in the corner was Elena's most prized possession, a housewarming gift from the twins. It was an older space with soft, glossy dark floors and a slightly cluttered floor plan that was so at odds with today's open-style living spaces.

I loved it.

But it felt unspeakably strange to be in the belly of the beast, the place Sinclair and Elena shared as a couple. Especially after my previous night with him and the wonderful afternoon I had just spent at his office. As he introduced me to more members of his team and joked with Candy about my distracting capabilities, it felt almost as if I was his girlfriend. Candy had tried to emphasize exactly that point, but I'd convinced her to move the conversation along to less complicated things like her new boyfriend, Gregory, whose Russian accent was so thick that sometimes she could barely understand him. Apparently, it had made for some confusing situations in the bedroom.

Sinclair had stood silently by as I explored the place, but now he stepped forward to slide his hands down my arms and link them through my fingers.

Pressing his nose to my hair, he murmured, "Is it terrible of me to say that I like seeing you here? In my space."

I shrugged helplessly. "I think it is safe to say that we are not the best people."

His hands tightened in mine. "You are very good, Elle. Your lightness, your kindness are what drew me to you in the first place."

"I don't feel like a good person," I said and felt him stiffen behind me, knew that my words hurt him. I spun around to place my hands on his cheeks, my thumbs against his cut-glass cheekbones. "I feel selfish and gluttonous, but I can't help myself. Whenever I'm without you, I trick myself into thinking I can survive without *this,* and honestly, I know if I was strong and good, I could. But I don't want to, and it's getting hard to remind myself why I should care."

Sinclair's electric eyes blazed down at me. I wanted to fidget or drag my gaze away, but I forced myself to stay still, willfully trapped in his snare.

"What are you saying?" he said roughly. "Tell me I am not insane, *d'accord*? Tell me you mean what you say."

My mouth was beyond parched. I felt as if I had swallowed a pound of sand, and when I parted my lips to speak, I could hear them rasp apart like Velcro.

The rattle of a key in the doorway had us springing apart before we could even rationally make sense of the warning. Sinclair cleared his throat and shoved his hands through his hair before turning on his heel toward the kitchen while I quickly settled onto the stone suede couch by the fireplace.

That was how Elena found us when she came through the door, looking as beautifully put together as always.

"Giselle, I'm so sorry that you had to go through that today. New York is wonderful, but unfortuantly it is filled with unsavory characters. I'm sure it was just some deviant who took a liking to you then got bored," she said immediately, making her way over to me after carefully hanging up her coat, scarf, and briefcase.

I accepted her soft kiss on the cheek and hoped she couldn't hear my hammering heart. Immediately, she made her way to the sound system and plugged in her phone. A moment later, Chet Baker's smooth tones spilled into the room, and I was reminded of how much Elena loved music. As a girl, she had spent hours at Signora Donati's house playing the piano, and I'd often trailed her, ducking in the dry brush beside the window to the living room to hear the music that pooled beneath her eloquent fingers.

"I decided to host dinner this year," she continued, moving around the room to straighten the already immaculate pieces of furniture. "It's Thanksgiving tomorrow, Daniel. Did you remember to take the day off?"

"You've reminded me every day this week. Of course, I did," he called from the kitchen.

She turned to look at me, narrowing her eyes as she took in the swell of my breasts in the brightly patterned neckline of my dress and the mass of curls that fell artlessly around my shoulders. I took the time to admire how beautifully ladylike she looked in her high-necked lace blouse and black pencil skirt. I tried not to compare her to Lady and me to the Tramp.

"Is that what you wore for your date with Ulrich?" she asked with a surprisingly playful pout. "No, don't frown, this is very much my fault. I should have lent you something. Not that I don't love the whole Parisian artist look, but Ulrich works on Wall Street."

"Trust me, I know," I muttered as Sinclair came back into the room carrying three wine glasses and a bottle of Pinot Grigio. It was the same label we had shared together just last night. I wondered if he knew, and if he did, why he had chosen to drink it now.

"You had a date with Ulrich Wick?" he asked after he had placed the glasses on the table and a brief kiss on Elena's proffered cheek.

I caught the amusement in his eyes as he popped the cork on the wine and began to pour. With my chin tilted high, I replied haughtily, "I did, indeed."

"Elena, how could you?" he scolded lightly.

She sat down beside me on the couch, perched on the edge with her hands in her lap like a princess waiting to be served. But her eyes smiled too, sparkling back at Sinclair with warmth and good humor.

"What? Ulrich is a very intelligent and kind man."

"He is also extremely dull, darling."

Darling. I so clearly remembered him calling her that while we were in Mexico. I had wondered what kind of woman she was. Though I couldn't have known Elena was Darling, it was eerie how close my imagination had come to conjuring her exact image based on the little I had known in Los Cabos.

Elena was laughing, her true light and trilling giggle that made her eyes squinty. "He is not boring, Daniel. You think any man without knowledge of fishing, art, or travel is a bore."

He shrugged one shoulder and handed her a glass of wine. Her fingers brushed lingeringly over his, and he bestowed her with a beautiful smile.

It was hard to listen to their conversation over the roar of blood rushing through my head, but somehow, I managed to.

"It is not so specific. A man, or a woman for that matter, must have passion, or else they are a shell of themselves," Sinclair said.

He was looking at me now, but I couldn't bring myself to meet his gaze.

"Passion is messy," Elena said, waving a dismissive hand through the air. "I think this was one of the first things we bonded over."

He nodded his agreement, but his lips were tight over his teeth with restraint. I fought not to let out a bitter little laugh. Passion was the first thing Sin and I had bonded over too.

"Yes," I managed to say. "How did you two meet?"

"Cosima introduced us." I watched Elena's features melt under the warmth of her recollections and felt my lungs tighten. "I was infatuated with him on sight, I think. He was wearing this gorgeous navy blue bespoke Brooks Brothers suit, and it was before he let his hair get so long and unruly. He looked like such a gentleman."

A wolf in sheep's clothes, I thought.

"I offered to help with her English," Sin explained. "It was as good an excuse as any."

"Well, I certainly couldn't resist my gorgeous tutor, now could I? After our 'study' date, I was hooked, and the rest is history."

It was a cute little story, one that they had obviously shared countless times. I thought about my meet-cute with Sinclair, how I must have looked after puking for hours on the plane. The relationship that followed wasn't exactly picture perfect either.

Once, making the comparison between the perfection that was Elena and little old me would have induced coma-like melancholy and self-doubt, but I knew myself better now. I loved myself more. And I knew that despite our imperfect origins, Sin was inexplicably drawn to *me*.

For the first time since I found out who he really was, I wondered if that was enough to make him choose me over her.

"Oh, by the way, we have an appointment with Miss Hertz

this weekend. One o'clock on Saturday. I already let Margot know, and she said it wouldn't be a problem with your schedule," Elena said.

Sinclair grew exceptionally still beside me, the kind of immobility that somehow seemed more obvious than a shout in an empty room. I found myself unconsciously clenching my muscles, freezing in the act of bringing my wineglass to my lips. The air grew static as a storm began to brew.

"Elena," Sinclair said softly. "I thought we spoke about this."

As if to make up for his lack of movement, Elena stood and became a flurry of activity, placing coasters under our glasses and fluffing already plumped pillows.

She didn't look at him when she said, "I know we did, but one conversation that came from absolutely nowhere should not derail our plans to have a family."

Oh, *my God*. I was paralyzed by my urge to flee, the rush of adrenaline through my blood causing some kind of overload in my nervous system. I prayed fervently, with a passion that would have rivaled Mama's, to any god who would hear me, that they wouldn't talk about this in front of me.

I'd never been a very lucky woman.

"We should discuss this later when we can be alone. For now, please call Miss Hertz and cancel the appointment," Sinclair said, so reasonably that even I wanted to punch him.

But Elena didn't rage against his condescension. Instead, she retracted into herself like a threatened sea anemone. It was almost amazing to watch her grow cold and distant, mostly because Sinclair reacted to conflict precisely the same way. I wondered, horrified, how they ever overcame difficulties when both of them gave in to the urge to flee instead of fight.

"I will not. It took us months to get this far, Daniel, and I will not cancel this appointment on one of your whims."

"One of my whims?" Sinclair asked with one eyebrow raised.

Elena stuck out her delicate chin.

Slowly, he rose out of the chair with such controlled discipline that I imagined his joints clicking into place like an automaton. There was something so absurdly terrifying about the calculated movements and the way he cocked his head just slightly to the side to study her. This was the businessman, the Dom, the predator. Someone who dared you to fuck with them so they could have the pleasure of ripping you to shreds.

Suddenly, I felt terrible for Elena.

"We aren't happy, Elena. That is no atmosphere to bring a child into," he said.

"Speak for yourself," she snapped, hands on hips. "I am happy."

He only stared at her. I'd never met anyone who could use silence as a weapon like Sinclair could.

"I want a baby."

"Do you want me to say yes only to please you?" he asked in that cool, quiet voice.

My heart was beating so loudly that it was a wonder they didn't hear it.

"You agreed, Daniel. You agreed years ago when..." She paused, and sadness flared across her features, "When we first got together. You promised that one day we would have kids. It's important, isn't it? That you agreed? I know you never wanted them. You don't think I don't know that? You don't want kids, you don't want marriage, but you want me, don't you? And I *need* this."

My eyes swiveled in my frozen face just in time to see Sinclair deflate. His features softened, and his eyes took on that electric glow that I had once thought was reserved only for me. Wordlessly, he breached the space between them and took Elena into his arms, one hand locked firmly on her neck as he tucked it into his shoulder. Almost immediately, she let out a gusty sigh and wilted into his arms.

I stared at their embrace for a long moment, cataloging the way she fit against him like a tailored suit, how beautifully and tenderly they clutched each other. When I finally wrenched my gaze away from my worst nightmare, my eyes overcorrected and flew to the opposite wall of the room, where a portrait picture of Éclair hung over the mantel. In it, Elena sat in a rigid chair with Sinclair standing behind her, one hand on her shoulder. It was the kind of painting I expected to find in a royal museum, and the sight of it punched me right between the eyes.

I might have murmured something as I peeled myself off the couch and zombie-walked down the hallway to my bedroom for the night, but I couldn't be sure, and either way, they didn't notice me leave. I closed the door softly behind me and felt my way toward the bed in the pitch dark. I flopped on top of the many-pillowed bed and stared into the darkness as if it was a prophet sent to deliver answers. When none proved to be forthcoming, I turned on my side, clutched my knees to my chest, and cried and cried and cried.

Chapter Sixteen

After finally falling into a tear-soaked coma, I woke up the following morning before the crack of dawn in order to escape the apartment without having to face either my sister or her boyfriend.

Her boyfriend. That was how I was going to refer to Sinclair from now on. Not my Frenchman, not my friend, not even Sinclair but as Daniel, Elena's boyfriend. If I could force myself to think of him as this other person, as I might have known him had I met him properly, I might have a chance in hell of getting over him. I imagined meeting him for the first time at a family dinner and found it easy to believe I would have found him haughty and remote, condescending and one-dimensional. His beauty would have imprinted itself on my psyche—it simply couldn't be helped—but I wondered if the chemistry between us would have remained caged and hidden behind the bars of acceptable social norms.

As of this morning, I was turning over a new leaf. It didn't erase the sins I had already committed, but it would keep Elena happy, my family intact, and Sinclair firmly embedded in the kind of lifestyle he coveted. As I straightened the bed and vainly tried to smooth the wrinkles from my slept-in clothes, I considered moving back to Paris. Christopher had found me there, but by now, he might have moved on.

My thoughts were still spinning with possibilities as I tiptoed out of the bedroom and into the living room. I was just peeling open the front door when the overhead light flicked on, freezing me like a thief in the spotlight.

To my surprise, when I turned around, it wasn't Sinclair who stood there, silently contemplating me, but Elena.

She wore beautiful black silk pajamas with white piping and a matching eye mask pushing back her softly tousled curls. There were dark shadows beneath her eyes, and she wrung her hands in an unusual display of nervousness.

"Morning," I said into the awkward silence.

She blinked. "You look like you are getting ready to do the walk of shame. If you have to leave right now, at least borrow a jacket."

My spine straightened painfully under her casual censure. "I'm fine like this, Elena, but thank you."

"You look like a siren. Do you want men propositioning you on the street?" she snapped.

You look like a siren. It took monumental effort not to collapse into tears right there on my sister's living room floor.

"Fine, if you don't mind, then I would love to borrow a jacket."

Elena nodded curtly and went to the closet to pull out a long Burberry trench coat, the same one she had been wearing the night of my welcome home party. I let her help me into it and tried to breathe through my mouth to avoid the aroma of her Chanel Number 5 perfume. She lingered over the collar, turning it up against my throat and smoothing my wayward hair around my cheeks.

"You are very beautiful," she said, almost as if it pained her.

"We have good genes."

To my utter surprise and dismay, Elena's lower lip curled into a pout and wobbled.

"Daniel doesn't want to be with me anymore," she whispered so quietly that I was almost sure I had imagined it.

"*Scusi*?" I asked, my muddled brain devolving back to Italian.

Her dark eyes shone like polished graphite. "He doesn't love me anymore."

My heart hiccupped in my chest, but I fought down my own feelings with a Herculean effort and gently took hold of her limp hand in order to lead her to the couch.

"First of all, where is he now?" I asked.

"Work. He went in around four thirty this morning. To get away from me." She sniffed wetly and tugged her knees to her chest like a little girl in need of comfort.

"I'm sure that's not true."

"It is. He always goes in to work when he needs to get away. Even on Thanksgiving."

I actually knew that was the truth, but I kept my mouth shut.

She placed her pert little chin on her knees and looked down at her perfectly painted toes. "Things were fine before he went to Mexico. I swear. I mean, we weren't having sex much, but he never seemed to mind before."

"What?" I cleared my throat and fought to be there for my sister despite the absurdity of the situation. "Why do you think things changed?"

She shrugged. "I honestly don't know."

"Have you asked him?" It was too surreal to be having this conversation with her, my sister and his Darling. A small nefarious part of me wondered what would happen if she ever found out that it was *me*, that her belittled younger sister was the one who changed things between them. Would she think back to this conversation and hate me even more for guiding her through a storm of my own making?

The obvious answer was a resounding *fuck yes*.

"He said Mexico woke him up, that he had been numb for years, and he missed pain." Elena scrunched up her perfect nose. "Who misses pain?"

I shrugged as if I didn't understand. "Some people think that pain amplifies life, that it heightens pleasures that would otherwise seem mundane."

My elegant sister snorted.

"If you think about it for a second, it makes sense," I tried to explain, suddenly eager to make her realize how pivotal hurting was, that it was an essential part of the human experience. Maybe if I was eloquent enough, she could finally understand me. "Why would God give us so much misery if it wasn't for a reason?"

"We aren't religious," she argued with the second-nature exactitude of a lawyer.

"I was just trying to help."

"Yes, well, as pretty as the words are, they don't work. Not when I'm in so much..." She waved her hand around, unable to even articulate the messy, passionate mass of feelings clogging her system like so much hair in a drain.

"I think you should call Cosima or maybe even Mama."

I clearly wasn't the one to talk with her about this.

She looked off over her shoulder into the city beyond the windows. The apartment overlooked the meticulously maintained Gramercy Park, a private garden accessed by fewer than 350 keys and one of New York's first attempts at city planning. I knew it was the reason Elena had been drawn to the house even though she hadn't told me. The beautifully tempered greenery and exclusivity of the place would have appealed to her obsession with prestige and control.

"I want you to paint me."

"Pardon me?"

"I want you to paint me," Elena reiterated, turning to face me with a face made of granite. "I want you to paint me like this, like I am right now."

"Elena..." I hesitated, not only because of the space she was in at the moment but also because I didn't know how to depict this sister on canvas. She was an enigma to me, something unknown and frankly terrifying. I could paint her in four hundred different ways, and it still would not do justice to the contrary nature of her personality. I only understood one thing about Elena—she was so desperate to be everything at once, perfect in all ways, that she had no definitive identity.

She visibly deflated at my hesitation, but my sympathy, my *villainy*, wasn't enough to make me paint her. I refused to dishonor my art and us both by combining the three.

"One day soon," I promised. "When you are feeling better. You obviously had a terrible night's sleep, and I would need you to hold a pose for hours."

She pursed her lips but seemed to believe me, sagging back into the couch cushions like a discarded wind-up doll. My heart throbbed with the echo of hers, a sympathy beat that made it difficult to catch my breath.

"Are you all set for Thanksgiving tonight?" I asked, fully expecting Miss Organized to have everything ready to go.

"I ordered everything from Dean & Deluca. They should be here by four o'clock to deliver it."

"Did you order dessert?"

"A pumpkin pie. Why?"

I stood and walked over to her, offering my hand with a smile. "Come on, why don't we make tiramisu?"

Her lips wobbled before forming a smile. "We haven't made one of those since we were teenagers."

"Exactly," I said, strangely happy with the idea of spending the morning baking with my sister. "Why don't I call Mama, and we can make one together?"

Elena took my hand, coming to her feet before me. We smiled shyly at each other for a moment with our hands clasped.

"Thank you," she mouthed.

I wanted to say *I'm sorry*.

Instead, I squeezed her hand and asked, "Do you remember the recipe for the homemade ladyfingers?"

hen Sinclair entered the kitchen, Cage and Santiago were close on his heels, and the morning had passed into the late evening. The gorgeous mahogany dining table, which I couldn't help but notice was the same shade as Sinclair's hair, was laden with flower arrangements stuffed into pumpkins Elena, Mama, and I had carved ourselves that morning. Lindi Ortega's bluesy country music threaded through the speakers, lending itself to the candle-lit atmosphere and the heady scent of Dean & Deluca's Thanksgiving dinner warming in Elena's underutilized double wall oven.

I knew he was in the kitchen the moment he crossed the threshold even though we hadn't heard the front door open over the swell of our voices raised to sing along to "Desperado." Elena froze beside me a few seconds later, bent over the open oven to check on the turkey. She shot me a frantic look as Mama warmly greeted the men, and I nodded at her because I didn't know what else to do. She took comfort from the gesture and straightened, self-consciously patting her frilled apron. She hadn't changed into something formal yet, and I knew that bothered her.

"Daniel," she greeted quietly before going to place a soft kiss on his cheek.

He wound his arm around her waist and tugged her into a quick hug. "The place looks beautiful."

"Thank you." She blushed. "Mama, Giselle, and I spent all day decorating."

"We also made tiramisu," Mama said, beaming proudly at the sight of Elena and Sinclair together.

"Oh, where?" Cage asked, darting forward to open the fridge in search of the treat.

Mama *tsk*ed him and slapped at his hand as it shot forward to taste the cocoa-covered mascarpone top. "You wait!"

He pouted dramatically, batting his eyelashes at her. "But I promise to share with Iago. You know, Caprice, he has never had the privilege of your cooking."

"We helped too," I reminded him.

He made a disgusted face. "In that case, I hope you ordered something else for dessert too. Just in case, of course."

"Of course," I repeated mildly.

I squealed when he lunged at me, pulling me into his arms for a smacking kiss on the lips.

"In any case, you look good enough to eat, so I could always have you for the last course," he growled lasciviously.

I laughed and tugged at his thickly braided hair. "You rogue."

"You flatterer."

"Put her down, Cage," Sinclair ordered with his arm still looped around Elena. "And try to behave tonight, will you?"

Cage pursed his lips and stared at me with sparkling eyes as he lowered me slowly to the ground so that our bodies brushed intimately. My eyes flicked over his shoulder to Sinclair, whose jaw was clenched as he played with the ends of Elena's hair.

"Stop it," I whispered to Cage. "Don't make this harder than it already is."

"It's not nearly hard enough, or one of you would have made a change," he retorted, but he released me nonetheless.

"What time will the others be here?" Santiago asked me as he came forward to press a kiss to my cheek.

His fingers brushed lightly over my neck, reminding me of our conversation yesterday about how pretty I would look in a collar. I shivered.

"Cosima should arrive around eight," Elena said.

"This is quite late for Thanksgiving dinner, no?" Sinclair asked.

"We're European, Sin," I reminded him. "It's basically blas-phemous to eat before eight."

Humor tightened his lips, but he didn't smile, and I wondered if it was because he could feel Elena's anxious energy pulsing like a warning beacon.

"You're right, of course, Daniel. Happily, though, Sebastian should be here shortly, so we can start with some drinks and appetizers," Elena said. "I'll just go change."

"*Ragazzi*, you follow me into the living room for drinks," Mama ordered with the grace and confidence of a woman who had been beautiful all her life.

Santiago and Cage happily complied, each already trying to charm her with stories from their childhoods living abroad.

When I turned around, Sinclair was leaning against the island counter with his shirt stretched taut between his lean shoulders and his russet head hanging low. I stepped up behind him to place a gentle hand on his back.

"It will be okay," I said, despite my nerves and despite my resolve to treat him with indifference.

"*On a des casseroles au cul,*" he muttered without turning around.

I pursed my lips to buckle in the pain. "You really think our affair is haunting you?"

He sighed. "It is the haunting I take issue with, Elle, not what I did to warrant it."

We were silent for a long moment. I didn't have anything new to add to the conversation. The affair had happened and, arguably, was still happening. It was deeply immoral, not only to deceive another person—in fact, my entire family—but because we were actively, consciously betraying my sister. I loved Sinclair with a severity that obliterated all obstacles in its path, and he, at least, was enchanted enough with me to heed my siren's song over the practical call of reality. Apparently, he had even voiced his reservations to Elena.

I knew the components. I just couldn't make out the full equation.

Sin spun around, one hand plunged into my hair and the other on my hip, pressing me up against the fridge. He pressed his forehead hard against mine. "I'm not going to do this anymore. Do you understand?"

I didn't, so I remained quiet.

"I will not put the people I love through this for one second longer. Regardless of you and me, what kind of person would do this to their partner?"

Again, I didn't know, so I remained quiet.

He sighed heavily, then ran his thumb across my cheekbone to take the sting out of his anger and impatience. "I'm not going to do this anymore, Elle. Do you understand?"

This time, I nodded even though I still wasn't certain what he meant.

The delicate chime of the doorbell sounded, and Sinclair's jaw clenched fiercely when I moved to answer it. His hands flexed against my skin painfully before letting go.

I answered the door to find Sebastian speaking with the young woman delivering the alcohol Elena had ordered. Sebastian was speaking to her easily, taking the bags from her and handing them off to me so that they could take a selfie together. I watched as he whispered something in her ear that made her burst into unattractive and beautifully genuine laughter. Mama and I smiled at each other as they said their goodbyes.

"You charmer," I teased Sebastian as he leaned down to give me the customary kisses.

"Yes, Seb, are all the older ones taken?" Elena said as she breezed into the living room, now wearing a lovely black sheath dress. I could smell her Chanel perfume as she swooped in to give him a kiss.

"Elena," Mama chastised while embracing Seb herself.

She shrugged one delicate shoulder. "It was a joke."

"It's all right, Mama. Elena has never had a very good sense of humor," Sebastian said as he swung off his leather jacket, tossed it onto the side table, and grabbed my hand to tug me farther into the apartment.

"Hang up your coat, you ape," Elena called after us before we disappeared around the corner into the kitchen.

Sinclair was still there, decanting the mandatory red wine while he listened to someone on his phone.

"I want at least three options by the end of next week, Margot," he was saying as we swept into the kitchen.

Sebastian grabbed the extra bottle from Sin's hand and poured himself an overfull glass.

I raised my brows. "Tough day?"

His shoulders were nearly at his ears with tension, and I watched as he tugged his hands through his hair so that it stuck up at funny angles. "Tate wants to produce my film."

"And that's a problem because?"

He didn't answer me immediately. Instead, he leaned against the fridge and stared out the window into the darkening cityscape.

"Rumor is, she's sleeping with Jace Galantine."

I winced because even I knew who Jace Galantine was, award-winning actor, modelizer, and all-around stud. He graced the cover of so many magazines, gossip rags, and movie posters that I hardly went a day without seeing his gorgeous face plastered to something.

"I'm sorry, Seb," I murmured, placing a hand on his tensed arm. "I mean, she is married too, so how much more can this hurt?"

I knew it was the wrong thing to say as soon as it left my lips.

He swung his vibrant gaze to me and glared. "Well, I guess I know where you stand on infidelity."

I bit my lip and focused on not looking over at the silent Sinclair currently assembling the meal from Dean & Deluca's on to serving plates.

"I'm sorry," Elena said as she came into the kitchen with Mama's arm tucked through her own. "I wouldn't have invited Savannah if I knew you two were fighting."

"What?" Sebastian snapped, rounding on her like a provoked bear.

I placed a gently restraining hand on him again and spoke softly, "Why would you invite Savannah Richardson?"

"She is a good friend, no?" Mama asked. "She used to come for the dinners always, and now, we never see her."

I peered up at Sebastian. His face was deeply etched with pained anger, and I suddenly understood the need for Sinclair's perfectly composed mask. How horrible it must be for Sebastian to have his emotions so clearly displayed for others to see.

Elena noted it with triumph, a sly smile corrupting her pretty mouth. "Should I call and ask her not to come, Sebastian? Her husband is away on business, so she would be banished to a Thanksgiving dinner for one..."

I squeezed his bicep and watched him swallow hard before saying, "You've already asked her. We wouldn't want to be rude by uninviting her now."

Elena nodded curtly, but her lips twitched down, and I wondered, not for the first time, how she could be so callous toward her own family.

"Why doesn't everyone sit down?" Sinclair suggested. "The food is hot, the wine is breathing, and the last of our party should arrive soon."

As if on cue, the doorbell rang, and Sebastian shrugged off my hand to go answer it. I followed him, eager to escape the messy atmosphere leftover like an oil spill in the kitchen.

"Cosima!" I cried out when I saw her step through the door and into Seb's enthusiastic embrace.

Despite my cry, the twins hugged silently for a long minute, dissolving into each other more and more with each second as the tension they had both been holding dissipated. There was that deep understanding of another person that I so badly craved. It didn't need to be romantic, but the closest I had ever come to elementally knowing someone like that was with Sinclair, and as I thought of him, a yawning abyss of loneliness blossomed in my heart.

I noticed someone emerge from the other room in my periphery and turned slightly, surprised to see Elena standing mute in the other doorway. Her expression was soft, almost soggy with longing, and I knew it reflected the same emotions in my own face. I didn't feel a kinship with her over our mutual exclusion, though, mostly because I had spent years wanting the same closeness between us and only been met with failure.

"*Mia famiglia*," Cosima cried as she stepped away from Sebastian and grinned at the rest of us. "It wouldn't be quite the party without me, would it?"

She stepped forward to embrace me next and spoke softly for my ears only. "And I had to rescue my sister from spending another night here, hmm?"

I tried not to stiffen at her insinuation, but she only laughed and squeezed my frozen shoulders reassuringly before moving on to kiss the next family member.

Within minutes, everyone was listening raptly to the story she told about a frazzled mother's young children asking to braid her hair into cornrows on the flight, and the previous uneasiness in the apartment was banished by laughter.

Dinner proceeded without a hitch, and I didn't know who was most surprised by it. Savannah Richardson arrived demurely. Sebastian was able to keep his calm and react neutrally, even excellently, to her presence by becoming the life of the party. After an initial comment about the food not being as excellent as her own, Mama settled into her matriarchal spotlight with good grace and bantered hilariously with Cage and Santiago, who both seemed to delight in flirting outrageously with her.

Even Elena was quiet, smiling instead of contributing, even though I knew Cage's outrageous arrogance and bawdy humor grated on her nerves. She sat beside Sinclair, and at one point, she reached over to take his hand, but otherwise, the two didn't talk. It didn't give me much hope because Sinclair barely looked my way. Instead, he spent most of the evening talking to Cosima. I felt a curious kind of jealousy when she made him laugh.

We had already presented the pie and tiramisu when the first bomb dropped.

"Katarina would love to be here for your showing, Elle," Santiago said to me, his grin wide with pride as we spoke about my upcoming showcase. "I will have to fly her out specially."

"I would love to see her," I admitted. "And not just because she would make sure you didn't wear this awful chartreuse blazer again."

He laughed, drawing attention to our side conversation.

"How do you know Kat?" Elena asked casually.

And that was when I realized we should not have been talking about Mexico at the dinner table.

"Um..." Sweat broke out across my brow, but surprisingly enough, Cosima stepped in to save me.

"They met in Mexico," she exclaimed with just enough enthusiasm. "Giselle was feeling a little lonely so I sent her Iago's information."

"Where did you stay, Giselle?" Savannah asked.

My mouth opened and closed, but again, Cosima saved me by saying, "I recommended the Westin. Sinclair, weren't you there too? I'm surprised you two didn't cross paths."

Savannah laughed lightly. "It's a small world we live in."

"Yes," Elena said immediately, leaning forward in her seat to smile sweetly. "Savvy, did I hear that Tate is producing Seb's new film?"

I watched Savannah's round eyes widen with shock. "I wasn't aware he was interested, but I'm not surprised. Sebastian is wildly creative."

My brother snorted softly but refrained from retorting. I

tried to curb my selfish relief at the turn in conversation, but I couldn't resist looking over at Sinclair, who was looking at me with those fathomless blue eyes.

"Weren't you considering Jace Galantine for a role?" Elena continued, casually taking a sip of her wine.

Sebastian grew still, his fists clenched in his lap while Savannah's comically wide eyes blinked owlishly.

"Giselle, how is the exhibition shaping up?" Cage asked, his black eyes sparkling with rage as they swept over Elena and on to me.

Elena pouted slightly, her attempt to derail the evening once again rerouted, but I had no doubt that she would find something disparaging to say about my artwork too.

"Very well, thank you. I'm nearly finished. Sebastian was one of the best little brothers a girl could ask for. He sent me Kayla Kensington, and my friend Stefan Kilos is visiting specifically to be a part of the showcase." I laughed. "He was offended that he wasn't my first call."

"Stefan Kilos, the Greek shipping magnate?" Elena asked with her eyebrows raised in a haughty semblance of respect as if she couldn't believe her dubious bohemian sister could have such a connection.

"Exactly the one."

"Will he stay with you?" Sinclair asked coolly, his eyes focused on Elena's hand as he ran his thumb along the back of it.

My heart twisted painfully, but I fought to keep my expression neutral. When had the dinner table turned into such a passive-aggressive war zone?

"What the hell are those?" Sebastian asked loudly, leaning over the table to grab Cosima's outstretched hand as she accepted a new bottle of wine from Santiago.

She tried to wrench her hand out of his grip, but his other

hand snatched her wrist and shoved down her long sleeve to reveal deeply purple bruises encircling her forearm.

Everyone gasped, but Cosima stood without embarrassment and snapped her arm away. "Nothing that concerns you."

"*Nothing that concerns me*," Sebastian mocked in a high imitation. "You are kidding me. I think my sister wearing such ugly bruises would obviously concern me."

"It's nothing," she insisted between clenched teeth.

I could see the anger rise in her like a tsunami, the receding calm before the rush of vicious fury.

"Cosima," Mama tried, "who does this to you?"

"No one."

"Cosima–" Elena said.

"No. I do not want to talk about this. I'm fine. Nothing was done against my will."

"What can you mean?" Mama asked.

My eyes snapped to Sinclair, and the same horrified understanding dawned in his eyes.

"I liked what was done to me, understand?" Cosima explained haughtily. Her chin jutted forward like an arrogant boxer's, daring someone to hit her with censure. "These are reminders of pleasure, not abuse. It is no concern of yours anyway, but especially because these"—she bared her bruised wrists—"do not concern me."

Awkward silence reigned at the table as her meaning sank in. Despite my own experience with mild pain in the bedroom, the livid color of her markings scared me. Sinclair had never deliberately hurt me, his spankings were just firm enough to entice, and I couldn't imagine true pain ever entering into our partnership. The idea of Cosima brutally bound as she must have been to incur those bruises made me angry despite myself.

"I will kill him," Sebastian growled.

"You will not. You cannot find him, and I do not want to

choose between you or him," Cosima retorted calmly. "Now, if we are done discussing *my* sex life, I think we should all get back to this delicious treat, hmm?"

I was surprised when Savannah Richardson was the one to clear her throat and swallow a large mouthful of tiramisu. "It really is delicious."

There was a smattering of agreement from Cage, Santiago, and me before everyone decided to take her lead and tuck into the cake.

I was so concentrated on acting normally that it took me a moment to notice the tension between Elena and Sinclair. She had removed her hand from his and angled her body fairly obviously away from him. As for him, his face was immobile, his body perfectly rigid. He was furious.

Finally, after a few minutes, he couldn't take it anymore.

"Jesus, Elena, I'm not going to bite." He reached over to tug her seat closer to his once again.

Elena flinched.

"For fuck's sake," Sinclair swore, his face morphing into intense disgust. "I'm not a monster, Elena. I didn't do that to your sister."

"No," she murmured, genuine fear in her eyes, "but you could have. You like that kind of thing."

"I do not!" he roared, heedless of the half dozen other people at the table. "I have never hurt a woman like that in my life. I would never do that to you."

"Only because I don't allow it," Elena whispered.

Sinclair pushed to his feet, his face slack with horror as he stared down at his partner. I couldn't imagine how he must have felt, faced with a girlfriend who was disgusted by his sexual proclivities and who flagrantly denounced them in front of her family. I was just as horrified by Cosima's confession as the rest of them, and I could even vaguely understand Elena's irrational terror, but to fight with him like that in front of other people? I shuddered with sympathy and revulsion.

"I am not Christopher," Sinclair said softly after a long minute of silently staring down at her. She still didn't face him. "I am not that man, and I have never treated you with any degree of violence. I worshipped you, Elena, and still it is not enough."

He sighed, his hand lifting to tug at a lock of hair that was no longer there. "All these years and I still disgust you. I, for one, am tired of it." He stared at her, waiting for her to respond, but she only stared off into the distance. Finally, he turned to the rest of the table and smiled thinly. "I'm sorry for disrupting dessert, but if you'll excuse us, I think Elena and I need to be alone."

"Don't be dramatic, Daniel." Elena straightened, suddenly remembering her aversion to drama even though she was so often the cause of it. "Everyone, please stay and finish the cake. It's Thanksgiving, for goodness' sake."

Everyone remained seated, paralyzed by the frozen air between Elena and Sinclair.

"Yes, I'm sorry. Of course, stay and enjoy the cake. I have business at the office, so I have to go, but..." Sinclair tried to smile, but the result was more of a grimace. "Please, stay and enjoy."

Without another word, he crossed to the front door, unhooked his overcoat, and left, closing the door softly behind him. All heads swung from the closed door to Elena, finding her dark eyes filled with tears.

"Oh, Elena," Cosima scolded softly. "Why do you do this to yourself?"

"You don't understand," she tried to explain.

"No, I think we do," Cage said, standing up to look directly down into Elena's face. "You are a coward, Elena Lombardi, and you do not even try to hide it well."

She opened her mouth on a gasp, but Cage was already bending down to kiss Mama on the cheek and say his good-byes. I accepted a kiss and a shoulder squeeze from him as well before he was out the door, Santiago following quickly in his wake.

Savannah was just standing up to do similarly, I think, when Elena finally croaked, "Please stay, Savvy. I know I'm wretched, but please, stay for a while."

The older woman looked quickly at Mama, who was thoroughly shocked into silence, and then at Sebastian, who seemed to teeter between disgust and sympathy for his older sister.

"Okay," Savannah said slowly. "But only if we can play charades."

Elena's lip trembled fiercely before she finally gave in to a weepy laugh.

Chapter Seventeen

I played one game of charades with the rest of the guests, but my mind was hazardously preoccupied with thoughts of Sinclair. After one too many confused glances my way from Mama and Cosima, I said my goodbyes with the excuse of a stomachache.

And it did ache, a deep churning that twisted my gut up like a coiled snake, ready to strike out against my impure thoughts. I couldn't help replaying the dinner over and over in my head —Elena's intense disdain and Sinclair's utter defeat. The perfect couple I had constructed of them in my mind was far from reality, but the fractured nature of their relationship— very much like my own with Elena—didn't make my love for Sinclair any more *okay*. We were still two people actively deceiving someone we had promised to love and care for; Elena's bad behavior did not justify our own.

I self-flagellated myself during the entire cab ride, each stroke harder than any Sinclair would ever land, yet I still told the cabbie to take me to the Faire building, still walked the steps to the wide glass doors and buzzed in with the night receptionist who thankfully recognized my name from the gallery. I watched my reflection in the shiny chrome of the elevator doors as they closed and ferried me up to Sinclair's sixtieth floor, and instead of running away from the villain I faced in the mirror, I smiled sharply at myself and strode from the elevator with the confidence of a seasoned sinner.

He knew the moment I entered his office even though I didn't make a sound, and he didn't change his position, angled away from me as he stared out the glass walls behind his desk at the glimmering city rolled out before us. I stayed close to the door because despite my determination to see him, I didn't know how to articulate my desire to comfort him. More importantly, I didn't know if he would even accept it.

"I love you."

That was what I wanted to say. I wanted to smooth it like salve into the wounds Elena had inflicted with her scared and bitter words, wanted to coat him in it until he shone with it for everyone to see.

How many times in the past few weeks had I imagined hearing those words from his lips? Imagined how the power of them would ignite the latent fire in my heart until it raced through my veins, eviscerating everything heavy and dull, the boulders of rationale and pain, the horrors of guilt and yearning. Burning it all clean until I wasn't even a vessel anymore, maybe not even human, just red, smoldering flames feeding on shiny, weightless air.

"I love you."

Sinclair turned to face me, but I tucked my chin in so that

the long curtain of my hair would conceal the grotesque longing on my face. He didn't need to see that. I didn't *want* him to see that. It was bad enough that I saw it every day in the mirror, felt it in every single pore of my skin like old sweat and grime. I wanted Sinclair to see me differently, supple and shiny with love.

"Giselle." His cold tone cracked through my simmering thoughts, and I jerked toward him unconsciously. We were suddenly so close that I could see the texture of different blues in his crackling eyes.

"Are you going to say something?" he asked.

He was grinning, but it was twisted badly like a misshapen paperclip rendered useless.

"I'm sorry, I must have been zoning out." I clamped my sweaty palms together in my lap. "What did you say?"

"I love you."

Blink.

Pulse.

Blink.

Pulse, stutter, and pulse.

One hand ran through his hair, and he looked away, slightly over my shoulder as if he couldn't bear to look at me.

"I love you so much that I'm clumsy with it. There are so many times when I stared at you and waited for some sort of poetry to form, words that were worthy of my love for you, the intense, nonsensical, filled to the brim way that I feel about you. I pride myself on being an elegant man. I wasn't born that way, but I was raised it, and when those words won't come, others do. The crass, dirty, and poor part of me emerges like a fucking animal, and all I want to do is claim you, put my scent onto every inch of your gorgeous skin, scream like a psychopath at everyone who looks at you that *you are mine*."

He was almost panting, his chest heaving and his features cracked wide open to reveal the massive crater I had unknowingly excavated. A yawning darkness filled with his love for me. The heavy sound of his breath and the sight of his pulse fluttering desperately in his throat reminded me to breathe.

"Do you understand, Elle? What you do to me? I want to brand you and fuck you and marry you and breed you and do any goddamn thing I can think of to bind us together so that no one, not one single fucking person, can get between us. Because, *fuck*, ever since I saw you pale and needy and so gorgeous my bones ached on that plane, there have been things between us. Damn important things that just won't go away." He sucked in a deep breath and ran both hands through his hair before his eyes finally landed on mine, sliding into place like a key turning in a lock. "I know you don't want to hurt your sister, and you don't want to cause any more turmoil in your family, but, Elle, my siren, my love, I am being ripped to pieces every day knowing I can't have you."

These words were better than anything I could have possibly thought to long for, to imagine, and they settled around me like fine silk, the softest satin. But instead of luxuriating in the feel of it, I tangled myself up until I couldn't breathe.

"You don't mean it. I mean, not really. It's the excitement, the novelty and mystery of being with someone new, someone so different, and I don't know, maybe younger?" I turned away from the slow freezing of his features; I couldn't bear to watch the ice creep over my favorite blue eyes. "You *think* you want me, but maybe you just don't want Elena, especially right at this moment when she was just so cruel to you, or maybe you're having a midlife crisis, or maybe you just want a submissive or—"

His hand on my arm was firm but not painful as he pulled me around to face him, our hips flush and his breath on my cheeks. "That is an awful lot of maybes, Elle."

"We barely know each other," I lied, and it felt like blasphemy.

"I will tell you anything you want to know. You have free rein to dissect my soul. It is yours to do with as you please."

My heart beat rapidly at the back of my throat, so fiercely that I almost gagged. I had never pictured a declaration of love like this. Everyone spoke of softness and ease as loving words spilled from their lips, of euphoria and the miasmic shift as a yearning heart clicked into place with its soul mate. So why did I feel sick and aching, poised on the edge of an abyss so gargantuan and dark that I could see no means of escape? My fears lived within that crater, the deepest and darkest of them, and as I looked down at them, I knew the decision I had to make—to love Sinclair or not—would mean the difference in facing them.

"They'll hate me," I whispered brokenly as tears slipped over my cheeks and seeped into his fingers.

He pressed his forehead to mine so hard it almost hurt. "They might."

I was both furious and relieved that he agreed so easily.

"How can you know it's worth it?"

His face spasmed with hurt, but he recovered quickly. "I've never been so certain of anything. *Mon amour pour toi est plus grand que le monde.*"

My love for you is bigger than the world.

I sucked in a breath and choked as it fractured in my lungs.

"I just got them back, Sin," I tried to explain.

He lifted his head and stared down at me with eyes that were half-shuttered. He was beginning to understand that I could seriously be rebuffing him.

"They will forgive you. They are your family, and they also understand the ways of the heart. I think they will know that we tried to stay away, but..." He shrugged in that Gallic way that made huge issues seem ridiculously easy.

"They won't."

He stared at me for a long time. I watched his eyes shift through ten different shades of blue. I watched as his heart calcified, and I felt mine crumble in my chest.

"So you will not," he finally said.

I bit my lip, but it was answer enough for him.

With a suddenness that made me gasp, he grabbed my shoulders between his hands and shook me slightly. His beautiful face was twisted into a snarl, his habitually cool mask shattered.

"Why are you choosing heartbreak? It will not stop when you wake up tomorrow, Giselle. It will not stop in a week or a month. This pain will *haunt* you until it devours you whole. You are saving your sister, you think? You are wrong. I had to choose between you and Elena, and I have. I made the right choice. But you had the same choice, and now," he snarled and took an abrupt step away from me, "you are choosing wrong."

He turned on his heel without giving me a chance to speak and disappeared into the darkness of the unlit building behind me.

Chapter Eighteen

I woke up hollow as a dried reed, my brittle limbs creaking in protest as I awkwardly swung myself out of bed. The light slanting in through the gap in the curtains was winter white and dim in the gloom of the early afternoon. I'd slept the day away. Recovering from a crying jag was the worst kind of hangover. The throbbing pulse in my head was stronger than the weak one of my fractured heart.

I tried not to think about him, but everything—from the way the scalding shower water pounded against my skin in a parade of pained and pleasurable sensation to the leftover crepes I ate for breakfast—reminded me of my Frenchman. Finally, after I absentmindedly put dish soap into my coffee for the second time, I succumbed to the cyclone of Sinclair-related thoughts that threatened to dominate my psyche.

I remembered all the beautiful things he said to me that I hadn't been aware of at the time, the many moments he might as well have declared himself to me that I was too stupid to see. I cut myself with memories, strangulated myself with the recollection of his touch. It was easier to wallow in the pain than to conquer it.

When I finally emerged from my bedroom, I was perfectly turned out. I had even painted my nails, something I never did because the chemicals from my paint solutions always dissolved the polish.

I didn't want anyone to have a reason to point out my heartbreak.

Even though it hit me like a punch to the kidneys, I wasn't surprised to see Elena in the living room drinking tea with Cosima.

She looked up at me when I entered and smiled sadly as if I could understand what she was going through. It disgusted me that I did.

"He's done it. He broke up with me," she said.

Cosima didn't say anything, and I had the feeling she hadn't in quite a while. She was perched on the edge of the deep leather chair, her arms braced on her legs as she leaned forward to stare into the bottom of her mug. She looked like she was trying to read her future in the tealeaves.

"I'm so sorry," I said because I was.

She nodded again, her movements heavy with weariness. Despite that, though, she looked even more put together than me in a gorgeous coal gray blazer and matching skirt with every curl perfectly held in place. I noticed the suitcase leaning against the couch and frowned at it.

"I have business in LA for the week."

"Awkward timing, can't you reschedule or send someone else?"

"Why would I? This is perfect timing. I fully expect Daniel to come back to his senses after a week without me."

"Lena..." Cosima murmured, shaking her head as she continued to look into her mug. "You said some terrible things about his character. His pride would take more than a week to recover, not to mention his emotions."

Elena sniffed. "As always, you underestimate Daniel's level-headedness. I apologized to him, and when I get back, I'll show him how sorry I am. Honestly, I didn't even say anything until he acused me. I was just shocked and upset about your wrists and then it all...snowballed."

When Cosima didn't respond, Elena's mouth rolled into a pout. "You don't think he'll forgive me, truly?"

Cosima lifted her head on her hunched shoulders and looked at me for a long second before turning to our sister. "I really don't know. I don't even know if this breakup is about forgiveness. You may hate me for saying this, but really, Lena, are you passionately in love with him?"

She opened her mouth to protest, but Cosima held up a hand and qualified, "I mean the kind of love that sucks all the air out of your lungs so that the only hope of getting your breath back is by kissing the man who owns it."

"Of course," Elena said, too quickly.

I wondered for a wild minute if what Cosima implied was true? Could Elena really not be in love with Sin?

It wouldn't eviscerate my wrongdoings, but it would go a hell of a long way to making my selfish self feel better.

"We've been through a lot together, and in a few months, this crazy period of our lives will be just another thing we over-came. I won't lose him. We are perfect for each other."

Maybe that was the problem. Elena and Sinclair were so perfectly suited on paper that there was no room for improvisa-tion, for growth or movement.

"How did you leave things with him?" Cosima asked.

"He's staying at a hotel, and he says he is moving out." Her lower lip trembled, and she bit it viciously to stop it. Then in a softer voice, she confessed, "I've never lived alone before."

The three of us shared a moment of silence, all staring into the distance absorbed by our own reflections.

"I have to get going," Elena said, standing abruptly.

Cosima nodded, standing too in order to embrace her. I watched Elena step eagerly into her arms, and I wondered at my younger sister's ability to coax the best and most beautiful qualities from everyone. I wondered for the millionth time how she and Elena could have such a better, healthier relationship.

"I'll cab with you to the airport, *si*?" she murmured to Elena, who closed her eyes and nuzzled closer.

My heart squeezed painfully with the keen awareness of betrayal. At this point, did it matter that I had turned Sinclair down when I had already done so much to orchestrate Elena's heartbreak?

My phone lit up from where I'd place it on the coffee table, Sinclair's name flashing like a neon sign. I grabbed it hastily, aware of Cosima's eyes on me, and read the text message.

The Frenchman: Meet me at Devereaux's restaurant in one hour.

I looked up at Elena, small and doll-like in Cosima's arms, and felt the ugliness of my sin saturate my soul.

I texted him back immediately—*okay*.

He was at the same table Cage and I had occupied a few weeks ago when we had run into Elena and him on a date. It was cyclical and so totally Sinclair to have chosen it. He stood to greet me with a kiss on the cheek but remained silent as the waiter held out my chair, and I settled in. His quietude left me jittery and intoxicated on the emotional fumes I kept bottled up inside myself. I couldn't even begin to guess at why he had invited me for lunch, especially because he had been too angry, so atypically expressive last night.

"I didn't handle that well," he began, and I wondered for the millionth time how he could do that, switch from human to robot in under a second. "The affair and the secret of it, but specifically, last night when I tried to express my feelings for you."

"Oh?"

His eyes narrowed slightly at my composure. Inside, I was as nonplussed by it as he was.

"The first time I wanted to tell you, we were in Mexico, and you weren't even awake. I had just netted that enormous fish, and I flew up to the second deck to rub your nose in it. You make me feel like a boy, and boys do that kind of thing to girls they like. But you were asleep, sprawled out on your stomach with all that coppery hair spilled around you. I quite literally couldn't breathe as I looked at you and something fundamental shifted in my chest like tectonic plates." He shook his head, shearing himself from the memory. "I was ready to heed your siren song, jump off the side of the boat and into the promise of your arms. But I didn't know if you felt the same, and maybe even more importantly, I take my obligations seriously, and I wasn't ready to entertain the idea of leaving Elena."

He cleared his throat and brought a glass of ice water to his lips. I watched his Adam's apple bob as he swiftly drank half the glass, and I tried not to be endeared by his nervousness.

"Then you told me that you loved me." He laughed harshly. "Or rather, I ordered you to tell me, and as always, you obeyed beautifully. I have never witnessed anything so stunning as the sight of you giving yourself to me, heart and body, with your skin covered in starlight."

God, he was poetic.

My starving soul absorbed those devastating words before I could remind it that we were on a hunger strike.

"After we returned to the hotel and you fell asleep, I called Cage and made a plan."

He waited for me to swallow back the mass of hope that rose like bile in my throat.

"After I broke things off with Elena, I would stay with him while I looked for another apartment. It would take a few months to get all my affairs in order, but then I was coming for you. Robert Corbett had already recommended an excellent private investigator, and I was fairly sure you had told Stefan Kilos who you really were. I was so determined, I even wrote out a to-do list," he admitted with a mocking twist of his lips.

"You didn't," I breathed because this was too good to be true.

"I did. It took a bit longer than I may have liked, and obviously, there is even more in the way than I had originally planned on, but now I'm doing it. I've contacted an attorney to help us negotiate the separation of our assets and told Elena unequivocally that our relationship is over."

"She doesn't think it is." I remembered the determination in her eyes that morning and shivered because there was a storm coming and the clouds rolling across the horizon were the exact color of Elena's eyes.

"To me, it is. It has been for a while now."

"I don't think that changes anything. Elena is still my sister. You are still her boyfriend –"

"Ex-boyfriend."

"Fine, ex-boyfriend. But Sin, you still stayed with her for weeks even after you knew who I was," I pointed out.

Until I said it out loud, I hadn't really known that fact had bothered me. I could focus all I wanted on my reasons for staying away from him, but my heart focused on *his* reticence at the end of the day.

Sinclair adjusted his cuff links, twin circles of silver engraved with the Percy family crest. "I did, and whatever excuses I give you will be exactly that, excuses. But I want to give them to you nonetheless. The first was simply selfish. When I met you on the plane, I told you that I didn't like the idea that you could change my life, and I meant it. My life pre-Giselle was a well-oiled machine. I had a lovely, intelligent girlfriend who loved me and whose aspirations perfectly suited my own. After years of work, my business was firmly established in the city, and I was finally expanding internationally. My parents were proud of me." He shrugged as he said it, but I knew that last point was the most important.

"When I saw you in Caprice's kitchen the night we returned, I wasn't prepared. Mostly because you fucking left that morning before I could tell you how I felt, and I spent the rest of the day searching for you, trying to track down that damn Kilos to beat your information out of him if I had to. When that didn't work, it dawned on me that maybe you didn't want to be with me. It might have had something to do with Margot's incessant scolding on the plane ride home, but by the time we landed, I had already convinced myself that you were just a holiday affair."

"I didn't want to leave you, but..." I trailed off because I didn't know how to explain, in any language available to me, how I had felt that final night, tucked into his arms with so much love to give but no future to give it to.

He sighed raggedly. "There is one more excuse, and it is a big one. In fact, it's the mainstay of why I have been with Elena all this time, maybe even why she feels so dependant on me when she is a capable, independent woman all on her own."

His pause felt cruel, like a commercial break at the climax of a television show.

"About eight months into our relationship, Elena got pregnant."

I choked on my spit and started to cough.

Sinclair waited for me to stop before continuing, "I wasn't thrilled about it. I wasn't ready for children or even sure that I wanted them. But you know Elena. She was thrilled."

I could imagine her excitement, her face made uncharacteristically soft with joy, her voice high and bright and accented because she would forget to modulate her speech. My sister had always wanted children more than anything else. My hand curled into a fist over my heart because I knew the story wasn't going to end well.

The waiter came, having lingered long enough on the sidelines waiting for a break in our conversation, and I happily let Sinclair order for me.

"I adjusted. There wasn't really anything else to do but accept it. Elena wouldn't get an abortion, and even though I wasn't sure if I wanted it, I didn't want her to get one either. The only thing I remained firm on was the fact that I didn't want to get married. She seemed okay with it then, I think, because she was already too preoccupied with being a mom.

"She had a plan. Finish her first year of law school and then take a year off to care for the baby. We moved in together, and she began to buy little things for the baby, onesies with baby animals on them and this little pair of sneakers, each shoe smaller than my fist."

"She lost it," I blurted out because I couldn't handle it anymore.

"She lost it," he confirmed in a hollow voice that matched the emptiness in his eyes.

"*C'est tellement triste*," I murmured as unbearable sadness flooded through the suddenly open door of empathy I felt for Elena.

"It was horrible," he agreed, unable to look at me. "Only Mama and Cosima knew. Sebastian was away on location, and Elena didn't want any of her friends to know about the pregnancy until the second trimester."

Sinclair sighed and raked a hand through his hair. "The thing is, she had an ectopic pregnancy. It ruptured her fallopian tube."

"She can't have kids," I concluded in horror. "She always made adoption sound like a choice, not the only option."

Sinclair nodded jerkily.

Fuck.

I couldn't understand why Sinclair would have brought me here to tell me this. I'd already rejected him. Why did he need me to feel the true weight of this guilt? Was it to alleviate some of his own or merely so that I knew all the facts? For one moment, my passion for him flared into hatred so pure I felt electric with it. How could he have done all of this to my sister?

I glared at him with my teeth clenched so hard my head started to pound. He looked back at me, his expression perfectly neutral, his mouth slightly open as if he was willing to breathe in my toxic breath, to house all of my self-hatred and shame within himself so that I wouldn't have to.

He reached across the table to place his hand parallel to mine. I couldn't have withstood his touch at that moment, but his gesture of togetherness was just as comforting.

"I hesitated to tell you because it is really Elena's secret to share, and she is very guarded about it. There is a small chance she could conceive again, but the doctors have assured her not to count on it. She feels defective even though that is far from the truth. The ordeal brought us closer, and I felt compelled to stay with her, to protect her and care for her because I had done that to her. I took away her dream, and the worst part is, I was secretly happy about losing the baby."

"I told you we aren't good people," I said softly. "But not wanting the baby didn't make the miscarriage happen. You aren't to blame either, Sin."

"I know that now. I know a lot of things now." Finally, for the first time since I had sat down across from him, he looked into my eyes and let his pretty, composed mask fall away.

I wanted to reach out and touch that astounding, angular face. Instead, I touched the edge of my pinky finger to his where it lay on the table.

"I know that staying with Elena because I feel that I owe her my love after what happened isn't fair to either of us. I know that it will take a long time to completely separate my life from hers, and I know that she will likely never forgive me. It hurts me to know that, Elle. To know that a woman I have spent the past four years of my life loving will always hate me. I think that pain will stay with me forever, and it's going to ruin me at the most inconvenient times. I may not have been madly *in* love with her, but she was my best friend, my partner, and confidant.

"But I also know that I have never loved anyone the way I love you, and I honestly know that I never will. I understand that this is hard on you, that it's unfair of me to ask you to choose me over your family, but I'm still asking you to make that decision."

I opened my mouth to say something, then didn't.

The waiter arrived with our dishes. When he placed a beautiful plate of seared Dorado in front of me, I blinked up at Sinclair. I felt so vulnerable. I was afraid a slight breeze would dissolve me, scatter me across the air.

"I'm asking you to make the decision, but I don't want you to make it right now, and I don't want you to make it lightly. I want you to know what I know. I have never been so serious or sincere in my life when I say that I want to be with you. I meant what I said in my office. I want to live with you, Elle, and one day, I want to claim you as my wife. Someday soon after that, if you don't mind, I want to have children with you."

"Sin," I said as I tore into the fish with the prongs of my fork but didn't eat. "You can't expect me to think you've done a complete about-face on marriage and babies."

"You're right. That is why I invited you here today. I wanted to give you fair warning that I am going to woo you, Giselle Moore. I am going to show you who I am and how much I love you every day, and I am not going to stop until I've convinced you that I am the only family you need."

"You're killing me."

He nodded curtly and competently cut into his steak, utterly polished and confident once more. "It's part of the process. This is going to kill you. This *has* been killing you all along, but I'm going to pull you out of this hellish situation, and I'm going to love you more than anyone ever has every day after to prove to you how much that pain was worth it. We are going to resurrect each other."

I stared at him numbly. Sinclair's self-assurance might have drawn me to him originally, and his aloofness had tempted me to linger, but it was evidence of this, his boundless passion, which lay waste to my resolve. I tried valiantly to digest every-thing that he said, but it felt as if I lacked the education, the fundamental principles needed to answer this mathematically, reasonably. Maybe because there was no way to respond reasonably to such a tangled conundrum.

Sinclair finished his steak in silence. A detached part of my mind wondered how difficult it was for him to restrain himself from ordering me to eat. My food grew cold and congealed, ravaged by my nerves but untouched. Still, I stared, my mind so full of thoughts that it shorted out and left me blank.

Finally, after paying for the bill, Sinclair offered me a small, genuine smile.

"I know this is a lot to take in, which is why I am more than willing to give you time to make the decision. The only thing I am not going to do is give you space."

He reached into the breast pocket of his blazer, concealing something shiny in his palm. My skin sizzled uncomfortably under the heat from his touch as he gently took my wrist in his and secured something to it. He raised my hand to his lips, brushing his mouth against my fingertips before releasing me.

I was too caught in his gaze to look at the heavy piece secured to my forearm.

"I own you as you own me, and I'm not going to hide it anymore. When you are ready to stand beside me and tell the world, I promise I will protect you from its censure. And I promise to work hard every day to repair our relationship with your family. I don't want you isolated from them."

We looked at each other, and I felt like his puppet brought to life, a creature with its own will but still tied fundamentally, irrevocably to him.

"I'll be seeing you soon, my siren," he said with a full-fledged grin as he stood and buttoned his blazer. "Oh, and make sure you eat something, *si*? It is hard to make life deci-sions on an empty stomach."

It took me a few minutes after his departure to clear the fog of my thoughts enough to look down at my wrist. The gorgeous silver and turquoise cuff I had admired in the Cabo San Lucas market with Candy winked at me under the noon sunlight. I told myself it was the glare that brought tears to my eyes, but as I looked down at the gift, all I could really think was *I'm fucked.*

Chapter Nineteen

Sinclair was true to his word.

The following day, a Saturday, I was discussing my finished paintings with Rossi and Eddie in the kitchen of Cosima's apartment when the lavender arrived. Eddie had offered to answer the door because my hands were full of canvases, and the next thing we knew, a team of men and women were carrying arrangements of fragrant purple stalks into the apartment. There were arrangements with white roses in delicately etched glass vases that they placed on every available table, four huge clay pots of it mixed with gorgeous golden grass that swayed in the breeze flowing in from the little balcony, and little silk embroidered sachets filled with the dried flowers that Eddie happily, and nosily, placed in our clothing drawers and closets. By the time they had finished, the apartment smelled like heaven. There was no note with the flowers, of which I was grateful because Rossi and Eddie were forced to accept that it was from Ulrich, the odious man I brunched with at Prune.

I opened the door Sunday to a smiling Santiago who had graced me with a kiss before handing me a brown paper wrapped package. I'd known somehow without opening it that it would be Frida Kahlo's 1926 sketch *Accident*, the very one I had admired with Katarina at Santiago's house party in Mexico. It seemed that Sinclair was calling everyone in my life in his quest to woo me. I wanted to be annoyed by it, but as I hung Kahlo's gorgeous conflicted work of art beside my bed, it was hard to be bothered by such thoughtfulness.

Monday was a framed picture of Sinclair and me from the Romani International Gala with a note that explained how he had paid the photographer for exclusive rights to the picture. I could understand why as soon as I studied it; we looked very much in love, or at least in lust, as I smiled up at him while accepting his hand. It was the moment he had asked me to go outside with him, and I could clearly remember the swirl of apprehension and giddiness that had coiled my stomach into a sailor's knot. Later that day, another picture arrived, this one tucked into an unmarked envelope. It was of me, captured when I was exiting the gallery. My hair was caught in the breeze, the curls fanning out behind me, and my dress pressed intimately to my curves. I didn't know when he would have taken this or why he sent it to me, but I carefully placed it in my nightstand all the same.

Cosima had been deliberately avoiding me, but on Tuesday, when she accepted a delivery of five packages from Dylan's Candy Bar, including their Ultimate Chocolate Sharing Sweet Treat Tower, she finally confronted me about the unmarked gifts.

"The apartment smells like Provence, that sketch in your

bedroom is worth thousands of dollars, and now all this candy from your favorite shop?" Cosima stood before me with her hands fisted on her hips, and her yellow eyes narrowed. "Who the hell is this secret admirer, Elle? This is more than a casual crush. Though he clearly doesn't care about cavities..."

I shrugged and tucked my tongue beneath my teeth as I adjusted the shading on the painting of Candy's mouth sucking suggestively at an oversized cherry red lollipop.

"Giselle, talk to me."

"There's nothing to talk about."

"*Cazzatte*," Cosima said, calling me on my bullshit.

I sighed and carefully placed my brush on the palette before putting them both down. "Fine, I should say I don't want to talk about it."

"Giselle –"

"Hey, if you don't want to talk about the Mafia-eyed Dante, then I don't have to talk about this. Okay?"

Hurt flashed across her features before she screwed them shut with a twist of her mouth. "Fine."

I was happy she wasn't home on Wednesday to see the two tickets to watch Miles Davis play in the Rose Theater at Lincoln Center for his ninetieth birthday. I clutched the tickets to my chest and tried to temper the rapidity of my heartbeat with deep breaths.

When that didn't work, I called him.

"*Bonjour, ma sirène. Ça va?*"

His cool voice flowed over my skin like water, immediately cleansing me of my anxieties even though he was the cause of them.

"Sinclair," I said after clearing my throat and affecting a pretty badass professional tone. "I'm calling to return the tickets."

I could hear the smile in his voice. "I'm sorry, I thought I was speaking to the woman of my heart, Giselle Moore. Not some ungrateful...stewardess is it?"

"They aren't called that anymore, old man," I grumped, charmed out of my demeanor before I could help myself.

"And you've forgotten your manners, young lady."

I shivered at the image his words imparted, picturing myself over his lap for a spanking. He chuckled as if he knew what his words had done to me.

"Why did you give me two tickets?"

"I thought you could take a friend."

"Don't you want to go?"

"Yes. The tickets were originally for me, but I thought you would enjoy it more. I've seen him play twice before."

I shrugged into my gray coat and grabbed my keys from the hall table, unwilling to end the conversation even though I needed to leave for Terry Paulson's apartment.

"I didn't know you liked jazz," I said even though if I had taken the time to think about it, I might have guessed as much.

"We grew up listening to it in the orphanage. Cage actually considered being a jazz singer before the lure of rock stardom called to him."

I laughed, picturing the sexy, leather-pants-wearing Cage Tracey crooning soulfully over a piano.

"I love that sound," Sinclair said casually.

I stopped laughing.

"I won't take the tickets back, Elle. I want you to enjoy the experience. The Lincoln Center has magnificent acoustics, and I like to imagine you there, dressed up in some purple dress with your eyes closed to absorb the music. I only wish I could be there to watch you."

Watch *me*, not the legendary musician.

I swallowed hard and spoke before I could stop myself, "Come with me then."

My words were followed by silence, and I was just about to

blurt out something for the sake of speech when he cleared his throat.

"I would like that very much. I have to work until the last moment, but if you could meet me at the office at seven, we can walk to Lincoln Center together. It isn't far."

My smile cut brutally into my cheeks. "Okay."

"Okay."

I knew without confirming that we were both smiling into the phone.

"I'll see you soon then, Giselle."

I nodded even though he couldn't see me and hung up.

I was still smiling when Terry Paulson opened the door for me twenty minutes later. She was clad in a bright floor-length kimono with her voluminous hair twisted into riotous curls. Huge hoop earrings adorned her ears, and her acrylic nails were a bloody red. My fingers itched to capture her particular brand of brazenness, a sexual appeal that was almost crass it was so bold.

"You look happy," Terry said, ushering me into her opulent

top-floor apartment. "I hope I am at least partially to blame. Or am I the only one who has been excited for this all week?"

I laughed at her enthusiasm, immediately at ease despite the intimidation of our surroundings. A crystal chandelier the size of a Smart car hung from the foyer ceiling and nearly blinded me.

"At the risk of sounding like a pervert, I've been looking forward to painting you since we first met."

She laughed loudly, throwing her red-tipped hand out to playfully push at my chest. "You are delightful. Now, I hope you don't mind, but I've set things up in the master bedroom. Let Gus take your things for you. Did you take a cab here? I should have sent a car."

"It was no problem," I assured her as I handed off my cumbersome easel and wooden travel kit to the stoic-faced liveried butler who appeared beside me. "It's the only workout I get, so I actually look forward to it."

"You can't be serious." Terry's bright red lips parted over her white teeth, and I found myself wondering what that wide mouth would feel like against mine.

Sinclair had turned me into some kind of sex machine.

"I will have to take you to my tennis club. It's great exercise and good fun. Plus, I think you would look wonderful in a little white skirt." She winked at me, laughing lightly at my blush as she took my hand to lead me through a large corridor, up a set of marble stairs to the second floor and finally, into a bedroom painted a deep, lusty red.

A tarp covered the Persian rug before us, and Gus the Butler had already set up a small table and my easel. I moved over to the station, relieving him of his duties so that I could set up everything to my tastes.

"I did some research," Terry explained as she perched on the edge of her massive four-poster bed, "about sex in the modern-day art world. Pauly loves art, and he's been teaching me about it for the last couple of years, but I didn't really get into it until Elena mentioned your project. It seems like you are doing something similar to Jack Vettriano, yeah?"

I nodded. "There is definitely a similar theme, though there are actually quite a few contemporary painters who explore sexual themes. I really admire Lisa Yuskavage and Jenny Saville too."

"So it was the trendiness that got you interested in sexual fetishisms and fantasies?"

I bit my lip and moved away from the easel with my large draft book and pencil case. Taking a seat on a conveniently provided stool, I began to loosely sketch vignettes of Terry's long face, the deep contours of her collarbones, and the vulnerable recess between her breasts.

"Not exactly. I probably sound cliché, but I recently had a pretty torrid affair that opened my eyes to how many indecent things there are to indulge in. Afterward, I couldn't help looking at people and wonder at their sexual secrets." I looked up at her through my eyelashes, feeling strangely coquettish. "What are yours?"

Terry smiled slightly and edged herself slowly to the head of the bed. "I'm so glad you asked." I watched with lowered lids as she reclined against the heap of silk pillows, legs bent at the knee and braced open to reveal the deep shadows at the apex of her thighs. There was a barely imperceptible rattle as she retrieved something from behind the velvet curtains and produced thick metal and leather cuffs attached to the bed frame. "Would you mind helping me into this?"

I painted the New York socialite like that—bound to the headboard by leather handcuffs, legs spread, and torso raised like the Queen of Sheba languishing on her throne—for nearly four hours. She was a beautiful model, barely a fidget in sight and only one bathroom break. We chatted as I traced her curves across the thick paper and then even thicker canvas. Her

New Jersey accent was at odds with her elegance, and I came to realize that even though her husband, Pauly, had taught her the finer graces of high society, Terry was still proud of her Jersey shore roots. She laughingly relayed that Paulson had suffered from insta-lust when they'd locked eyes at a function she was catering.

"He liked my nails and big hair," she explained, wriggling her fingers. "And I may have unbuttoned my top a teensy bit more than was respectable."

I found myself infusing the painting with semblances of her humor, the glimmer within the depths of her brown eyes, the tilt to her harlot red lips. My forehead was hot with feverish excitement, and even as my hand swirled across the canvas, I was thinking of other poses for her.

"Tell me more about your sex life," I coaxed. "Obviously, you enjoy restraints."

"We enjoy a lot of things," she purred, stretching sinuously as I released her from the cuffs.

Without thinking, I gently rubbed the ache out of her wrists. She ran her tongue along her teeth as she watched, her gaze heated. Despite the fact she was fifteen years older than me and, of course, a woman, I was inexplicably attracted to her. Something about her intensity and assuredness reminded me of Sinclair.

"Why don't you come with me to get my daily snack?" she asked after studying me for a long moment.

"Okay."

I let her lead me from the room by the hand after gathering my sketchbook, pencils, and camera.

"I'm so happy we did this," she said, her thumb stroking over my palm. "Your sister called both Pauly and me to discourage us, but she was worried for nothing."

Acid filled my gums. "Excuse me?"

"Hmm? Oh maybe I shouldn't have mentioned it. I think

she was nervous that you would scare us off the deal with Daniel Sinclair. Honestly, I can't blame her. Pauly comes across as a real stick in the mud, and he is always bothering them about getting married." She looked over her shoulder to roll her eyes at me as we descended the stairs. "I swear that man could have grown up in Victorian England, all stuffy on the outside but a real perv deep down."

My laughter burst forth before I could help it, but Terry just grinned. We arrived at a large wood-paneled door, and she knocked three times in a strange rhythm.

"She's a nice woman, your sister, though obviously not very supportive. Do you think it has something to do with that gigantic stick up her ass?" Terry asked me with wide eyes.

I laughed again even though the fact that Elena had once again tried to thwart my project made my belly heat with rage.

A murmur came from inside the room.

"Now, you may come inside and document, but try not to get in the way, okay? Pauly and I have a ritual, you see."

I nodded, my curiosity piqued, and my arousal already high.

Paulson was sitting behind a huge mahogany desk, talking on speakerphone to someone with a Southern accent. His helmet of silver hair glinted in the low light emitted from the antique brass fixtures, and his stern face was tight with frustration. Still, he didn't seem surprised when I entered behind his wife. He even gave us a nod of acknowledgment before turning back to his computer screen.

Terry squeezed my hand before dropping it and stepping farther into the room. I watched her approach the desk with her head bowed and her hands clasped demurely in front of her. When she reached his side, she dropped to her knees in a position of subservience as beautiful as origami.

Paulson ignored her, even when her robe pooled in a small puddle of blue silk around her knees.

Silently, I placed my bag of supplies on the ground and brought my camera to my face. I wondered if I should ask Paulson for permission, but just as I was opening my mouth to do so, he inclined his head at me.

I raised the camera and framed them in the shot. Paulson reached out idly to pet Terry's riotous curls.

Click.

My shutter closed over the sight.

My body digested the image of them like a shot of burning liquor. I placed my hand on an end table to steady myself. This was a real moment in the lifestyle I could have enjoyed with Sinclair. I didn't know how I missed it when I met them; maybe Terry's bold personality had distracted me. I had always assumed that meekness was at the cornerstone of submissiveness, but as I gazed on the couple before me, it occurred to me that personality outside the bedroom had very little to do with it.

Paulson continued to speak on the phone, jotting down notes on a large legal pad with his free hand while the other pulled viciously, casually, at Terry's nipples. I moved unobtrusively around the room, close up to record the way her skin pulled and released like taffy, far away to mark the contrast of the power dynamic.

Finally, he gave Terry some kind of hand signal, and she quickly crawled beneath the desk. From my vantage point, I could only see her bare ass perched almost daintily on her crossed high-heeled feet. There was the soft clack of a belt being undone and the sexual gasp of a zipper.

I zoomed in on Paulson's face, but his jaw barely clenched as Terry paid homage to him. I hastened to take out my sketchbook. For a few long minutes, the only sounds in the room were Paulson's low voice as he spoke into the phone, the infrequent wet suck from Terry's busy mouth, and the scratch of lead over the toothy paper of my sketchbook. I drew ceaselessly, squeezing my thighs together to ease the ache at their center. My mind wheeled with fantasies of performing a similar task for Sinclair, of having an audience the way we did by the side of the pool at the Westin in Los Cabos. A shockwave of arousal pulsed through my body at the idea of Sinclair taking me, using me—however he wanted, whenever he wanted.

Even then, immersed in a real-life D\s scene with another couple, I was thinking of him.

The click of Paulson hanging up the phone brought me out of fantasyland just in time to witness the tensing of his features as he came down Terry's throat. He stared at me the entire time, his expression as forceful as a hand on my throat. I knew next time he would have me on my knees beside Terry in a heartbeat. The thought thrilled me but not more than the realization that I wasn't ashamed by it.

I smiled demurely at Paulson, my tongue peeking between my lips because Sinclair had taught me to be unashamed. He had pried open my reserved cage and exposed the delicious heart of sensuality that now pulsed like a beacon in my belly. He had given me the key to unlock things within myself that I had never known needed to be opened, and that was such an amazing gift.

I knew if I decided to be without him that I would survive. His gift had been unconditional, without strings just like our weeklong affair. But I also knew that if I chose to be with him, I would continue to unfold and bend into beautiful new formations of myself, like origami paper under his artist touch. Thinking about him, about *us*, like that made the prospect of our shared future less selfish and beautifully possible.

Chapter Twenty

He took my breath away.

Standing at his panoramic office window in three-quarter profile, Sinclair had never looked so unattainably gorgeous. His mahogany hair waved back from his broad forehead in a perfect sweep that I was already dying to run my fingers through, and the tailored midnight blue suit highlighted the depth of his tan, the startling blue of his eyes when he turned to look at me. But it was his smile that seduced me completely, the slight but genuine tilt of his firm lips and the way it pleated the skin beside his eyes. That expression meant more than all his gifts combined.

"*Mon dieu*, you are a vision."

I smiled at his breathy compliment, smoothing a hand down the deep plum-colored dress. It was short with a flirty hemline and a high-collared neckline. The torso was sheer, and I wore only a flimsy purple balconette bra beneath it.

"You look like a very classy schoolgirl."

That was the goal, so I rewarded him with a smile and a small twirl so that the skirt floated out and above my lace-topped stockings.

He groaned.

"You make it incredibly hard for a man to behave himself, Elle."

I lifted one shoulder. "You once told me that you were neither a saint nor a gentleman."

He crossed the room in three massive strides so that he was only a breath away from touching me. "With you, I feel like a savage. I want to throw you over my shoulder and have my way with you. I want to handle all that creamy skin with rough hands and brutally push into you before you're quite ready so that you'll feel my mark for hours after I've left your body."

My head tipped back on my weak neck, lips blooming open to make way for my heavy breathing. Less than a minute in his presence and I was already soaking wet.

He stared down into my eyes, looming over me in a way that was both threatening and incredibly sexy. The tension between us grew unbearably taut and vibrated like a struck wire. I was just about to push myself into him, unable to endure the physical space between our bodies, when he broke into a gorgeous smile and began to laugh.

At first, I frowned, but I quickly followed him into giggles when his arms snaked around my waist, tugging me into the air and up against his chest.

"You crazy, sexy, amazing woman. You intoxicate me." He laughed against my cheek as he pressed our foreheads together.

I wrapped my arms around his neck and leaned back in his

embrace to smile into his face. "That's probably an apt description. Like alcohol or drugs, I'm not the best choice for you."

His features slammed shut, but I smoothed his frown with my fingers so that he would know I was in a good mood despite my words.

Carefully, he set me down and ran a hand over my hair. "Do not talk like that tonight, *d'accord*? I want this evening to be about you and me only. No ghosts or skeletons from the closet will be joining us. Can you do that for me?"

I nodded because he was asking me for what I was desperate to have.

"Good."

His hand slid down my arm to lace with my fingers, and he tugged me toward his desk. "If we were dating, we would meet here often. I work too much, usually until seven thirty to eight or nine every evening Monday through Friday and frequently over the weekends."

He stopped us both before his desk, pressing my thighs into it and his front into me. I sighed as his hands came around to clasp over my belly.

"That would stop. Or, at the very least, I would work from home so that I could look up whenever I wanted to and watch you paint or sleep or just breathe."

I tilted my head back against his shoulder, settling into the fantasy.

"But at least once a week, we would meet here before I took you out on the town. I want to show you off, do you understand? I want to show the world that I am the man who captured a siren."

He pressed a chaste kiss to my cheek and squeezed me closer to his body.

"Sin," I breathed, not because I had anything to say but because I was full to the brim with emotion, and the only way I could think to release it was by saying his name.

"I wanted to show you a new acquisition I made," he said, tipping my chin up with two fingers so that I was looking at the previously empty space between the two wide bookcases behind his desk.

One of my paintings, *Solitaire du nuit*, now occupied the space. It was a large canvas dominated by a purple-black sky over the tiny lights of Montmartre and the moonlight-gilded dome of Sacre Coeur. A waxy, opalescent moon hung in the deeply bruised night sky like a grotesque pearl. It was one of my first paintings under the mentorship of Odile Claremont at *L'École des Beaux-Arts* and the first to be sold at my opening gallery showcase. Stefan Kilos, the gorgeous Greek I had met in Los Cabos, had informed me that he owned the piece, yet now it hung here in Sinclair's office.

I turned in his arms to gape at him.

He was smiling slightly. "You mentioned that Kilos had bought it. I didn't like the idea of him staring at it while he slept, and I wanted something of you close to me."

I swallowed convulsively.

Sinclair had just made my painting the only personal touch in his office.

"You are very good at this whole wooing thing."

The left side of his smile lifted further. "Thank you."

"I don't know if it's a compliment. I feel overwhelmed by you," I admitted.

"And you didn't before?"

"Touché."

He took my hand, bringing it to his lips in order to kiss my fingertips. "These are very talented fingers. They move my body with your touch and my soul with your art."

I pressed my hand to his chest. "Stop. I don't need pretty words."

"Just because they are pretty doesn't make what I'm saying

any less true," he said, reminding me with my own words of our conversation on Tuesday when I'd called him a god.

"But okay," he conceded, sensing my discomfort. "Let's go see the amazing Miles Davis. We can talk afterward."

He held my hand.

In theory, it seemed like such a trivial thing. People held hands all the time. Friends held hands, mothers and daughters, linked lines of camp children and people assisting the elderly. It was really no big deal. But I fixated on our clasped hands the entire evening, and not even the incredible Miles Davis nor his bold, brassy music could pull my gaze away from the sight. Sinclair's hands were beautiful, broad palms topped with long, lean fingers all covered in golden skin and lightly dusted with reddish hair. There was a scar on the back of his right hand, a small whitish burn mark that I compulsively ran my thumb over.

We parted for ten minutes at intermission so that I could use the restroom, and for those few minutes, my hand felt almost alien to me. I imagined what it would be like to let myself acclimatize to him the way my body so clearly yearned to do; how it would feel to greet him at the door of our shared apartment at the end of each day and wrap my arms and legs around him koala bear-style, to wake up in bed with my body pressed like a flower between his body and the bed.

His hand was waiting on the armrest, palm up and fingers unfurled when I returned. He smiled at my involuntary sigh when we reconnected and gave me a reassuring squeeze.

Afterward, we were both quiet as we filtered out of the theater and stood before the iconic fountain. I had a feeling Sinclair had things to say, but our companionable silence had created a bubble around us, and we were both happy to stay in it for a while yet.

So of course, some asshole had to come and pop it.

"Daniel Sinclair," a loud voice boomed from behind us.

Sin clenched my hand hard in his before letting it go to slowly turn around. I took a deep breath before doing the same.

An older man with graying blond hair and a beautifully gray cashmere overcoat was striding toward us with a tight smile and a very unhappy Margot on his arm. I sucked cold air in through my teeth, bracing myself for the confrontation.

Sinclair's hand found the small of my back in a surprising show of togetherness.

"Dean, Margot, it's a pleasure to see you. Did you have the gratification of seeing Miles Davis tonight in the Rose Theater?"

Dean looked down at Margot, expecting her to respond. Instead, she continued to glare at me.

"Not a fan of jazz music, to tell you the honest truth. We were watching the ballet." He leaned closer conspiratorially. "Fucking hate the ballet too, but this one loves it, and you know what they say, happy wife, happy life."

Sin and I laughed politely.

"Now, who is the gorgeous redhead on your arm?" Dean

asked, dropping the bomb into the middle of our tiny group as if it was a discarded gum wrapper.

I stared at the ground where I imagined it to be, a huge ticking machine with an angry red count down to explosion. Two minutes thirty seconds.

"This is Giselle Moore," Sinclair said smoothly. "She is a Parisian transplant and a very talented artist at the gallery. Her showcase is coming up in January. I think you would be a fan of her work."

"Oh wonderful. You know how I'm always looking for the next big thing. Are you it, Giselle Moore?"

I smiled, but I could still feel Margot's crushing censure, and it took everything I had not to flee from it. "I'm happy to be the next thing, if not the biggest. I'm incredibly grateful for the opportunity."

"The accent, it's not quite French."

"I was born in Naples, actually."

"Enough," Margot spit, finally roused out of her murder plotting and into action. "This is ridiculous small talk. Sinclair, what are you doing here with *her*?"

Her. If I decided to be with him, this man I loved, I would have to get used to hearing that. There were a lot of words for a woman in my position: slut, whore, home-wrecker, mistress, and adulterer. Yet until now, I had never known a pronoun could be so vicious. *Her;* that woman who stole her own sister's boyfriend.

Revulsion rolled through me.

"I enjoy spending time with Giselle, as you well know," Sinclair was saying in that implacable way of his.

It only made Margot incensed.

"Fuck *that*."

"M," Sinclair reproached at the same time that Dean gasped, "Margot!"

She shook off her date's arm, stepping forward to press a

finger to Sinclair's chest. She vibrated with righteous indignation. "I was supportive of you in Mexico. I stayed away and let you have a torrid little holiday fling. But we are living in the real world now and fantasies like this"—she waved her hand in my direction as if indicating shit on the sidewalk—"they don't exist in real life for a reason. Sure, she's pretty, but have you even thought about the consequences?"

She wasn't finished, I could tell. But something had shifted in Sinclair's posture, a subtle broadening as his own anger infused him with strength and superhuman intimidation. His anger wasn't even directed at me, and I felt my knees weaken under the pressure of his gaze.

"I wasn't living in reality, M. I was living in the fucking matrix. Nothing had meaning to me but the next meeting, the next deal, how people perceived me in the business world. Have you ever known me to make a decision lightly? Don't come at me like a scorned woman for falling in love with someone other than you or Elena. I'm fully prepared to reap the consequences but only from the people who were really wronged. You can't plan for something like this. It happened. It's done."

There was a pregnant silence. Sinclair's hand slipped from my back to the curve of my hip. He tugged me close to his side where my body settled easily like a puzzle piece. We both sagged slightly into each other.

"I'm happy with my decision," Sinclair said softly.

Margot stared up at him with large unblinking eyes. Sinclair's words had cracked open her hard exterior, leaving her open and vulnerable beneath our scrutiny. I could see the truth of her love in the glazed stare, the trembling lower lip, but I could also read her determination to support him in the way she squared her shoulders and nodded her head curtly at him before turning to me.

"I hope you're half as brave as him. He deserves a lot."

"I know," I said because she was right on both accounts. Sinclair was the bravest man I knew, pursuing what was right for him—which was somehow *me*—despite all the obstacles, moral and physical. Being with him, taking that final step in the betrayal of my sister, wasn't about me being a villain. It was about me being a heroine, his heroine.

This is going to kill you. This has been killing you all along, but I'm going to pull you out of this hellish situation, and I'm going to love you more than anyone ever has every day after to prove to you how much that pain was worth it. We are going to resurrect each other.

Sinclair's words from our lunch date reverberated through my head.

Straightening my spine, I skated my hand under his coat and around his back so that we both clutched each other. "I've always appreciated your take on the situation, Margot. What you've said, what you are saying, isn't wrong. But neither is this."

Her lips rolled under, but after a long moment of intense staring, she shifted on her feet and nodded at me. "Okay. Good luck then."

She turned back to Dean, who was standing with soggy shoulders a couple feet behind her. She hesitated before reaching up on her tiptoes to press a kiss to his cheek. "I'll meet you at the car."

He nodded, but his eyes were on Sinclair. After Margot moved out of hearing distance, he took a step forward to extend his hand to Sin, his eyes sad despite his smile. "Sorry about my girl. You know how she can be, fire and ice and all that."

"I don't know," Sinclair said firmly, deliberately. "But I'll take your word for it, Dean."

The older man smiled again at both of us, dropping the handshake tiredly before putting both hands deep in his pockets and taking off after his wife.

Sinclair and I stood there for a minute or two after they left before he wrapped me up in both arms and hugged me tightly. I giggled into his coat because his affection made me giddy.

"You are so beautiful to me," he said into my hair.

I smiled when he buried his nose in it and inhaled, knowing I smelled like lavender.

"Did you mean what you said?"

I pulled back within the span of his arms so that I could stare up into his electric eyes. "Yes. The affair was wrong and keeping it a secret compounded that, I think. A lot of people—our friends and family included—are going to hate us, and they might never stop." I reached up to run my fingers through his lush hair like I had wanted to do all night. "But I would take all the hate in the world if it meant your love."

Sinclair's face broke into a colossal grin, his teeth exposed and shining in the city lights. I grinned back at him, my happiness rushing through me, pushing against my tongue so that I almost gagged with it. Instead, I laughed. And after a moment, he laughed with me, great rolling guffaws that shook our bodies and made my belly ache. It was silly, and it made me feel like the teenager I had never been, impulsive and full of impossible fire.

I moaned when Sin swooped down to capture my smile between his lips. My body melted against him, his strong hold the only thing keeping me steady as he kissed me deeply. I tried to pull away slightly, aware we were in a public, albeit fairly deserted place, but he only brought me closer with a low growl. He gathered my wrists behind my back into one of his hands and pulled me tight against him. I wiggled against his hold, tilting my hips back and forth over the erection I could feel against my belly.

"Come back to my hotel room," he murmured against my skin. "I have a surprise for you."

I giggled, thrusting my breasts into his chest as I wiggled

my eyebrows salaciously. "I don't think it's much of a surprise at this point, Sin."

He blinked blankly before chuckling. "Your dirty mind always surprises me."

A few weeks ago, I would have blushed. Instead, I pried one hand out of his hold in order to cup his rigid length through his slacks. "Pleasantly, I hope."

He groaned when I squeezed him. "Most definitely. But that is not actually the surprise I was referring to."

When I pouted, he smiled. "I promise it will be just as fun."

I widened my eyes comically and grabbed his hand to drag him along behind me as I marched to the curb to hail a cab. "Just as fun as sex? Okay, this I have to see."

Chapter Twenty-one

Sinclair had the Royal Suite at the St. Regis. It was ridiculously beautiful with heavy velvet drapes, a black marble fireplace, and luxurious furnishings. Yet I could barely take my eyes off Sinclair as he competently removed our coats, hung them up in the closet, and called reception for a bottle of wine to be brought up. He moved through the world with a confidence and discipline that awed me, especially given the way he had grown up before the Percys had found him.

"Please take a seat," he said with a wave toward the two sofas.

"Did you take finishing classes?" I asked, plopping onto the couch with a smile of glee at how comfortable the fabric was beneath my palms.

"Excuse me?"

"I was just wondering if you took finishing classes, or the male equivalent, whatever that may be. You went from a French orphan to a governor's son practically overnight."

"I had a private tutor, and I was enrolled at Trinity." At my blank look, he explained, "It's the best prep school in the country. The summer they brought me over here, I spent every day perfecting my English, learning Spanish, and improving my standing in every other academic arena. Willa took me through the more delicate etiquette of high society herself."

"I am so sorry," I said somberly.

I was rewarded with his small smile. "So was I, at the time. I lived on a carefully constructed schedule Willa had created for me: schooling, modeling, and dating. Until you, I hadn't realized I'd never stopped living like that even after I rebelled and moved out."

"Dating?"

"Willa and Mort have always expected me to marry well." He hesitated. "They weren't even pleased with Elena at first, but she worked tirelessly to impress them, and now she and Willa are as thick as thieves."

I looked down at my hands so Sinclair couldn't see how those words scrambled my compartmentalized thoughts.

He sat down beside me and tipped my chin up with two fingers so that I had to stare into his intense eyes. "Elle, don't leave me."

"I'm here."

His eyes narrowed, the fingers under my chin turned over to pinch it firmly. "I can't have you checking out of this relationship every time we talk about Elena. We need to talk about her. She's a part of your family and a huge part of my past. If we don't normalize discussion about her, she will come between us."

"I'm sorry. There is just so much... stuff."

I leaned into his hand as he cupped my cheek.

"I know, which actually leads perfectly into the surprise I have for you. I have to be in France on business next week. When we met on the plane to Mexico, I was just returning from an inspection of a recently acquired property in Paris. It's time for me to go back to check on the finishing touches and interview the short-listed interior designers."

My heart sank at the thought of being apart from him just when we had decided to be together but I knew Sinclair's job was his number one priority, and I respected him for his dedication, lusted after him for his drive.

"I completely understand. I'll miss you, but we can talk when you get back," I said.

He was smiling when I looked back up at him. "I hoped you would come with me. It will give us time to figure out how we want to... proceed without the anxiety of lying to our friends and family. But mostly, I love the thought of having you to myself for another seven days, of walking through the streets holding your hand, kissing you when the urge strikes me— which, I'm warning you, will be often."

The idea of being with Sinclair in Paris made me dizzy. My mind rebelled against the image because it was too good to be true. How was it possible that despite everything, I could visit the city I loved by the side of the man I loved? Wasn't the villain in stories like this supposed to end up with nothing and no one?

"When do we leave?" I asked.

"Tomorrow morning. I thought we could stay here tonight."

"I would need to go back to Cosima's and pack."

"I had Candy go over earlier to pack a bag." He grinned at my incredulous look. "Just in case you said yes."

"You are so arrogant." I laughed.

"You love it."

"I do."

"You love me."

"I do." My eyes filled with tears. "I can't believe this is happening."

Sin framed my face in both his large hands and stared at me with complete sincerity, business-like seriousness. "Believe it. Say you'll come."

"I'll come."

"Good girl," he murmured before descending on my lips for a thorough kiss. "Now come here."

He swung me onto his lap to straddle him and gripped my face tightly beneath his hands so that he could maneuver me to his liking as he plundered my mouth. I groaned as he bit into my bottom lip sharply.

"Who owns you, Elle?" he husked against my damp lips.

"You, sir."

I shivered as his hand moved possessively over my curves to land on my flared hips. Just saying the word *sir* triggered my submissive nature, and I found myself edgy with the need to show him how good I could be. I wanted to bend and break under his hands, be reformed into something new and stronger.

"Yes," he hissed, seeing the glazed look in my eyes. "Strip for me. Show me what belongs to me."

I rocked once along his erection, slowly dragging my panty-covered core over him so that he gritted his teeth before I stood, sashaying a few feet away to the space in front of the fireplace. I took a moment to breathe, to absorb the tingling electricity that flowed through our connection. When I looked over my shoulder at him, there were no insecurities or guilt—nothing existed but Sinclair.

I pouted slightly as I swished my hips back and forth for him, the flirty skirt of my dress flipping up to expose my lace-topped stockings and the ends of the purple garters I wore. His eyes burned against my skin.

Suffused with desire, I bent over to bare my ass to him, the two plump cheeks bisected by the thin wedge of my satin thong. I straightened slowly and turned around to stare at him with my lip between my teeth as I painstakingly undid the buttons on my dress. When the fabric gaped open, I rolled my shoulders one at a time until my torso was free of the garment.

Sin made a primal noise in the back of his throat.

I reached back to undo the clasp of my bra and the little zipper on the skirt at the same time. When they fell to the ground, I lifted both breasts in my hands and pinched my nipples hard. I tilted my head back on a ragged moan.

"Show me your pussy."

I shuddered. Framing my hands beneath my breasts, I slid them slowly down my stomach until my fingertips slipped beneath the edge of my underwear. My hips swayed languidly as I bent my knees, dipping low to peel apart my legs and briefly flash the damp gusset of my panties at him.

"Show me," he ordered, and his fierce words hit me like a whip.

My sex throbbed, but I wanted that look of frustrated need on Sinclair's face more than I wanted to relieve the ache. I braced myself on my hands and knees, facing away from him, and reached back to run my fingers lightly over my seam from ass to clit.

"Feels so good," I breathed, rocking my hips into my touch.

"Don't make me ask again."

I bit my lip as I moved my panties to the side, giving my questing fingers access to my cleft while keeping it from his gaze. I groaned loudly as I sank two fingers inside myself.

Pain lashed out across my raised buttocks. I jerked forward to absorb some of the shock, my hand flying from my sex to the ground to brace myself. Another blow landed on the other cheek. I whimpered but kept my head lowered, my body still as Sinclair spanked me hard for my disobedience. When he was done, ten blows later, he looped my hair around his fist and tugged until my back and neck protested the angle.

"Who owns your body?" he whispered harshly into my ear.

I could feel the edge of his massive erection against the hot skin of my ass, and despite myself, I rubbed against him.

He pulled back tighter on my hair so that my eyes watered and a fresh flood of arousal coated my inner thighs.

"Answer me."

"You, sir. You own this body."

"Yet you disobeyed me?" His fingers began to trace back and forth over my swollen sex, just hard enough to stimulate. I tried to rub myself harder against him, but he only chuckled and, releasing his grip on my hair to still me with one firm hand on my hip. "What happens when you disobey me, siren?"

"I have to be punished, sir."

His hand smoothed over the sensitized skin of my ass teasingly. "You want to be punished, don't you?"

When I didn't answer quickly enough—too absorbed by the connection between his hand and my burning flesh—he spanked me again, three quick, powerful slaps to each cheek.

I whimpered and shamelessly ground myself against the air.

"Be still," he barked.

I locked my arms and legs, but I quivered with lust, my swollen breasts swinging beneath me.

His hand dipped into my sex again before he grabbed my hair, lifting my head to paint my lips with my wetness.

"Taste yourself. See how aroused you are?"

I licked my lips, caught his lingering fingers with my tongue, and drew them into my mouth to suckle. He withdrew them too quickly, and I made a noise at the loss.

I wasn't bereft for long. Before I could even process it, Sin ripped my panties off with one violent tug and thrust three fingers deep inside me. I cried out as he began to pump them in and out while his thumb drew tight circles over my clit. My knees began to quake, and unattractive sounds leaked out of my mouth as I lost my mind to the pleasure.

"Sin, Sin, Sin," I chanted between whimpers.

"Yes, siren?"

"Please, please, please…"

"Use your words."

"Please," I burst out as the burn of my impending orgasm rushed like a brushfire over my skin. "Let me come."

"The only way you come is on my cock."

I tried to find the words in my vacant mind to make him understand that I was on the edge, dangling over it, desperate for the final push. "Fuck me then, please sir."

His fingers left me suddenly, and the cool kiss of the air-conditioning made me tremble. If he blew on me, I'd come. But he didn't. In fact, he waited for so long that I finally looked over my shoulder to find him disrobed, sitting on his haunches as he stared at my exposed core, one fist pulling firmly at his cock.

"Please sir," I whispered because my strength had deserted me.

"Are you begging for my cock, siren?"

His eyes were bluer than I'd ever seen them as he stared at me, his face impassive. It turned me on so much to see his tightly leashed control. I wanted to rip his mask off with my nails and teeth, impale myself on him, and rock and rock until he shattered underneath me.

I nearly snarled when I said, "I need you to fuck me. Please, fuck me hard, fuck me like you hate me."

Immediately, he rose and pushed down on my lower spine so that my hips were hitched further into the air, and I was splayed open for him. The tip of his erection burned my wet lips as he placed himself against me. He reached around to grab me by the throat, lifting me onto my knees as he thrust up into me. I groaned as I settled back against him, basically in his lap. He pressed his chest to my back, tightened his grip on my throat slightly so that my airflow was just barely constricted, and bit my ear. "I'll fuck you, Elle. Because you asked so nicely and your pretty pussy is desperate for it. But I'll fuck you like I own you because I could never hate you."

My open mouth clanged shut as he lifted me with one hand and held me securely in place as he began to pound into me. Each time he bottomed out, our skin slapped together. I loved the sound. I bucked back against him, throwing myself into it so that it hurt. I wanted the pain. I needed it, needed *him*, to kill the remaining pain in my heart with physical pain.

"Please," I panted.

He wound my long hair in his hand and tucked it tightly under his arm so that my back was bowed and I couldn't escape the brutality of his thrusts. His hand found my slick clit and clamped it tight between his fingers. It didn't seem possible, but his pace increased.

"More, more," I begged, even though I was already incoherent and my orgasm was looming so large, I was actually a little frightened of it.

"When you come, I expect you to thank me," he ground out.

"Yes, sir."

"Then come."

His fingers released my raw clit, and blood flooded back to it painfully. I screamed. He slapped down once, twice on the abused flesh, and I exploded. My mind fractured, crumbled into ash, and disappeared so that I was only body—throbbing, hot, slicked, and panting, a pink thing of desire. Yet I remembered to scream out, "Thank you, thank you, thank you!"

When I came back to myself slightly, Sinclair was still buried inside me, unwilling to move despite our climaxes. His hands shifted over my scalp where it lay on his shoulder, and I moaned at the comfort of it.

"You are perfect," he murmured against my sweaty cheek. "And somehow, you are mine."

I smiled slightly, too weak to talk. He laughed at me.

There was a gentle knock on the door. Sinclair shifted carefully underneath my prone body until I was in his arms. He stood and swiftly took me to the bedroom where he pulled back the covers and slid me into bed.

"I'll just deal with room service and be right back," he said, pressing a kiss to my forehead.

I nodded, but he had already left the room.

I snuggled deeper under the covers and smiled. In twenty-four hours, I would be in my favorite city with a man who I had loved for months and that now, somehow, I could finally call mine. My upcoming showcase was shaping up to be something I was monumentally proud of and I had friends whom I loved in the city. I knew a wealth of pain and animosity awaited us, but for now, I could afford to languish in the beauty of being newly in love. I tilted my head into the soft pillow and sighed, utterly blissed out.

That was, until I heard the voice speaking to Sinclair in the other room.

"Daniel, we need to talk," Elena said. "I don't care if it's a bad time. I'm not leaving until you hear me out."

The End.

The Sinners (The Evolution of Sin Trilogy, #3) Excerpt

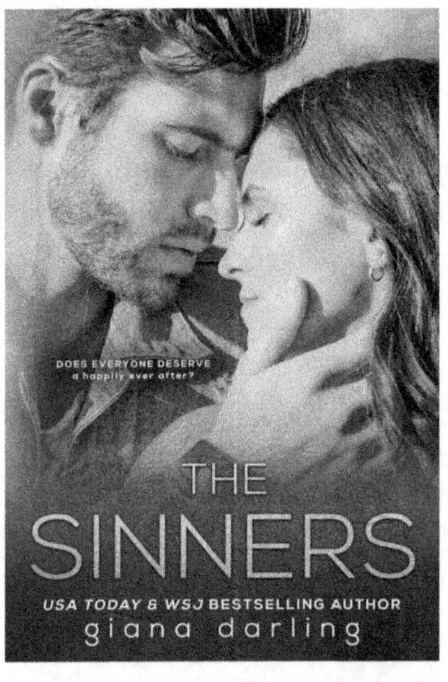

Does everyone deserve a happily-ever-after?

After years of turmoil, my life was finally looking up.
I was launching my career as an artist at one of the hottest
galleries in New York City, I'd reunited with my family, and
most of all, for the first time in my life, I was in love.
In love with a man who was never really mine to have even
though our feelings told us otherwise.

There was only one thing that could derail my happiness and
that was my guilt over my forbidden love for my sister's
boyfriend.

After finally confessing our feelings for each other, Sinclair and

I left for Paris to experience what our relationship could look like if we were ever free to be together.

Before long, tragedy strikes at the heart of my family, beckoning us back home to face our demons: my sister, a sinister man from my past, and the scrutiny of everyone we know condemning our happily-ever-after.
Sinclair always said our love was bigger than the world, but is it big enough to eclipse all of our sins?

The Sinners: Chapter One

SINCLAIR

Le cœur a ses raisons que la raison ne connaît point.

The heart has its reasons which reason knows nothing of.

Blaise Pascal was a fucking genius. Then again, he was French and my countrymen knew a thing or two about being in love.

Therefore, it should stand to reason that I may have inherently known a thing or two about love as well but the idea that love could outweigh logic had never occurred to me. It could have been because I couldn't remember much about my birth parents, my Roma mother and her French husband who both died mere months apart when I was seven years old. Willa and Mortimer Percy had adopted me when I was sixteen but our family was one of deliberate choice, calculated divination. They loved me in their own way, I think, but it was a secondary emotion. A result of pride and cultivation, the way Frankenstein might have loved his monster.

Then there was the love of Elena Lombardi.

She loved me for the reasons I loved myself: my drive and work ethic, my reasonability and sophistication. I enjoyed her company and coveted her mind; the twisted turns it took to shortcut the obstacles in our road to success. She was dark beneath the veneer, hiding away the same inherent ruthlessness I had been born with, and even though we never spoke about the deep-seated ugliness that poverty had wrought on our souls, it was a comfort to both of us just knowing it existed.

The truth is, we saw in each other the ideal partner for our ideal selves and for years, it was enough because it never occurred to me to ask for more, for the kind of love my kinsmen waxed poetic about...

... and then I saw her.

It wasn't love at first sight. That implies my response to her was subtle and warm, something easy and quintessentially human.

No, the moment I saw Giselle Moore sitting curled up and vulnerable with sickness and fear in the first-class cabin of that plane, my humanity - the class and refinery that I had cultivated for years - sloughed off me like molted skin and revealed the heart of the animal I secretly knew myself to be.

My heartbeat roared in my ears and my groin tightened with a desire so fierce, I almost doubled over. Only one thought reverberated through my head like a fucking mantra.

Take her.

Take her.

Own her.

I felt the pulse of the words in my blood as it scorched through my body and ricocheted off the walls of my heart. I wanted her. It was primal and fiercer than anything I'd ever experienced before. It took every ounce of civilization I had left in me to approach her politely, to keep my twitching hands in my lap instead of spreading them all over her luminous pale skin.

At first, she was reserved with me, barely allowing her eyes to slide my way. I took the time to visually devour her, noting how the golden freckles across her shoulders and cheeks contrasted with the olive tint of her complexion, how her auburn hair glowed like copper under the dim cabin lights. And when she finally met my gaze, I stared hard into her eyes, wide and pure as silver dollars.

I found myself jealous of her smiles, wanting to own them for myself. When I leaned over her, the smell of her lavender and honey fragrance intoxicated me. The soft brush of her aroused breath against my skin nearly made me lose control.

I knew even as I left her behind on the plane that meeting her had changed my life but I never could have guessed how much.

I wasn't a man that believed in fate but when she showed up at The Westin in Los Cabos, I couldn't say I was surprised. It solidified the proposal that had waited poised on the tip of tongue since I had first laid eyes on her – a weeklong affair to purge myself of this egregious need for her. Those torturous hours while I had waited for her answer were some of the longest of my life and they set the precedent for the weeks of indecision that followed, horrific bouts of self-loathing peppered with moments of such clear, bright joy that they obliterated all memory of shame and hatred.

Now, here I was, rearranging everything I had always known and thought I wanted, to make space for my siren, my Elle. The mantra that had infiltrated my head like a siren's song from our first meeting had only intensified, sunk into my bones and saturated my blood. I couldn't take a breath without feeling her in the previously unused muscles of my heart.

Look at me; she'd even turned me into a fucking poet, a true Frenchman when I'd forsaken my homeland years ago.

I was jeopardizing my reputation and therefore my career, and polarizing the only family that had ever really cared for me. Worst of all, I was forcing the love of my life to choose me over her sister.

Do you want to know the worst thing about this cluster fuck of a situation?

I didn't care.

Everything I had loved before Elle paled in comparison to my need for her. The thought of anything getting in the way of being with her both incensed me and perversely excited me because I knew I would eviscerate it.

It wasn't rational and it was completely out of character but as my compatriot Blaise Pascal said, "*the heart has its reasons which reason knows nothing of.*" And since the moment I met Giselle Moore, my heart had stopped being mine to reason with.

Which was how I found myself opening the door to my suite and temporary home at the St Regis with a completely idiotic smile on my face - high on my courage, exhilarated for the first time in my life at the prospect of my future because a gorgeous redhead by the name of Giselle Moore had just promised to be in it indefinitely - only to find my ex-girlfriend at the door.

It was obvious that Elena had come directly from the airport by the large canvas bag she carried over one shoulder. She was still wearing one of her power suits, an inky black ensemble from head to toe that was meant to detract from her femininity. Instead, it highlighted her delicate beauty like a neon pen. She looked polished and gorgeous, not at all heartbroken.

"Daniel, we need to talk," Elena demanded. "I don't care if it's a bad time. I'm not leaving until you hear me out."

It was a bad time.

The worst.

It was fucking *awful* because I had just shared the most extraordinary night of my life with the woman I had finally convinced to be mine and she was currently tucked away within hearing distance of this very conversation, wearing only a post-coital smile and the scent of our sex on her skin.

Anxiety pricked my skin like a thousand hot needles. I couldn't afford to lose her, not after tasting, however briefly, the possibility of a future with her.

Giselle Moore was mine. And I wasn't going to let anyone get in the way of that.

Not even her sister.

"I appreciate that we need to talk, Elena, but now isn't a good time," I said, widening my stance so that I blocked most of the doorway.

"Don't be ridiculous. It's eleven thirty at night, you can spare ten minutes to talk to the woman you devoted the last four years of your life to," she snapped.

I gritted my teeth against a brief flare of guilt as she brushed pass me into the suite. She stopped in front of the couch, delicately placing her coat, bag, and Prada purse there before facing me again with her hands clasped before her. Even in her righteous indignation, Elena comported herself like a princess. She was heartrendingly beautiful, with a face like a renaissance painting and a spine made of titanium steel. If I had never met Giselle, I knew I would have stayed with Elena for the rest of my life. It would have been so much simpler that way.

And yet, the thought was singularly depressing.

Giselle brought my ordered black and white life into color with her passionate strokes and exceptional love. There was no going back from something like that.

I crossed my arms. "I leave for Paris early tomorrow morning."

"I just got back," she said, as if that made it unacceptable for me to leave.

I didn't say anything.

"Fine, that just means it is even more imperative that we talk now."

Stuffing my hands in my pockets, I considered the wisdom of either just kicking her out or hashing it out with her. I was well aware that Giselle was in the bedroom listening to our every word. It might do her good to realize how serious I was about leaving Elena, to hear some of the things I needed to say. And a large part of me realized that Elena needed the opportunity to discuss her feelings with me. When I had ended things with her last week, she barely spoke, barely even moved. She just sat perched on the edge of the couch with her hands demurely held in her lap. I deserved a thorough tongue lashing at the very least, even a good hard slap or two across the face. It was, pathetically, the least I could do to ease her pain.

"Okay, take a seat. Can I get you some water?" I asked, moving forward towards the bar to pour myself a much-needed drink.

I had briefly tidied up the suite before answering the door, more out of habit than anything else and I was intensely grateful for my compulsion now. Still, I cast my eyes about the room, spotting the neat pile of Giselle's clothes partially hidden under the coffee table on the other side from Elena.

Fuck.

I composed my features and carefully slid my gaze to her. Thankfully, taking her seat and smoothing the immaculate black pants over her thighs preoccupied her.

"A whiskey, please."

I nodded curtly, two cold glasses of liquor on the rocks already in my hands as I skirted the coffee table. I kicked Giselle's purple garter belt further into the shadows as I moved past to sit on the chair adjacent to Elena.

She accepted the tumbler with a tight smile and a sincere 'thank you' because her politeness wouldn't allow for anything else.

"What is it that you would like to say?" I asked, leaning back in my chair and crossing one leg over the other.

Elena's eyes flickered over the bare skin of my torso as my muscles contracted with movement. She had never been overly effusive about my looks, something I had always been thankful for, but I knew that the sight of me unclothed affected her. Strangely, perhaps, the knowledge did nothing for me.

I wished for Elle's sake that I was wearing a shirt.

"I want to better understand this early mid-life crisis you seem to be having. I've had time to think about it and I can see that your company's expansion could be putting too much stress on our relationship." I opened my mouth to speak but she held up her hand. "We both have one-hundred-hour work weeks and even though our professions have always come first, we need to remember to take time for us."

I knew she must have taken the time to read articles and books about our situation: what-to-do-when-your-partner-leaves-you-unexpectedly and how-to-breath life-back-into-your-relationship psychology dissertations and magazine findings. When Elena was faced with a problem, she researched the hell out of it so that when the opportunity arose she could beat it to death with thought and theory. I knew all of that because even though we weren't married, for the last four years we had lived like husband and wife. I knew all of the things that made Elena Lombardi frequently intolerable and constantly brilliant. I could see the despair she tried to hide in the lines around her pursed mouth, the helplessness she held tightly in her clasped hands. I was actively destroying her and it was killing me.

It helped to remind myself that it was the least that I deserved.

She offered me a small, shaky smile.

Putain, I was such an asshole.

"It's too late for that, Elena."

"It doesn't have to be. There is no *deadline* on a relationship, no expiration date. We can work this out. A co-worker recommended an excellent couples' councilor."

"Not interested."

"Don't be so closed minded," she urged, her voice still pleasantly modulated even though her hands had unconsciously curled into fists.

"It's not a matter of obstinacy. Counseling wouldn't work for us."

"How can you know that?"

Because I'm savagely in lust and irrevocably in love with your sister, who, coincidently, is laying naked about fifteen feet away from us in my bed.

"Because we don't have any issues to work through. We've never been passionate with each other, which I always thought was a good thing," I tried to explain.

"It is," she agreed eagerly.

I scrubbed a hand over my face, caught the scent of Giselle's sex lingering on my fingers and fought the urge to lick her off my skin. "It isn't a good thing for a couple. How can there be erotic love without passion?"

Elena's lips twisted, then went lax. "Are you saying that you aren't attracted to me anymore?"

Yes.

Instead, I said, "Have you ever head the Greek term, *philia*? It describes the love between two warriors or best friends, a partnership based on unswerving loyalty and respect."

Elena blinked at me. "Are you kidding?"

I spread my hands and shrugged. "The Greeks actually valued it more highly than romantic love."

Her eyes, just shades darker than Giselle's, narrowed dangerously. I sounded callous and cruel, as I often did when discussing emotional issues. It was difficult for me to marry the empathy I felt with the logical methodology of my thoughts. Giselle was the only one who gave voice to my mute soul. I wished, irrationally and unfairly, that she was beside me.

"I," Elena cleared her throat. "I thought we both valued

those characteristics. You make our relationship sound so... unfeeling. Maybe I didn't do a great job of showing it, but you mean the world to me, Daniel."

Her words pressed around me like a cold iron fist. Was it possible to feel heartbroken even though I was the one ending things? I wanted, no, I *needed* to be with Giselle but in doing so, I was effectively antagonizing my best friend. Elena and I had never been as perfect as we thought, but we were still a team. I was losing my right hand man and despite how unromantic that may have seemed, it was fucking devastating all the same.

"You mean the world to me too," I said.

But my love for your sister is bigger than the world.

Elena stared at me. She was still waiting for the punch line of a bad joke, for me to laugh and tell her it was all a ruse.

I sat taller in my chair.

It would be unkind to allow her to think she stood a fighting chance of winning me back so even though doing it sickened me, I slaughtered the last of her hope.

"But I'm not in love with you and I'm not going to change my mind about this. I want you to have the Gramercy apartment and the furniture. I've moved out the things I wanted to keep and had them put into storage. We never had shared bank accounts, or any other permanent assets."

A choked sob escaped her lips like the whistle from a punctured balloon. She clapped a hand over her mouth, cleared her throat and resumed her enforced dignity.

I had never wanted to hold her more than I did in that moment.

I cleared my throat too. "I am sorry, Elena. It makes no difference, I know, but I need to tell you that you are my dearest friend. Hopefully, after the dust has settled, we can find that again."

Elena stared at me impassively for a long time. It was utterly silent throughout the hotel suite but I didn't allow myself to linger over thoughts of Giselle and what she thought of the entire conversation. That would come later. For now, I owed it to Elena to be present.

I tried to relax the muscles in my face, open my posture up so that she could see how much I was grieving and even, if she was perceptive enough, how little I deserved her understanding.

"You are serious," she finally breathed.

I nodded.

She took in a deep, shuddering breath and let it out slowly through a mouth I had kissed a thousand times. It was indescribably strange to look at the woman I had thought myself in love with and feel so devoid of feeling. I was sure it made me a horrible person. I let myself drown in it for a minute.

"Okay," she stood up swiftly and strode forward to offer me her hand.

I stared at it before clasping it within my own. She had long, lean fingers that stroked piano keys more passionately than they had ever stroked me. I rubbed the back of them with my thumb and it felt absurdly *final*.

"I don't want to see you for a while but I don't see why we can't be amicable about this. You've become a fixture with my family and friends," - I fought the urge to wince - "and I can accept that sometimes, people just grow apart."

"They do."

She nodded curtly and dropped my hand. I watched her pick up her bag, carefully cross her coat over one arm and begin the slow walk to the door. It was the most surreal moment of my life to watch my former partner walk out of the same space she unwittingly shared with my new lover. If it hadn't been so fucked up, it might have been a little poetic.

So, it took me a second too long to realize that Elena had tripped on something and was bending over to examine the purple scrap of lace caught on the sharp edge of her high heel.

It then took me a half-second more than that to register the aberrant look of horror on her habitually placid features and the venomous bite of her words as she whispered, "you fucking cheating bastard."

Get The Sinners now!

Thanks Etc

I couldn't have written *The Secret* without the loving support of my friends and family.

Many thanks go to Najla Qamber of Najla Qamber Designs for another gorgeous cover and teasers.

To all those bloggers who took the time to read and review my book thank you from the bottom of my heart!

My beta readers Eliza and Angela Plumlee, and my incredible proofreader and virtual friend Patricia, I can never thank you enough for your support!

Also, thank you to Jenny Sims from Editing 4 Indies for giving this book new life.

Last but never least, thank you to H, who taught me everything about love, loss, and the importance of communication.

The Fallen Men Series

The Fallen Men are a series of interconnected, standalone, erotic MC romances that each feature age gap love stories between dirty-talking, Alpha males and the strong, sassy women who win their hearts.

Lessons in Corruption

Welcome to the Dark Side

Good Gone Bad

Fallen Son (A Short Story)

After the Fall

Inked in Lies

Fallen King (A Short Story)

Dead Man Walking

Caution to the Wind

Asking for Trouble

A Fallen Men Companion Book of Poetry:

King of Iron Hearts

The Evolution of Sin Trilogy

Giselle Moore is running away from her past in France for a new life in America, but before she moves to New York City, she takes a holiday on the beaches of Mexico and meets a sinful, enigmatic French businessman, Sinclair, who awakens submissive desires and changes her life forever.

The Frenchman

The Sinners

The Evolution Of Sin Trilogy Boxset

The Enslaved Duet

The Enslaved Duet is a dark romance duology about an eighteen-year old Italian fashion model, Cosima Lombardi, who is sold by her indebted father to a British Earl who's nefarious plans for her include more than just sexual slavery... Their epic tale spans across Italy, England, Scotland, and the USA across a five-year period that sees them endure murder, separation, and a web of infinite lies.

Enthralled (The Enslaved Duet #1)

Enamoured (The Enslaved Duet, #2)

The Enslaved Duet Boxset

Anti-Heroes in Love Duet

Elena Lombardi is an ice cold, broken-hearted criminal lawyer with a distaste for anything untoward, but when her sister begs her to represent New York City's most infamous mafioso on trial for murder, she can't refuse and soon, she finds herself unable to resist the dangerous charms of Dante Salvatore.

When Heroes Fall

When Villains Rise

<u>Anti-heroes in Love Boxset</u>

<u>The Dark Dream Duet</u>

The Dark Dream duology is a guardian/ward, enemies to lovers romance about the dangerous, scarred black sheep of the Morelli family, Tiernan, and the innocent Bianca Belcante. After Bianca's mother dies, Tiernan becomes the guardian to both her and her little brother. But Tiernan doesn't do anything out of the goodness of his heart, and soon Bianca is thrust into the wealthy elite of Bishop's Landing and the dark secrets that lurk beneath its glittering surface.

Bad Dream (Dark Dream Duet, #0.5) is FREE

Dangerous Temptation (Dark Dream Duet, #1)

Beautiful Nightmare (Dark Dream Duet, #2)

<u>The Elite Seven Series</u>

Sloth (The Elite Seven Series, #7)

<u>Standalone</u>

Serpentine Valentine (A Sapphic Medusa Retelling)

<u>Coming Soon</u>

My Dark Fairy Tale (A Mafia Romance)

The Moon & His Tides (The Impossible Universe Trilogy, #1)

About Giana Darling

Giana Darling is a USA Today, Wall Street Journal, Top 40 Best Selling Canadian romance writer who specializes in the taboo and angsty side of love and romance. She currently lives in beautiful British Columbia where she spends time riding on the back of her husband's bike, baking pies, and reading snuggled up with her cat, Persephone, and dog, Romeo.